DEATH ON A1A

A Perry Savant Novel

HERB SENNETT

Death on A1A

CIF Publications
West Palm Beach Florida 33406
www.cifpublications.com

ISBN: (pb) 978-0-9970231-6-9

CIF Publications date: October 2018

www.novelsbyherb.com

10 9 8 7 6 5 4 3 2 1

Contents

CHAPTER ONE

Central Park is a great place to run. During the summer months, the air is often crisp and cool in the early mornings. Never cold; just cool enough to keep the body from sweating profusely and soaking your clothes.

Every day, six miles. No change. No faster, of course—maybe a little slower these days. Just daily. It's the only way I can keep up with the younger officers. It took me nearly fifteen years to get to do what I do. It's only fair that they put in their time.

Running helps my thoughts to drift to nowhere in particular. I feel peaceful inside. I've earned my pension. I'll be retiring in a few more years. I'll move to Florida at the age of fifty-one and live well.

I might even get a nice gig with a small-town police department. Or maybe, I could do some part-time bailiff work just to keep from going start-raving mad.

I could never imagine myself sitting quietly on a beach somewhere soaking up the sun for days on end. There's nothing in that. In fact, it's quite boring. I know I could find something to do.

No family. Nobody to hold me here through long winters. I don't necessarily want to spend my time alone. I could learn to play tennis. No. I could learn to golf—that's what they do down there.

As I approached the park entrance on the south end, I slowed to a quick walk before reaching my usual morning eatery a couple of blocks away. At the front entrance, I stopped to grab a newspaper before heading for breakfast at the diner next door to my apartment building.

I sat down at a table and signaled to Roberta. She quickly met me with a cup of coffee. I look into her somewhat sad eyes.

"How do you always have my coffee in front of me before you have time to pour it?"

"Saw you coming, Perry. How was the run?"

"As usual; boring but healthy."

"I've been reading about the muggings."

"We've had a few."

"I feel safe having you around here," she said.

"I hope so."

"Your usual?"

"Of course," I answered finishing with the sugar in my coffee. I turned and opened the paper to read it. Part of my morning ritual: run, read, eat, shower, go to work. I slowly stirred the coffee hoping it would cool down before burning my tongue.

I dropped the spoon.

What I saw made my mouth malfunction such that the coffee fell into my lap, not in my mouth. The headline on the front page caught be completely off-guard.

NYPD CHIEF INTERFERES IN LOCAL POLITICIAN'S MURDER

"What the hell!" I yelled out uncharacteristically.

Everyone in the place looked up.

"Are you okay?" Roberta called from behind the counter.

"Yes, darling. Sorry about that, people."

It appears that one of the reporters in the crowd yesterday had done his homework and discovered my past with the alderman. He wrote a speculative piece. Since I had never married, I must be gay. The alderman was a closet gay, sneaking around in low rent hotels to meet up with young men for sex. The reporter put two and two together and came up with twelve.

I continued reading a list of accurate details about the murder. The only conclusion I could think of was he got his information from one of the investigating detectives. I felt my jaw drop as I continued reading:

According to a boyhood friend, the famous chief of detectives had been gay since grade school. Obviously, he was attempting to help his "gay" friend by attempting a police cover up of the murder and the sordid details of the deaths.

The reporter did not name the source. He claimed the man had grown up in the same neighborhood as me, went to high school with me, and knew me well.

Roberta brought my order to the table.

"Got to go, Roberta. Can you put it in a box for me?"

"Sure," she replied and took the food back to the kitchen. About two minutes later she returned with the box. I gave her a twenty-dollar bill and headed out the door.

"Chief!" She called out.

I stopped and turned around just outside grabbing the door to keep it open.

"The coffee cup."

I looked down at my hand.

"I'll bring it back in the morning."

I bolted toward the apartment building. Upstairs I quickly showered. Before I could finish dressing, my phone rang. It was my boss.

"Damn it, Savant! What's this all about?"

"I don't have any idea, Chief. I'm almost dressed I'll be there in about forty-five minutes."

"Make it fifteen!" He said and hung up.

I hoped he wouldn't see the newspaper before I arrived. Something must have gotten him to his desk early. Or he looked at his newspaper at home earlier than normal.

Usually he only reads it when he gets into the office; sort of like research on the crimes happening in the city. I never could figure that out. I usually checked the night desk reports when I got to work to see what was going on.

But then I don't pay much attention to the precincts outside of Manhattan. I may be the Chief of all criminal investigations in the NYPD, but my main interest is downtown. I have a chief of criminal investigations in every borough. I only respond to highly controversial or high-profile cases like yesterday. I'm sure my action is being taken badly—for me.

Who could this person be? I wondered. Who does he think he is that he decided to make up lies about me? The only thing I had ever wanted to do was to make my dad proud by following in his footsteps. I wanted to be one of the New York's Finest! I wanted to be a New York City Cop. That's all.

I had to think this through. Perhaps the job had so completely taken over my life that I had no time for a social life. I watched many of my colleagues go from gung-ho to bitterness. What we see almost daily is enough to turn anyone into a pessimistic and bitter old man.

Somehow, I escaped all that and had become happy, even contented with my life. My whole identity had been tied up with being a part of the NYPD.

I looked at my reflection in the mirror over the bathroom sink. I thought about what had happened. The events of yesterday seemed so innocent. *What went wrong? Where did I screw up?*

After I arrived at the office yesterday, the front desk sergeant informed me of a double homicide in the forty-fourth precinct. But, when he said it may involve an alderman, I figured I'd better get to the crime scene before all hell broke loose after the media finds out who the dead guy was.

I knew that the Public Affairs people had made a habit of giving out too much information. Too many NYPD detectives had been dealing with that problem for the past year or so.

I immediately dialed my bosses' office and got a message that he was out of and would be in meetings all morning. I dialed the Commissioner's office just to discover that he was in the same meeting with my boss, the Chief of Departments. I decided to head for the crime scene.

Looking back on it, maybe I made an unwise decision; but at that moment I thought I could help by deflecting the press and other gawkers. I thought I could help the detectives do their job without press interference.

Captain Mark Harris, a 6'-3" bald African-American detective from the forty-fourth precinct, was the man in charge. He was one of those guys who had a way of making sure every person within sight knew he was in charge.

I walked over to where he stood.

"Perry Savant!" he yelled in his gravelly voice that dripped with skepticism at my presence at his crime scene. "What the hell are you doing here?"

"Thought you might need a little help with the press. It won't be long before they show up like flies on an outdoor john. I'm sure the word's already out about who died here."

"I don't know, chief. You're the boss, of course. But I think we got this under control. The PR people can take care of this after they arrive. My boys will keep them at bay behind the tape."

"I won't interfere. I assure you. I'll stay here on the street and out of your way."

"Well," he said with a long drawl that gave away his Southern heritage. "I mean, you know, you and the alderman have a history."

"We went to the same high school for a couple of years. I barely knew him at all. Besides, you know the Commissioner's policy of having a representative from his office at high-profile cases. That's all. Besides, I don't think I need to remind you of the last time the PA folks tried to handle things."

"Oh, yeah. Right. Just—"

"I know the procedures, Chief."

"Just reminding you. I mean, it's been, what, five years?"

"Four years, seven months, and eight days. But who's counting?"

Out of the corner of my eye, I saw five reporters and a couple of cameramen approaching the police line.

"I'll take care of things down here," I said nodding toward the reporters. "You see to a sharp, neat, and clean investigation. Okay?"

"Okay, chief," he said then proceeded to fill me in on the details at that moment.

I thanked him and watched as he entered the old run-down building that pretended to be a legitimate hotel. I felt ill from the smell that permeated that part of The Bronx. I grew up in Queens. The smell over there has its own distinctive aroma. But, I was used to that smell.

Here? My stomach turned over several times.

I pulled out my handkerchief and placed it over my mouth. I took a deep breath and pushed the wad of cloth back into my pocket. I walked over to where the gaggle of reporters was growing by the minute.

As I made my way across the street I remembered how much I loved the details of detective work. I just never considered that dealing with the press would be part of my job. Otherwise I probably wouldn't have accepted the promotion.

Taking a deep breath again, I stepped up to the front of the reporters and video cameras, put on a serious face, and spoke as carefully as I could.

"My name is Perry Savant. I'm from the Commissioner's office," I began as politely as I could. "I'll be your contact this afternoon until the Public Affairs people arrive. As of an hour ago, two bodies were discovered in one of the rooms on the top floor. The guests were required to check out by 11:00, so when the cleaning crew opened the door a little after noon, they found two victims of gun-shot wounds."

I took a deep breath.

"The housekeeper immediately reported the incident and police officers were on the scene within seven minutes of the call. One of the victims has been tentatively identified. You'll be given all the pertinent information on both victims as soon as their identities are confirmed and next of kin contacted. I think you know the drill. Other than that, I have no further information. I'll return here in about an hour to update you on the situation."

As I turned away, at least a dozen people shouted out questions to me. But, one voice seemed familiar and caught my attention. It was the rattle in his voice from his COPD that I recognized. He was the one reporter I hoped had missed this melee.

"Chief Savant! Is it true that one of the victims is Alderman Josue Rodriquez?"

I stopped and turned around. It seemed like a hundred people were yelling at me to confirm what the reporter had asked. The moment felt like a conundrum of all sorts of chaos. To these reporters, this was big news. And each of them wanted to be the first to get that story out.

I held up my hand. The reporters quieted.

"I refuse to respond to rumor and speculation. The CSI unit, the coroner, and several of our best detectives are on the scene putting together the facts. I promise you that I'll let you know more just as soon as I know more. I can say now that the identities of the two men have yet to be positively identified. So, please, please, just calm down and let us do our job. Now! If you'll excuse me, give me a chance to gather more information for you."

This time I refused to turn around as dozens of voices vied for my attention. I walked into the building that looked as if it had its heyday in the 1870's. I was pretty sure it wasn't built until the 1950's or 60's. The smell of stale beer mixed with a hint of urine reminded me of the many crime scenes I had investigated over my sixteen years I was a precinct detective.

I climbed the four flights of stairs. I noticed where the wallpaper had peeled and languished in strips. At the top floor, several police officers held residents at bay about five feet to the left of the stairwell.

The officer standing guard at the crime scene looked very young. I did not recognize him. He was about an inch taller than me with a boyish face contrasting my own obvious advancing age. I wondered if I looked that young to the older officers when I joined.

"Go ahead on in chief," he said with a big smile and speaking in a deep, obviously conscious vocal sound trying to impress me.

"I think I'll stand out here until one of the detectives comes out."

"You want I should go and get one for you?"

"Naw. I'll wait. So, are you new on the force?"

"Yes, sir," he replied with a bit higher tone that more fit his youth. "I'm just shy of a year out of the academy. Uh, this is my beat. I mean my partner, Officer Keller, and I patrol this area. We were the first on the scene."

"It looks like you followed the book."

"We try, sir. I'm just sorry this had to happen on my watch. I think the alderman was a pretty good guy."

"Yes, he was," I replied as I watched him attend to a couple of children who were trying to get to the stairs. After a few minutes and after probably feeling a bit awkward, the officer asked, "It must be hard, huh, chief?"

"Yeah. I have to say I miss being in the middle of these investigations. I loved figuring out what happened and who might have done it, you know."

"I hear you. Damned if I would ever want to do what those guys are doing in there. I like walking my beat, talking to people, helpin'em feel safe. When something like this happens, I do my duty like now. But soon I'll head out and let people know that this was just a fluke and they shouldn't be afraid. You know, chief, I just want'em to know I got their backs."

"You're being a good cop. Nothing to be ashamed of."

Another young man I had never met stepped out into the hallway. He saw me standing nearby and walked over.

"May I help you?" He asked kindly, though I caught a bit of skepticism that gave way to an apparent bewilderment at seeing me.

"I'm Deputy Chief Perry Savant from downtown. I'm just checking to find out what I can do to help with the press outside. Any ID's on these people?"

"Sorry, Chief. I don't know much at all. Detective Lieutenant Browning keeps stuff like that close to the chest."

"That's fine. I don't think I caught your name?"

"Detective Junior Grade Miquel Chang."

"Oh?" I must have sounded bewildered.

"Yeah, I get a lot of that. Mom was Hispanic, and Dad was Chinese."

"How long you been on the force?"

"Five years. I made Detective about six months ago."

"Good for you, Miguel. If you don't mind, would you go back in there and see if Browning can talk to me?"

"Sure, Chief."

He walked back into the room as I waited maybe two minutes. Finally Browning came out, his eye brows furrowed over his well-tanned and wrinkled face. He looked at me shaking his head and spoke with some frustration.

"Hello, Chief. How'd you catch this one?"

"Just trying to keep the press at bay downstairs."

"Well, we've gotten a solid ID on the alderman. But we haven't a clue who the kid was."

"Kid?"

"Probably not even twenty, yet. He wasn't registered. The alderman signed in under an alias."

"An alias?" I queried.

"The manager downstairs says the alderman comes here often with some kid in tow; so, he lets him lie about his identity. Definitely didn't want anybody to know who he was with."

"Got it. Okay, I'll see what I can do to get rid of the mob outside. Oh, and, Browning, take your time. Do it up right. No screw ups anywhere on this one. Oh, and has anybody gone to contact his wife Betty?"

"No. You want that job?"

"Hell no. Betty hated my guts in high school. I don't want to bring that news to her."

"You went to school with the alderman?"

"Only knew him from afar. He didn't like hanging with us Italians. Betty was just like him. I think that's why they got married."

"I understand, man. We didn't get along with the Puerto Ricans on the East Side either."

"I'll let the commissioner know what's happened and see if he can get someone out to their house."

"Thanks, Chief. Oh, and go back to the office. You don't need to stay here any longer," he said as he turned away.

I walked back down the stairs and made my way over to where the press clustered together. Several of them yelled out my name. I stopped short of the police line.

"I still cannot confirm the identity of either of the victims at this point. Identification is in process as we speak. So, as soon as I get confirmation from the commissioner's office, I'll let you know. The detectives are still gathering evidence at the crime scene. The public affairs people will be here shortly. They'll handle briefings from here on."

I quickly turned away and walked back to my car. Once inside, I dialed the commissioner's office number and waited for his secretary to answer in that sensual voice she would use to impress people who called.

"Police Commissioner's office," she said.

"Is the commissioner in?" I asked.

"Oh, hi, Chief. No, he's down at Chief Heywood's office. I'll transfer you."

I heard the clicking as my call was being transferred. Chief of Police Departments Jonathan Haywood, my immediate boss.

Only a couple of seconds passed when I heard Heywood's sternly sounding voice.

"Perry, what's happening? How did you get there so fast?"

"You'd better put the Commissioner on the line."

A moment passed. I could hear a muffled conversation going on. The commissioner answered in that strictly business tone of his.

"Okay, Savant. What is it?"

"It's Alderman Rodriguez."

"Is it true that he was—"

"Yep. The kid wasn't even twenty. Peach fuzz, you know?"

"I know he liked that kind. But, I swear I thought he had stopped. I mean, Betty is going to have a cow."

"A cow?" I responded, "Naw. Total insane hysteria, my friend."

I heard the Commissioner laugh.

"I know. I'll take the chaplain out there with me. You don't have to worry about this one."

"I appreciate it."

"I'm sure she's expected something like this might happen someday. But no one expects something like..."

"Wait a sec, Chief," I interrupted. "I see the coroner bringing the bodies out of the building, so you might want to offer to take her to the morgue for a final ID. Give me a call and let me know if she does. I can throw some red meat to these press vultures out here."

"We'll take care of that," the chief said. "You get back here now. The Public Affairs people should be there any minute. And they'll be pretty upset about you being there doing their job."

"But I thought it would be good for you to have a personal representative here given the fact that an Alderman had died."

"Damn, Savant. You should have cleared it with me before you just showed up. We'll talk about this later."

He hung up the phone.

Me? I just sat back in my car seat and did some sweating. It was 97 degrees in the city. July can be brutal. I felt appreciative of having parked my car in the shade of a fifteen-story building.

At that moment I saw Detective Chang headed for his car. So, I jumped out and stopped him.

"Detective! A few more questions, please."

"Sure, Chief. What do you need?"

"How's it going in there?"

"It seems that they were shot while they were in bed; one bullet each to the head."

"Has Browning left yet?"

"No, Sir."

"Good. Go back inside and tell him that the alderman's wife will be at the morgue in about an hour. Maybe he should be there, too. He can fill in the Chief of Departments on the details. He'll be escorting her there."

"Wow," he said. "The Big Chief himself. Man. That would be cool to get to meet him. I'll give Detective Browning that message right away."

He rushed back toward the hotel and disappeared inside. That's when I knew my work there was done. Out of the corner of my eye, I saw the P.R. people arriving. So, I slipped quickly over to my car and left to go back to my office.

After thinking it through, I could see nothing wrong with what I did or said to anyone. But this news writer seemed to put a totally different spin on the events. I sat in wonderment as to just what I did that was so bad as to accuse me of interfering with an investigation.

I stood up, paid my check at the counter, and walked next door to my apartment. After showering and dressing, I headed down to the parking garage where I got in my cruiser. I took my time as I drove down to the south end of Manhattan to One Police Plaza. There I pulled into my reserved spot in the lower garage and headed up to my office.

As I walked in, Jonathan Haywood called out to me to come into his office.

"What the hell happened, Savant? I thought you had things under control?"

"What are you talking about?" I asked.

"How did the press get all the details of the deaths? My god, Perry, Betty had already gotten three calls from reporters and friends in the city government before the chaplain and I arrived to deliver the news. This is a total disaster!"

"I haven't a clue about that. Let me see what I can find out."

"You do that," he said in a dismissive voice.

I paused. He didn't look up, so I walked out.

Back in my office, I shut the door hoping no one would come in. I called one of the reporters that I knew who was there.

"Jamal Francis, may I help you?" came a cheerful, youthful voice.

"Jamal! My friend. Perry Savant here."

There was silence on the other end. Jamal's voice became hyper cautious.

"Oh. Hello, Chief. What can I do for you?"

"Well, for one thing, you can tell me the source of that story I read this morning."

"You're not asking me to do that, are you, Chief?"

"Well, yes I am. And my reason is simple. Everything that person said was a lie. I haven't had a thing to do with the alderman in nearly thirty years. We went to the same high school. But, he moved to The Bronx the summer after our sophomore year. I haven't seen him since."

"Okay, Chief. That's your side of the story. But, everyone in the press pool last night was wondering why you were there. You're not with Public Relations. Why you? This source made the whole thing make sense. The source said you were attempting to cover up the facts that your friend was having sex with teenage boys."

"I had no clue what was going on."

"You're trying to tell me that you just happened to be there by pure coincidence?"

"That's exactly what I'm saying. Everything you were told was speculation and BS. No truth at all."

"Well, I appreciate your call. I'll talk to my editor about this."

"Jamal, I've always been fair with you. I've even slipped you a tip or two along the way. So, if you should find your way..."

"I hear you, man. I'll ... I'll see what I can do."

He hung up.

I sat still for several minutes. I felt a slight shiver slide down my back. I looked through the glass door of my office. Two people on my staff were staring; they turned and walked out of my sight. I could tell they were talking about the story in the paper.

By now, just about everyone in the department believed the lies and distortions as probably true. And no one would hear my side. In the depths of my stomach, I just knew that my future with the NYPD was in jeopardy.

CHAPTER TWO

Sunny Isles, Florida, can hardly be called a city. Located on the same island as Miami Beach, it's little more than a couple-mile stretch of State Road A1A also known as the Intra-Coastal Highway.

This is one of those places where the population enjoys the convenience of living near the ocean. But, they are far from being in the middle of the fame and publicity of South Beach or downtown Miami.

Along the east side of the island town, condominiums climb into the sun-filled skies of South Florida. On the west side, a few hotels share the main road with numerous businesses of every kind. These shops make buying necessities convenient for the people who live in this up-scaled bedroom community northeast of Miami.

One of the tallest buildings along A1A is the Trump Tower Condominiums. That location has some of the most expensive steel-girder real estate in the entire nation. And despite all the rich and famous that visit or reside on this boulevard, Barry G, a homeless Vietnam Veteran, passed by the Trump-built condos every day as he made his way up Florida's most famous street. During the day, he begged for a handout or rummaged through the trash. At night he would slept in special hiding places.

First thing in the morning he would normally make his way to the Burger King across the street from the Trump Towers and buy a cup of coffee. If he had a successful day collecting change the day before, he would add a breakfast sandwich to his regimen. He would sit near the front and dream of the day he might own one of the expensive penthouse apartments at the top of the towers.

He was the third son of immigrants from the Castro revolution. Born in Havana near the end of 1952, his family fled the island for the United States after the Castro's took over in 1959. The Cubans settled down with many of their relatives and friends in a community west of Miami that came to be known as Little Havana.

Barry was fully Americanized by the time he graduated from high school. When he turned eighteen, he joined the army. After boot camp, he attended ranger school and scout training. He spent two tours in Vietnam. Now, in his mid-sixties, his drinking had taken its toll on both his body and his mind.

Barry G was the name that came to mind some ten years earlier when he woke up in a charity hospital in Boston. He had no memory of what he had been doing or even who he was. After his discharge from the hospital, he fled to Miami not because he remembered he had family there but because he hated the chilly winter in New England. His emaciated body suffered from a life of hard drinking and demanding work.

It took him about a year to figure out a route for his daily begging and sleeping so that he could avoid the police patrols. He would work his way across Sunny Isles Boulevard to A1A and north to NE 192nd Street. He would turn west to US Highway One and south to Sunny Isles and back to A1A, a route of about six miles total.

He walked that route as if it were his professional duty. He felt committed to that task as any full-time professional responsible for the lives of the people who worked and lived along there. He believed it was his job to make sure everything was okay along those streets. He would pick up the trash thrown from the shiny new convertibles that carted youthful looking children around like royalty.

It was a Wednesday, usually a poor day for handouts in the area; but it turned out to be one of Barry's best days ever. At least that was what he thought. A guy in a yellow Camaro handed him a ten-dollar bill.

He took the money to a local liquor store and traded it for a half-gallon of cheap wine. He hid it in his back pack until he could be alone and not feel compelled to share it with anyone else.

Later that evening, he found a shady spot behind a small strip-mall near Town Center Park. There he settled down for a nice quiet evening of drunken pleasure provided by the bottle of warmth. Around 11:00 pm, he awoke to realize he had passed out under the tree where he had settled down to drink.

Although unsteady, he pulled himself up onto his feet and relieved himself on the tree where he had been sleeping. After that he walked over to a place near a trash bin out of sight of the normal travel lanes of the local police and laid down with plans to spend the night there.

Even though this was not one of his regular bedding down spots, he felt the courage provided by the wine, and he drifted off into a total drunken stupor.

At about 2:00 am, he was awakened by a car driving through the alley. He stood up and stepped out from behind the trash bin that had shielded him from the breeze coming in off the ocean.

He looked around but could see nothing, so he walked behind a couple of bushes and relieved himself again. As he zipped up his pants, he turned back and walked toward the trash bins.

He stopped by another tree when he saw two large headlights meet him like the flaming eyes of a bull ready to charge. He stood paralyzed for a couple of seconds as the car speeded up and hit him, pinning him against the tree.

The car backed up allowing Barry to drop to the ground. The car wheels turned, and the vehicle seemed to be driving off when the right front tires swerved and rolled right over his head. The big, black automobile stopped, backed up crushing Barry's head as it rolled over him again.

A figure dressed in black stepped out of the car, bent over, and looked at the body that lay near the front wheels. The person's eyes stared at the disfigured face for what could have been more than a minute. The figure dragged the body to the wall of the building and left it there. The driver got back into the car, revved the engine, and drove off.

At seven in the morning a garbage truck pulled up to one of the trash bins in the ally. As the long metal arms from the truck raised the steel container from the ground to the top of the truck, the driver saw a horrible sight.

There on the pavement of the driveway behind the small pizzeria was the body of a male that appeared to be one of the homeless of the area.

The driver slowly opened the door to his truck and stepped out. He walked over to where the body lay. When he saw the blood and badly damaged head, he stepped back in shock.

"Damn!" He said as he pulled out a cell phone and dialed 911.

# # #

Newly donned Detective Junior Grade DeShawn Royce arrived at the crime scene to investigate. The initial reports indicated a possible accident. When he arrived, the coroner was just finishing up with the body. Royce unzipped the black bag and looked at the battered and bruised figure. Blood had soaked the dirty clothing.

The officer looked at the man's hands and saw nothing unusual. He looked at the man's face and noticed an unusual impression on one side.

He asked the coroner's assistant handling the pickup to look at the impressions and tell him what he thought they were.

"Officer, I'm only an assistant. I'm not authorized to give an opinion on anything here."

"I know that. I'm not asking for a professional analysis. Just your opinion. You know, just checking out my own gut reaction."

The young man stared at the face of the victim. He pointed to the impressions on the man's face.

"I don't know what that is."

"Was there any ID?"

"No, sir. His pockets were empty."

"Well, I'll identify him for you," said Royce. "He's known as Barry G. No last name that I'm aware of. Anyway, I think he has relatives over in Little Havana."

"Thank you, sir. I'll make a note of that."

Royce pulled his cellphone and took several pictures of the man's face,

photographing both sides and from the front.

"You can take the body," Royce said.

The coroner's assistant closed the back door to the van, got in on the driver's side, and drove off.

Royce spent more than an hour going over every possible inch of the area to make sure he had gathered everything he thought was important. He called it in as a possible homicide.

The shift captain responded less than ten minutes later.

"I looked at what you sent in, Royce. But, I still think you should mark it up as an accident."

"Sir, I know I'm new at all this, but the marking on this guy's face just doesn't seem right to be there. It looks like someone drove over his head after he was dead or unconscious. I mean, there was no blood on the skull; only around his waist."

"You'd better be sure about this, Royce. We don't want to make a fuss over some poor old homeless man who gets run over because he went to sleep in the wrong place."

"I understand, Sir. But, this man is not just an old homeless man, he's a Vietnam War veteran. He used to visit the homeless shelter in Overtown where I volunteered a while back. Yes, he did have his problems. But I knew him to be safe about where he slept."

"I don't know, Royce. I mean you're new to detective work. You haven't even been promoted, yet. Do you want to screw things up with this?"

"I'd feel better, Captain, if I could get someone else to look at this for me and see if I'm right or wrong."

"Okay, Royce. But remember this. If the chief comes down on us, I'm blaming you for everything, you hear?"

"Yes sir. I'll take it on the chin."

"Okay. You need to call Miami-Dade's detective division to get one of their people to look at what you've got. If they say 'no' then you gotta drop it, okay?"

"No problem, chief. Thanks."

When he called the Sheriff's office, he was transferred to Adolph Sanchez, the Chief of Detectives, who told Royce that the incident sure sounded like a typical hit and run to him.

"But if you feel so strongly about it," Sanchez growled, "you should call FDLE and ask them to investigate. I believe they're the next in line to support you in a case such as this."

Royce thanked the chief and called the number to the local office of the Florida Department of Law Enforcement. Laura Taylor, the supervisory agent in charge, answered his call. He briefed her on the unique features of the death.

"I have to say," Royce admitted. "My captain and Chief Sanchez both believe that this is a simple case of a hit and run.

The evidence I've gathered just doesn't add up to an accidental death by a driver who didn't see the man in the alley."

"Okay, explain it to me in such a way that I can see it from your perspective," Agent Taylor replied.

"Well, his injuries are consistent with being hit while standing; you know, blood all around his middle. Also, the injury to me seems to indicate that he was caught against something hard. And there's blood on a tree in the approximate location of where he would have been standing just a few feet away from where we found him."

"Hmm," said Taylor under her breath.

"And there's the fact that the body was stuffed behind a garbage bin. Someone tried to hide the body. Also, a car may have been sitting close to where the body was found. I'm not sure, of course, but it looks like a tail pipe blew exhaust down onto the grass."

"Mighty slim pickings there, detective."

"Actually, it's patrolman. I'm not a full detective yet. I just finished taking the course and test for detective. I haven't been officially designated as such."

"Well, almost detective patrolman Royce, do you have any evidence that you could give me that would convince me that this may be more than an accident?"

"Well, there are the markings on his face."

"Markings?"

"There were some impressions that look like tire treads on one side of his face. And it appeared like there were two different impressions like he had been run over twice. Oh, and I believe that it happened post-mortem."

"Send me pictures as soon as we hang up."

"Okay. So, one other thing. I've done some volunteer work with a homeless shelter in Overtown. I remember seeing this guy there. Anyway, I'd like to find out for sure that this is an accident; you know, for his sake?"

"Okay. I'll have one of my investigators meet you there within the next hour. I'll transfer you to the dispatcher. Give her the address and directions when we hang up."

"I will."

"And, Royce?"

"Yes?"

"Good job. I appreciate the fact that you're looking out for the people in your neighborhood. And some day, I've just got to hear how you made it from Overtown to the Sunny Isles Beach Police Department."

"I look forward to meeting you as well, ma'am."

Royce gave the information to the dispatcher, got into his car, and sat back to wait for the FDLE agent to arrive.

CHAPTER THREE

Carolina Brown, an attractive, light-skinned African-American woman in her late thirties, sat at her desk in the Southern District office of the Florida Department of Law Enforcement.

She was finishing up the paperwork on a recent case file. It involved a suspect who had just been convicted of kidnapping and killing his own children.

The case was draining leaving her exhausted and ready for some time off. She was looking forward to a week's vacation which was to start as she got off work on Friday afternoon.

The phone rang on her desk. She looked at the small screen on the set and saw that it was Laura Taylor calling her. Whenever Laura called, Carolina could expect another case to hit her desk. So, she answered the phone without much enthusiasm. "Hello, Laura."

"Carolina, I need you to run over to Sunny Isles Beach and see what's happened."

"Why doesn't Miami-Dade take the case? I would think it was their jurisdiction."

"They called Sanchez first, but he had them call us."

"Sounds like Sanchez dodging another political bullet."

"Could be; but I don't know."

"What is it?"

"I'm not sure. Something about a homeless man being run down by a car, I think. I believe what he said was run over and over or something like that."

"What's that supposed to mean?"

"I don't know, Carolina. Just get over there and see what's going on."

"Laura, Please! I'm leaving on vacation Friday. You know that. Can't you get someone else?"

"No one is available. Besides, there's probably nothing. I mean, Sanchez wouldn't have passed it off to us if there was any possibility that it would be a high-profile case."

"I can't believe this …"

"Hey! You're wasting time."

"I'm gone, Captain."

Carolina rarely used the title "Captain" except when she was miffed at the assignment she was given. This wasn't the first time Sanchez had dumped an impossible crime into their laps.

Less than a year had passed since Sanchez talked Taylor into a possible death by drowning. It ended up being a major hate crime of a gay couple who bought a residence in a high-end, exclusive, Roman Catholic neighborhood.

She believed that if Sanchez figured that a case would be a political nightmare, he would get FDLE involved and blame the problems they would run into on their inefficiency and bureaucratic red tape.

He was the one always making the sheriff look good to the county commissioners. She just knew that one-day Sanchez was planning to undercut his boss and run for Sheriff.

So as Carolina arrived at the strip mall on A1A, the Crime Scene investigators and the coroner's people had already left. One lone patrolman stood guard over the scene which was taped off with the recognizable yellow "POLICE DO NOT CROSS" plastic bands.

Carolina turned off the ignition and opened the door. As she carefully removed herself from the plastic seat that had stuck to the back of her thighs, she looked over at the patrolman and sighed.

"This is going to be a wasted trip."

She noticed a young African-American man sitting in a police cruiser from the Sunny Isles police department.

She walked over to the car and flipped out a badge.

"Okay, I'm detective Brown from FDLE. I guess you're going to brief me on this case?"

The twenty-seven-year-old patrolman and almost detective had completed two years with the local department after graduating from the Miami-Dade College police academy.

Brought up in the projects of the city's Overtown district, DeShawn Royce looked intently at the long-legged and stunningly attractive woman standing next to his car. He reached out his hand with an attempt at being professional.

"I'm Patrolman Royce, and you're a good detective. I'm the one to brief you."

"Wipe that silly grin off your black-face, boy, and get at it."

Red-faced, Royce turned away, opened the car door, and stepped out. He pointed to the area where the trash bins were located.

"Over there is where the trash collector found the victim."

She stood there for a moment letting a long breath out of her nose.

"You just going to point, or are you going to take me over there and show me?"

"Right," he stuttered nervously led the way to where two trash bins had been separated and were sitting catty-cornered from each other.

"Right here."

"Had the body been tampered with in any way?"

"I don't think so, I mean, I'm not sure."

"What do you know?"

"A Waste Management team found the man when they emptied the bin in front of him. One of our rolling patrols responded to the call within about two or three minutes. The officer said he left everything like he found it and immediately cordoned off the place while he waited for the rest of the investigative team to arrive."

"You people sure made a mess out of the crime scene, didn't you?"

"I'm afraid that the others didn't take this man's death as seriously as I did. I'm sure they were thinking, what's another dead homeless man in this uppity white neighborhood, anyway? You know?"

"So, why did you call me?" she asked.

"Well," the detective drawled. "You see, when we were checking him out, I noticed he had tire marks on his face, like, it seemed to me from two different directions?"

"Are you saying that somebody ran over the guy a couple of times then stuffed his body behind a trash container?"

"That's what I thought. I mean, I almost got sick when I saw how he looked. Anyway, I figured it wasn't simply some old man that crawled up behind some garbage cans and died."

"Ya think?"

"Well, I mean, I thought, well it seemed to me--"

"Right. Okay. Who's the lead detective on this?"

"Um, I guess I am."

She stood silent. Her eyes narrowed.

Royce shifted from one hip to the other as he looked down at the ground.

"Look," Detective Brown said, "There's nothing here that requires FDLE's involvement. This is a local matter. If you can't handle it, call Chief Sanchez at Miami-Dade. They're your backup on matters such as this."

She turned away as Royce pulled out a card from his shirt pocket and handed it to her.

"Please call me if you hear anything that might pertain to this."

She turned back to him, took the card, shook her head slowly, and walked back to her car. She put the key in the ignition. She smiled. He seemed cuter than she had thought originally. She drove off.

The lone patrolman who had been helping keep the scene free of spectators scratched his head and cleared his throat.

"What was that all about?" he said. "She got a problem with you or something?"

"How would I know, Charlie?"

He turned and walked back to his own car, opened the door and got in. As he turned the key and the engine turned over loudly, he whispered quietly and under his breath, "Witch."

CHAPTER FOUR

At about two in the morning, Hard-luck Harry, as he was known to the other street people, was walking through one of the alleys near A1A checking out the various garbage cans and bins for something he might be able to salvage.

He hated pushing a grocery cart. Several months earlier he found a perfectly good back-pack sitting by a garbage can in a nice residential area. He took it and began to collect things that might help him out.

He had an old blanket someone had thrown away as well as a rather scratchy sweater that he found hanging on a gate next to several trash containers. He figured that if the people wanted the sweater, they would have come out and gotten it off the gate instead of leaving it there for anyone who came along.

He had also found a sturdy metal drinking cup with a top still intact which he would use to get free coffee from the manager at the Food Mart.

Harry continued walking along the alley for a while. When it ended he walked over to A1A and headed north to 192nd St. He thought he might find a nice warm spot under the bridge for the night with some of the regulars who stopped there to catch a few hours of sleep before the Sunny Isles police came by to run them off.

While he walked on the sidewalk, he could hear and see the cars as they passed. After several minutes, he felt a churning deep in his stomach. He thought a car seemed to be following him. He turned around and saw nothing.

The lights from the Golden Nugget Hotel sent an eerie glow down onto the highway helping him to see the street better than he would under the streetlights.

He paused for several moments and turned back around thinking that perhaps he must be imagining things that weren't there. But the dark sedan that was following him had turned off at 186th Street before he turned around.

The sedan moved along Atlantic in the darkness to 196th Street and stopped where the driver could see Harry. The headlights went off and the motor died as the sedan sat waiting, patient, quiet, for its next prey.

Harry walked further north along A1A convinced that nothing was wrong. He began to hum a tune as he headed for the bridge and the quiet place where he could get some sleep. As he stepped out to cross 196th, he heard a car screeching toward him.

Just as the car reached him, it slowed down just enough to strike Harry, knocking him with a thud to the pavement.

The car backed up and ran over Harry again. He lay huddled behind his back-pack hoping it would protect him from another assault. The car backed up, ran over him, and over him again, and again, and stopped.

The driver opened the door, walked back to where Harry was lying and kicked him several times.

After a moment or two, the driver looked around, walked back to the car, got in, and drove off toward the south. Harry let out the breath he was holding. He knew he was hurt bad because he could feel the pain in his legs, arms, and pelvis.

He could not move.

He attempted to pull himself to the side of the road. But he had no strength in his arms. He could feel the tears rolling down his face and across the bridge of his nose, to the ground below. After a few minutes, he lost consciousness.

At around 4:30 am, Marvin Mendelbaum left his house to do his morning run when he was stopped by what he thought might be a dark colored dog lying on the pavement near the end of the street.

So, he walked the half-block to see what he could do to help. That's when he discovered what he thought was an animal was a man grasping a back-pack in his arms.

He reached down and felt the man's pulse. He pulled out his cell phone and called 911. Within just a couple of minutes, an ambulance arrived, followed by two police cars.

A Sunny Isles Police officer got out of the first cruiser, walked over to the man on the ground and noticed right away several peculiar marks on the man's face. He ran back to his car and called the dispatcher.

"Better send Royce. I think we have another murdered homeless man."

CHAPTER FIVE

The hallway in front of the NYPD Commissioner's office is the best decorated and cleanest of all the halls inside the big, ugly, cubic building at the south end of Manhattan.

Since my promotion to Deputy Chief of Departments and Chief of all NYPD Detectives, I'd been here for so many reasons I had lost count. But, today was different. On this day, I was summoned by the Commissioner himself.

My stomach churned inside me like it was being run through a meat grinder. Although I had been a frequent visitor to the Commissioner's office during my tenure in this administrative torture chamber, there was something different about this summons.

I could even hear it in the receptionist's voice. This was not about some case that needed my special attention or even an issue with one of the detectives under my command. At least that's what I inferred from the tone of her voice.

When I needed to be a part of a meeting with the Commissioner, I would get a head's up from my immediate boss, Chief Haywood. And the protocol was to meet at his office down the hall.

We would make our way to the commissioner's office. But, not this time. So here I stood with my heart beating so hard in my chest I could swear people could see it beating.

My thoughts raced as I reached out to pull on the door handle: How bad can this be? It's probably nothing at all. I mean, I haven't broken any rules. I've stayed within the parameters of protocol.

What's the worst that could happen, getting fired? I've got a solid career with nothing negative. And I'm a third-generation NYPD cop.

Feeling a little better, I took a deep breath and opened the oversized wooden door with the title "Commissioner" emblazoned on it.

In the outer office, Dorothy, the attractive receptionist in her late-thirties, looked up with a smile.

"Have a seat, Chief. I'll let the Commissioner know you're here."

She stood and walked into the next office, closing the door behind her. Several minutes passed before she returned. It felt like an hour. When the door opened maybe three minutes later, she stood to the side and held it open.

She looked at me and smiled as she said, "You may go in." As I walked past her, I noticed that the smile disappeared.

Inside the office I stopped just short of the commissioner's desk. At that moment, I was unaware of what faced me from the other side of the massive oak desk that dominated the top cop's large office overlooking the East River.

The commissioner did not delay.

"Perry, you've done an excellent job for twenty-five years. And your boss and I have agreed that it's time for you to retire. You've done more than anyone could have ever expected. And you have served the people of New York in an exemplary fashion. I for one can say it has been a privilege to have served with you and known you for these many years."

"Thank you for that vote of confidence, Commissioner. But, I expected to be working here for another five years. May I ask why you want me to retire now?"

"I'm sure you know."

My stomach hurt like it did when I stupidly ate some bad ham and Swiss on a dare. I gazed hard at the man I had known since we were children. We even went to the police academy together becoming good friends and colleagues. Now this friend sat in the chair behind the boss's desk.

No matter how much I tried, I just couldn't make any sense out of what had just happened. I was being forced out! And over such a trivial thing as the word of a total scum-bag.

And that desk! It seemed to stand between us like a vast desert devoid of items except for a small name plate that seemed to brag the engraved words: Nathan O'Hara, Police Commissioner; and you're not. As I stood, all I could think was, *Who the hell works at an empty desk?*

And sitting in the chair on the commissioner's left was my mentor, a man I had admired and who was now my immediate boss. My blood seemed to be boiling. But I stood there with lips tight, eyes narrowing, my gaze focused on the commissioner. I didn't say a word.

I stood motionless as the sickening thought overwhelmed me that my successful, decorated, twenty-five-year career as one of New York's finest had ended with one simple statement from a loser in the Bronx. And it didn't make any sense.

I knew that loser. We were in the eighth grade together. I wondered why he told the press that I tried to protect a murdered alderman because I was gay too? And the press never investigated the allegations? Why investigate? The story would sell papers!

My mind swirled with questions such as: What am I going to do now? I'm only forty-four! Where do I go? How do I keep myself occupied? How do I protect myself from the thousands of criminals I put in prison?

And with no family to speak of and few friends, other than those on the job, I knew my future was bleak at best.

I noticed out of the corner of my eye, a mirror offering me a profile view of a man much older than I visualized myself as being. The lids on my deep-set steel-blue eyes quivered as my balding head glowed with what I knew had to be fire red.

For a moment, I contemplated the possible ramifications of simply pulling out my service piece and shooting the commissioner between the eyes.

In a moment of what I now think had to be incredible inspiration, perhaps like that of the mind of some ancient literary genius, I realized I had finally been set free. I could now pursue my own dreams. I no longer needed to do what I was always expected to do.

Since my father had passed away three years earlier, I felt … relieved. Now I won't have to face my old man and tell him about what had just happened.

A sudden movement in the mirror brought me back to reality as I saw Police Commissioner O'Hara looking down rubbing his hands together. He looked over at the chief then to me.

"I'm sorry about all this," he said. "I mean, I didn't believe you were gay. It wouldn't have mattered to me at all; really. But--"

He paused for several moments. I wondered if perhaps he was waiting for me to say something. The commissioner continued.

"But, come on, Perry! Inserting yourself into an investigation? You should have come to me before approaching the guys investigating the alderman's death. I mean, I didn't even know he was gay, not that it would have mattered to me. But with the way things have been since 9-11, and with the don't ask don't tell policy; I mean, if it were up to me, well, I mean, it doesn't matter to me you know."

My thoughts raced in a hundred different directions at once. How could this man say to me 'not that it matters to me?'

It always matters. The only clarity was in the few questions I wanted to ask the commissioner.

Questions like: how many times are you going to say, 'I'm sorry'? Why do you need my forgiveness for a decision you made? What difference was it going to make politically to anybody if I got my ass kicked out? Why should I care what you think about this if it doesn't matter to you?

All I wanted to do was reach across that desk, grab the commissioner by the throat and tell my 'old friend' to just shut up, say good-bye, and do something to himself that was physically impossible.

But instead, I reached into my pocket, took out the keys to the executive cruiser, pulled the badge and ID out of my inside coat pocket, took the holstered Glock from my belt, and laid them all on the desk.

As the biting pain of disappointment flowed through my body and caused a slight tremor, I looked hard into the commissioner's almost colorless and expressionless eyes. With those words 'not that it matters to me' ringing in my mind,

I turned my back on my two oldest friends and walked out through the office door and breezed past the secretary into the hallway.

The irony did not escape me that during the past five years whenever I would come to the commissioner's office, Dorothy would throw a flirting smile my way. This time, she kept her eyes fixed upon the book in her hands. Today there would be no smile, no flirt, not even a brief glance ... nothing.

I stopped in the hall as I heard the door close behind me. My body shivered as if a cold breeze hit me. I paused a moment and took a deep breath. I pulled my shoulders back and walked the twenty-five steps to the elevator.

When the doors parted, I got in, and rode down to the main floor. As I stepped from the small carriage, I turned right and stopped to look at the wall of fallen heroes.

Many of the men whose pictures were part of that memorial wall I had known. I had even worked with many of them side-by-side. My eye was drawn to the names of three men from my old precinct in Brooklyn.

Most of the men and women on the wall I did not know, yet I felt a kinship with them. I couldn't help but wonder if there shouldn't be a wall for heroes the department had screwed over the years; but I knew that would never happen.

Police departments don't easily admit to their mistakes. Nothing in it for them.

After standing there for several minutes in a posture of quiet reflection, I took another deep breath and walked out the front doors onto the large portico in front of One Police Plaza for the last time.

CHAPTER SIX

Exiting the front entrance to the police headquarters was a bit strange since I always entered and exited through the secure entrance that led to the parking garage below the building. But today I had to use the front entrance since I no longer held the credentials to allow me passage through the other doors.

Now I was just another civilian leaving the police station disappointed at how I had been treated by the officers inside. As I bypassed the screening gates that the public entered through, I could identify with those people who felt so disappointed over the years whenever I had been the one to say, "I'm sorry, but there's nothing we can do at this time. We'll call you if we have anything to report."

As I stepped into the bright sunlight I stopped to take my black generic sun glasses out of my suit coat pocket and place them over my eyes. I paused. I looked up toward the commissioner's office. Now I felt rejected ... deserted ... lost.

That's when I caught a glimpse of myself in the front windows: six-foot-two, a hundred and ninety pounds, dark suit, and dark tie. I smiled as I noticed why it was that people could spot a cop so easily.

You didn't need a uniform to be pegged in this town. All you needed was a cheap suit and tie, a well-worn white shirt, and cheap shoes.

With a sigh and a lingering feeling of rejection, I walked toward the parking lot to get my car when I stopped dead cold in my tracks. That beautiful, shiny, black, Crown Vic I drove every day? It was no longer mine to use. It belonged to the NYPD.

Standing in front of the police headquarters, I chuckled as I realized that I had thought the car was mine. I felt silly knowing I had fallen into the same trap that so many city workers fall into when given a car to take home.

A smile creeped across my face as I realized I had never owned a car. There was no need since the department issued one for me to use. At my promotion to detective, I was no longer considered a simple beat cop. Before that, I would take the bus, the subway, or just walk down the street to the station where I had worked when I started my career. Yet, I wondered just how it would feel to have a car that was mine and no one else's; one that I picked out for myself.

With a smile, I walked out to the street and hailed one of the cabs sitting nearby.

"Where to, buddy?" the cabby asked as the window on the passenger side slid to the open position.

"I, uh, oh. Wait a sec. Let me see," I felt embarrassment as I stumbled on my own words. I quietly pulled out my wallet to look at my driver's license for the address of my apartment. I laughed.

Even though I could easily wheel through the traffic right to where I live, I made it a habit of never giving anyone that vital piece of information. So, it was never implanted in the front of my mind.

Working to speak in a calm voice, I recited the address to the cabby and sat back in the faux leather back seat. I now understood why people would talk about how uncomfortable the back seat of a car was; especially a New York City Cab.

I shook off that thought as a hundred different feelings and thoughts popped into my mind, all of which made me want to scream bloody murder. But, I reminded myself that yelling such a thing might not be a clever idea inside of a cab.

I turned my attention to thinking about just how one little two-bit crook could spread a vicious rumor and be believed with no solid evidence. And do it in such a way that it would ruin another man's life. The possible answer to that question eluded my logical brain.

And the national newspapers, for God's sake, had published the rumor as fact. The Attorney General deposed the liar who swore it was true. And all this was done without my knowledge. Not one of the people involved talked to me about it. I was informed by a friend I knew in the AG's office after the investigation was completed.

Oh, there was the issue of inserting myself into an investigation of an alderman over in Brooklyn. I didn't do that; all I did was volunteer to help with the press until the PR people arrived.

I went over every detail of that day and could not find a single moment when I could be accused of interfering. All I ever did was attend the same school for two years that the Alderman attended.

Okay, so the murdered alderman was found in a compromising situation in a low-cost flop-house. And he was with a teenage boy, in bed, and naked. They had both been shot with a single tap to the head. I should have known that an inexperienced, young detective would wonder why the Chief of Detectives, a friend of the Alderman, was up to by showing up at the crime scene.

Of course, I was attempting to influence the investigation. I couldn't see it from the young man's perspective at that time. But that still didn't make what the kid did right by making a federal case out of it. And saying that the Chief of Detectives downtown was looking over his shoulder was an outright lie.

But, I still couldn't blame the detective captain at the precinct for being royally pissed off. I probably would have done the same thing if it had been me.

But of all the people in the city to believe the lies in the paper or believe I would interfere with an investigation, why the commissioner? Why would he believe it without ever talking to me directly about it? We had grown up in the same neighborhood.

We were just two Irish "Micks" in the predominantly Jewish section of Park Slope. We fought together, side-by-side, to make it.

But why no formal investigation, no deposition of witnesses, no formal inquiry? Just an inquisition of one irrelevant cop who had now become a political liability.

I just couldn't grasp what it all meant and why it happened so fast? Yet, politics being what it is, I knew my friend had little or no choice in the matter. His good friend had become an embarrassment to the department and therefore to the commissioner himself.

I also knew the two of us could have joined forces and fought the spurious charges and probably beaten them. But, I also knew the doubts and loss of trust would never be recovered. The commissioner might have lost his job before the next mayoral elections.

So, I sat in the cab with my blood pressure rising and my finger nails digging into my thighs. All I could do was think of how much I would relish the opportunity to strangle someone. As usual I shoved that feeling out of my mind. It was just an urge, not an action requiring initiation.

In a flash of unusual revelation, I felt a different urge: I needed to do something rash. No, spontaneous: a once in a lifetime event. The thought was freighting. My heart pounded hard against my chest. I could feel the goose-bumps fill my entire body as I continued to entertain the thought.

I never was what you would call a spontaneous person. I also was not a tough guy or ruffian. But, I wasn't soft either. In high school, I was a late bloomer. When all the other guys my age were going through the early stages of puberty, I wasn't.

In the ninth-grade gymnasium locker room I often felt embarrassed because I didn't have hair where many of the other guys were growing it. I thought that there might be something wrong with me. Sometimes I entertained the thought that I was not normal like the other boys.

Mother tried to reassure me that every person matures at a different rate. She would often say, "You'll become a man just like all your other friends. Besides, there's no need to be in such a big hurry to grow up." Those words didn't comfort me.

Dad, on the other hand, offered his own style of sage advice. He would say, 'Buck up, kid. You'll be a man one day just like your mother said. And you sure as hell don't want to be jealous of those idiots you run around with.'

I often wondered why it was that whenever adults talk to children they always say, 'One day you'll figure it out.' Why not just tell them the truth and help them? If I was old enough to understand plane geometry, why wasn't I old enough to understand why my body was slow in maturing?

But, again, I was now in my mid-forties and still unmarried with no children; what could I know about it?

I waited. Now I understand. But, of course, that didn't happen until after I had been brutally teased by the other boys in the gym class. The memories of the gymnasium at the old school flooded my mind. I shivered slightly as I remembered how that building was so typical for that day: no insulation and a ten-foot tall ceiling.

It seemed that I could still hear the laughter from the other kids as it resounded over and over in the air. Laughter haunted my ears and my head as I would run outside trying to get away.

Agony gripped my body as again I grabbed my thighs with the same vice grip I had learned in self-defense classes.

Something inside prevented me from pouncing on those boys and beating them to a bloody pulp. I knew that if I did I'd be the one to get into trouble. And those guys? Well, they would get away with persecuting me. So, I walked away holding back the tears that were welling up.

Now the back seat of this cab seemed more uncomfortable as I thought about how many times I had wanted to drop all inhibitions and just do something out of character for once.

I know I'm a straight-laced company man who had the responsibility to enforce society's rules and laws. I also know that in the end I would never carry out a single impulse.

Yet, I shifted on the cold leather seat as I remembered I never seemed to have the guts to be impulsive. Here sat a man who could run toward a gun fight without hesitation or dive into a burning car to save someone inside.

This guy sitting here could even shoot at the bad guys with little or no fear for himself. But, to do something just because I wanted to and not because I was supposed to? Well that would never happen. Yet I wondered: "Why not?"

"Why not what?" the cabby answered back.

"Oh, uh, nothing. No. Yes. Is there a Mercedes dealership near here?"

The Cabby had weaved his way through lower Manhattan and was headed north on Fourth Avenue just passing East Fourth Street.

"Yeah. I think there's one close to where you live. It's up ahead on Park. You want I should swing by there?"

"No. Yes! No. Drop me off there instead of my apartment."

"You got it, Buddy," he mumbled as he continued up Fourth Avenue another three blocks and merged onto Park Avenue South.

As the cabby drove the forty-something blocks to the Manhattan Mercedes Dealership, I sat back with a deep feeling of relief. I had done something impulsive. Deep down inside I felt something I hadn't felt in years. I felt excited, thrilled, nervous, delighted, and apprehensive all at once. The thought of buying a new car was scary. I had never done that before. I never needed to.

As the blocks flew by, I thought of every probable reason NOT to buy a new car, especially a Mercedes. I twitched and felt the power of the centrifugal force pulling me against the car door as the cabby made a U-turn at Fifty-Sixth Street. He stopped in front of the Mercedes dealership. I opened the door to get out.

"You want I should wait?" The cabbie asked.

"Naw," I replied as I handed the driver a hundred and said something I rarely ever said: "Keep the change."

I shut the cab door and turned toward the large glass window of the dealership.

The Cabby's face glowed like an over-charged flash bulb.

"Wow, Mister. Thank you."

He drove off with tires squealing for about ten yards.

Me? I looked through the clean glass window and stared at a brand new shiny black S-Class four-door sedan. I stood there staring at the car for several moments and walked into the showroom. I walked past several other cars as a slight smile crossed my lips. About an hour and a half later, I pushed back my pounding nervousness, wrote a check for the purchase price, and drove the car off the lot and onto the street. I made three turns and pulled into the parking garage of my apartment building.

For the first time since I had moved into the high-rise, I pulled my own personal car into the space I had been paying for all that time. And it felt so good to just sit for several moments enjoying the comfort that surrounded me.

I was sitting in a driver's seat that was more comfortable than the thousand-dollar recliner I had bought about two years before. As I sat in the darkened basement garage, my comfort became short-lived remembering that I had far more important decisions to make other than buying a car.

So, I opened the door, got out, and walked toward the elevator. The drab gray walls seemed to take on a brightness I had never noticed before. I even had a spring in my step as I walked across the concrete looking back about every four steps.

There was something about the polished gleam of the perfect paint job that only the craftsmen at Mercedes could create. It made me proud.

When I approached the elevator, I turned back to look at the car and walked backwards the last couple of feet to the elevator. I heard the doors open. I jerked back into reality when I heard, "You goin' up or something, buddy?"

I felt my face turn a shiny red with embarrassment as I stepped inside and pushed the button for the seventeenth floor. After the other man got off at the fifth floor, it took about a minute and a half for the old elevator to crawl the other twelve floors to seventeen. But, the ride seemed like an hour.

When I stepped out onto my floor, I felt a strange sensation tingling up my back bone. I knew I would be looking at those fake flowers in the bowl across from the elevator doors for only a few more days or perhaps a week. Nor would I look into the mirror that hung behind those flowers accentuating the collected years of dust layered on each flower pedal.

And, as usual, I grabbed my handkerchief as I sneezed twice my sinuses reminding me that I was allergic to household dust.

In front of apartment seventeen C, I put the key in the lock and opened the door as a soft breeze hit my face. It carried the fresh smell of auto exhaust and coolness brought by the northerly wind that often blew that time of year.

I always left the patio doors open so that when I walked in I would be able to see Central Park in the distance. And my apartment would be fresh smelling, rather than the normal sterile air conditioning smell of an office building.

After picking up the mail that lay on the floor awaiting my attention, I carried my postal booty with me out onto the patio, looking at each piece.

I dropped those I cared nothing about to the glass top table nearby. Recognizing that there was nothing in the mail that interested me at all, I dropped all the pieces to the table.

I looked up and out over the landscape of steel structures. I felt appreciative of the fact that even though it was not a "scenic" view of the park, at least I could see the park. And that was good enough for a simple man who had never asked a thing of anyone.

Standing silent for several moments, I took in the view from the seventeenth floor of my apartment building making a memory for the future. I stood there staring out as the sun began its slow descent toward the horizon spraying the sky with a plethora of colors reflecting off the glass windows of the many high rises between me and Central Park.

I had earned every promotion, every award. I fought my way almost to the top of the heap within the best police department in the world. I oversaw all the detective in every borough and every precinct in every part of this glorious, massive city.

And yet, I had just been forced to retire: early. Now I was nothing, a nobody. *But a nobody with a brand-new Mercedes!* I thought as a big smile crossed my lips.

My gut seemed to tell me that I should leave New York City for good. There was no way I could stay with this nasty business hanging over my head. I have talents. I could go somewhere and start over maybe as a private detective. I'd be good at it.

But, all I could do at this moment in my life was wonder: what do I do now?

CHAPTER SEVEN

Adolph Sanchez was in his office before seven hoping to catch up on the work he had left sitting on his desk. His face squeezed his eyes shut when the phone rang. He relaxed as he heard the voice on the phone.

"Chief, my name is DeShawn Royce. I'm with the Sunny Isles Police. We've had another incident over here. I tried to get FDLE involved yesterday, but they turned me down. Could you have someone come look at what's happened here and see if it's more than just an accident?"

Rubbing his eyes and forehead, he let out a silent sigh, "I'm pretty busy here--"

"Sir, I think we're way in over our heads here. Miami-Dade is supposed to be our direct support and--"

"Tell me where you're located, and I'll meet you there in about a half-an-hour."

Royce relayed to Sanchez the address and directions for the quickest way to get there.

"I do appreciate your time, Chief. I think this is extremely important."

There was a long pause as Sanchez decided just what he should say.

"Okay," he managed.

As he hung up the phone, he looked at his desk with the huge pile of paperwork to be completed sitting in front of him.

"To hell with all this," he shouted causing a woman walking down the hall to stop short and turn around to head in the opposite direction. He stood up, put on his jacket, walked out to his car, and drove east toward Sunny Isles.

As Sanchez drove across town, all he could think about was how excited and disappointed he was at the same time: excited because he might be facing a real mystery to solve, but disappointed because he just did not have the time or energy to tackle a major case right now.

While he drove, he tried to cheer himself up, so he wouldn't appear so negative. He was to face what seemed to be a young, inexperienced, yet enthusiastic detective. He would be the adult on the ground and needed to find steady legs for this one.

As Sanchez pulled up to the crime scene, Detective Royce met him with his hand held out and his face smiling in the morning sun.

"Chief Sanchez? I'm Patrolman Royce. I'm so glad you came. You see, night before last, I investigated a similar death less than a mile south of here. We called FDLE and they sent an Agent Brown here. She told me to call you next time and quit wasting her time."

Sanchez allowed a slight grin and chuckle.

"Carolina's a hand full. You're lucky she didn't leave you unconscious on the ground for calling her."

"Really?" Royce said as his eyes widened broadly.

Sanchez looked at him wondering: is this guy was for real?

"Show me what you've found."

Royce led Sanchez over to where the chalk outline was still visible, illustrating where the body had laid on the street. There were several numbered orange cones about fifty feet away marking fresh skid marks.

Sanchez took his time walking past the first cone. He walked another fifty or so feet and looked at some impressions on the grass.

"Bring over another cone," he yelled. "And we need to get pictures of this."

Royce walked over to where Sanchez was kneeling and looked at the grass.

"I can't believe I missed those."

"The car sat here for several minutes before running down the vic."

"What? How do you know that?"

Sanchez pointed to a darkened spot on the grass.

"See how the grass here has a slight discoloration? This is where the exhaust blew out. He sat here with the car running for several minutes. The car had a tail pipe that was pointed down rather than straight out; probably a higher end vehicle. Also, the grass shows where the driver pulled over to keep from blocking traffic."

Royce looked at the various markings in the grass marking each one, so the crime scene technicians could get their pictures.

Sanchez continued staring at the grass and turned to Royce.

"Take me to the other crime scene. Let's see what we can find there."

"Follow me," Royce said before walking the half-block to his car. While he pulled out onto A1A, he moved slowly to make sure that Sanchez was following him. The two men drove a little over a mile to the driveway behind the small strip mall.

The two detectives parked and walked over to the area where the death had occurred two nights before. Sanchez walked around the area within about a hundred feet or so in several directions. He signaled Royce to join him.

Royce made his way to where Sanchez stood and looked down.

"Exhaust?"

"Exhaust," Sanchez answered. "Probably from the same car. Have your C.I. techs take samples at both places and have them send the samples over to the lab. Be sure to put my name on the evidence bags as a contact."

"Will do," Royce said.

He pulled out his portable radio and called for the technicians to meet him there.

Sanchez noticed the chalk marks still visible behind the garbage bins. He looked around and saw a small piece of what looked like black plastic. He pulled out a zip top evidence bag and placed the item in it and made several notes on the bag dating and signing it as evidence.

"I think I've seen enough," he noted. "Give me your number and I'll see if I can free up one of our detectives to take on this case. I think we can help you with the investigation. Your instincts may have been right about this."

"I knew it," Royce said with a childish glee.

"I guess I screwed up by having you call FDLE instead of letting my office handle this day before yesterday. I'm sorry about that."

"No problem, Chief."

He handed Sanchez his card and watched him return to his car and drive off.

"Wow," Royce said in a low whisper. "Chief Sanchez himself. Helping me!"

CHAPTER EIGHT

It was four weeks after that horrible meeting with the commissioner. I slowed down as I passed the Hollywood Blvd. exit off I-95. I checked the GPS on the dash and followed its directions around Miami taking the Palmetto Expressway.

I headed around the downtown area toward Florida's Turnpike which would take me down to Florida City and to the Keys.

As I drove along, I enjoyed the music from a local 60's station on the radio. I looked around thinking how nice it was to be driving in such beautiful weather.

I remembered when I emerged from the tunnel to Jersey two days earlier, winter was beginning to remind everyone in New York that it was definitely on its way, ready to wreak its havoc with snow storms and sleet. I felt my heart race as I thought about never having to deal with that stuff ever again.

Now in Florida, the outside temperature gauge on my dashboard read eighty-five degrees. For a fleeting moment I wished I had bought a convertible instead of this big sedan. Florida seemed to be the perfect place to own a convertible.

I had heard a lot about Miami from an old friend. I guess I was looking forward to living in the southern paradise of the U.S. So many people I knew from Manhattan and Brooklyn moved down here after retiring.

As I drove, I realized just how good it felt to do something impulsive. That's when I thought maybe I ought to surprise my old friend.

Nearly ten years had passed since he moved down south to work for the Miami-Dade Police force. I also remembered how much I had missed him after working together on the NYPD.

"Why not?" I shouted aloud.

And with the words barely out of my mouth, I pulled off the expressway and stopped at a service station. I walked over to a telephone booth and looked up the address and phone number of the Dade County Sheriff's Office. I saw it was located on NW 25th Street less than a mile from the Palmetto.

So, after using the restroom, I bought a Diet Coke and a candy bar, and drove off to see if I could find my old friend Adolph Sanchez.

As I pulled onto the 25th St. exit, I pulled off the road, grabbed my cellphone, dialed the number for the Sheriff's department.

"Chief Sanchez, please," I said.

The extension phone rang.

"Chief Sanchez," my old friend's voice sounded.

He heard a gruff voice made tinny by the phone speaker.

"Detective, what are you doing about stopping all those murdering idiots in Miami?"

"What is this all about? Who is this?" Sanchez snapped back.

"Well, I know an idiot from Park Slope. You know him?" I said in my regular voice.

There was a pause.

"Perry Savant! Where the hell are you?" Sanchez yelled.

"I'm about ten blocks from your office."

"Why didn't you call?"

"What do you think I'm doing?"

"I mean … never mind. I'll be in the lobby waiting for you."

"I'll be there in about five minutes."

The smile on my face seemed to stretch from ear to ear as I hung up and headed toward the Sheriff's Office. All sorts of memories rushed back to mind. I remembered that it was I who had helped Sanchez get onto the force.

It was a couple of years after my friend had tried working at a bank on Flatbush Avenue. A much younger Sanchez poured out his frustrations at our favorite watering hole on Bergen Street near Fifth Avenue.

After listening patiently for an hour, I told him that if he wanted, I might be able to get him on at the local precinct where I was assigned at that time.

Sanchez had protested at first by saying he wasn't sure he wanted to be a cop. But after we had talked awhile longer and had a couple more drinks, Sanchez told me that the last thing he wanted to do was to sit in a bank for the rest of his life. So, he agreed to give it a go.

After all the paper work was done, Sanchez entered the police academy and was assigned to the street patrols in and around Park Slope. Although his beat included many Jewish establishments, this young Puerto Rican was able to build friendships with the owners and customers alike. The people learned to trust him. He was always the one who would respond to any call that came from the area.

The people were unaware that because of an up-tick in the crime statistics for that section of the city during the preceding five years, the department implemented the community policing concept.

The department assigned Sanchez and another patrolman to walk a beat that included about ten square blocks of the business district between Flatbush and Atlantic Avenues.

During his first two years on the job, crime dropped by half and Sanchez was awarded a special citation given by the people of the local Chamber of Commerce. He was named the coordinator for all walking patrols in the entire Park Slope area. And he was promoted to temporary corporal pending a review by the promotion board.

Ten years later, Sanchez was Detective Sergeant. After his wife completed her Ph.D. at CUNY Graduate Center in Manhattan, she was offered a teaching post at the University of Miami.

Adolph contacted the Sheriff of Dade County and asked if they might need a little help. He began working less than a week after they arrived in Miami.

He had spent ten years on the streets of Brooklyn as an NYPD beat cop and was turned down for promotion to Detective Lieutenant just before his wife got the offer to move. So, he knew that Miami would be their new home. And for the past fifteen years, he'd been happy as a cat with new ball of yarn.

As I approached the Sheriff's Office, I wondered if Sanchez had heard about what happened back in the city. Although I knew two weeks had gone by, I also knew the rumor mills at NYPD were not restricted to the boroughs proper but stretched world-wide.

I sat in the car for a moment to screw up my courage. Now I would find out just how much of a friend Sanchez was.

As I stepped out of the car I heard my old friend's familiar voice.

"Good Lord, Perry! How have you been?"

Adolph walked up to me and grabbed my hand and shook it with the familiar grip of a long-lost friend. At that moment, I looked into Adolph's eyes and knew everything was good.

Later that evening, I glanced across the table at Sanchez and his wife and felt a small ping of jealousy. My friend had found a brilliant, loyal, loving woman so many years ago in Brooklyn. Lourdes Sanchez had earned her credentials as a specialist in education while working full-time as an elementary school teacher. She later earned a doctorate because of her impeccable research skills.

Now she was a tenured professor teaching at the University of Miami. The couple lived in a beautiful home in a modest part of Coral Gables about a mile from the University campus.

I couldn't help but feel that maybe I had missed out on something along the way. Now at forty-seven, I was retired on a full pension from the city of New York. I wondered if I could still find love like Sanchez had.

I paid the tab for the dinner over Sanchez's way-too-loud protests. And even though the bill was well over $200.00, I felt it was no big deal. I mean, I could afford it. During my twenty-five years of service, I found that I could live quite comfortably on half my salary. The other half I invested and put some into savings.

Besides, I thought, I've just spent four hours with two wonderful people. And Sanchez never said one word about why I had left the department. That alone is satisfaction enough.

"So," Sanchez said. "What brings you to Miami?"

"I decided it was time to retire and move down south where the winters were a bit more tolerable," I answered. "Besides, with so many of our former NYPD colleagues in residence in and around Miami, my move here is a natural part of being an older New Yorker. Right?"

Sanchez just smiled and seemed to take that explanation without flinching in the slightest. Perhaps the opportunity would arise in the near future when I could explain to him-- well, tell him the truth.

Since I had spent several days in the car and was not looking forward to the three-hour trip down to Key West, after dinner I drove to Florida City where I found a comfortable motel.

I would sleep late in the morning and drive into Key West. That would give me time to look around before checking in at the hotel.

As I lay in bed, my mind whirled from how different my life was from two weeks ago. I guess I was still angry about all the things that were printed about me in the newspapers; and I hated the fact that all the reports were lies.

It hurt that people believed those stories. Or maybe they wanted to believe the worst about a worn-out old police officer.

I had done nothing wrong. Plus, I had done nothing that was described in the stories. But, if there was one thing I had learned as a veteran of the NYPD, it was that people will always believe what they want, no matter what the truth was.

I also wondered why it was that at my age I had never married or even thought about it. I had a great job for twenty-five years and had come so close to reaching the pinnacle of my chosen profession.

I owned a beautiful penthouse on the seventeenth floor of one of New York's up-scaled apartment buildings located two blocks from Central Park South. And yet the thought nagged me: *Why wasn't I married?*

As the memories filled my mind. I had to admit that I was never interested in women at all. But, not just that, I wasn't interested in men, either. I guess I just never had any time to think about sex or a relationship of any kind.

I was happy working twelve to fifteen hours a day at my job protecting the city I love from the bad guys. My basic attitude was this: if I'm not asleep, I ought to be at work.

Often as a rookie detective at the one-one-two, my captain would order me to go home and get some sleep. Instead of taking the long drive back to my home in Park Slope, where I still lived with my parents at that time, I would curl up in the back seat of my unmarked car and sleep for a few hours.

I would go back into the precinct, take a shower, and change clothes from the stash that I kept in my locker.

I knew full well I was married to my career. There was no time for anything other than catching the bad guys and putting them away. I didn't think I was gay, but I also knew I wasn't heterosexual. I was simply un-sexual, if there was such a thing.

And with that realization floating around in my head, I drifted into a deep and restful sleep.

The next morning, as I drove along the highway to Key West, I kept asking myself why I didn't buy the sports convertible rather than this huge sedan. The sky was a beautiful shade of light blue and the temperature was around seventy-five degrees with a slight breeze from the south west; the perfect combination for a marvelous convertible ride.

I drove along at about forty-five miles-per-hour with the windows down and the moon roof opened wide. I thought, *there's nothing like this in New York*. I was determined that nothing was going to spoil the feeling I had as I glided along the highway and up onto Seven Mile Bridge.

About an hour later as the clock showed two o'clock on the dashboard, I drove across the Stock Island Bridge and onto the island city of Key West. Feeling hungry, I looked for a restaurant where I would stop for lunch before I checked into the hotel.

As I approached the Old Town section, I saw a charming restaurant on the corner of Truman and Simonton that Sanchez had recommended the night before. I found an empty spot, parked the car, got out, and walked into what would become one of my favorite watering holes during the next several years.

While I sat eating an excellent Porterhouse steak, a gentleman who looked to be in his late fifties or sixties strolled up to the table and sat down across from me.

"I take it you're Chief Savant," he said as he reached over and extended his hand. "My name's Baxter. I'm chief of police around here."

"Very glad to meet you, Chief," I responded with a smile and cordial handshake. "To what do I owe the honor of this official welcome to town?"

"Well, to be honest, your friend Adolph Sanchez called me and said he'd appreciate it if I made you feel welcome to our little community. He also shared with me the reason for your early retirement. So, please understand that in this town, what you went through in New York City will be a badge of honor."

At that moment, I knew that he knew. And that knowledge gave me a deep appreciation and understanding of how lucky I was to have such a wonderful friend as Adolph Sanchez. I also had to smile as I felt thankful that I had decided not to spoil the evening by bringing that up during the dinner.

"Chief, I don't want any trouble," I said. "I think you know that."

"I know. And I won't be expecting any from you. In fact, if the word ever got out about your experience in New York, you'll be hailed as a hero to most of these folks."

"Are you?"

"Me? No. Mary and I've been married way too long to remember. Come to think of it, I believe it's been around forty-five years, I think. I got four children, seven grand-children and a great-grand-child in the warmer ready to pop."

"Wow. Congratulations."

"Thank you. No. I'm not gay. And no one's ever expected me to be."

"Sounds like a normal town to me."

"Of course, it is. But, I got a feeling that after I retire, they'll be looking for a gay, black, Hispanic, female to be chief. You know? Cover all the bases?"

"That was a good one, chief," I said laughing.

"Only difference between Key West and the rest of the country is our gay population doesn't hide it. You know? They just live it."

"Well, I appreciate the warm welcome, Chief. It was kind of you to take time out of your day to welcome me. And if you speak to Sanchez, tell him this is the last time I let him set me up so easily."

With that, the chief laughed out loud, stood up, shook my hand, and strolled out of the restaurant stopping at several tables to greet people as he left.

I watched the chief move through the restaurant just like the politician he needed to be to keep his job. Although not elected, his position always depended upon the city council's whim and they, of course, were influenced by what their constituency thought.

It was fun to notice how natural the schmoozing came to Chief Baxter as he glided around the tables inching ever closer to the door greeting pretty much everyone before he left the building.

It wasn't difficult to see the irony in comparing myself to this man. The main reasons I had reached my personal pinnacle as a chief of the detectives rather than becoming commissioner. I could never do what that small-town police chief did so well.

I never claimed to want to be police chief. I was not the type of political creature necessary to do that. Thus, deep down inside I knew I could never have fulfilled my dad's dream. I've always been an old fashioned, down and dirty street cop who was good at what I did.

That's why I became chief of detectives in the NYPD: I was a good investigator. It was everyone else, including my father, who thought I would one day be commissioner.

I placed two twenty-dollar bills in the small black pad containing the $19.99 bill for the steak lunch I had just enjoyed. I knew the waitress would tell the other staff members in the restaurant about the tip assuring that I would be welcomed as a king the next time I came in.

I stood up, glanced over at my profile in the window and realized that I was still virile and strong. I could also see that even at forty-four I was still physically fit and ready for whatever life threw at me.

And I knew deep inside that I had now reconciled to my situation and had nothing for which to be ashamed or embarrassed.

I weaved the big Mercedes down Duval Street, turned into the entrance to the LaConcha Hotel and parked at the doors leading into the lobby. A bell hop jumped up from where he was snoozing.

"Shall I get your bags, Sir?"

"Sure," I said as I popped the trunk and pointed to two large suitcases that the young man retrieved and placed onto a luggage carrier.

I pushed the key button and the trunk door closed automatically locking all doors to my car. I flipped the key ring to the valet as he approached. I walked into the lobby followed by the bell boy.

Approaching the front desk to check in, I saw the bell hop stop at the bell captain's desk to wait until being summoned.

"Perry Savant," I said.

The desk clerk checked the computer screen.

"Good to have you with us, Mr. Savant. How long will you be staying?"

"I'm not sure. I guess until I find a more permanent place to park my car."

The clerk smiled.

"Ah, a new resident for our fair city?"

"Yes," I replied. "I've decided New York was too cold – in more ways than one."

"Welcome to Key West. You'll be staying in suite six-o-two."

He pressed the bell just like an old fashioned 5-star hotel summoning the bell hop over. The clerk handed him the key and looked at me.

"This young man will show you to your room and put your things away for you, if you wish. And if you'll give me the keys to your car, we'll be happy to park it for you in a safe place and have your keys here at the desk whenever you need to leave. If you call down first, we'll have it waiting for you at the door."

"I gave my keys to the valet outside. Thank you for all your help."

I turned and walked toward the elevators. I felt a twinge of excitement about getting settled into my temporary residence in this little town at the end of US Highway One. I smiled and thought how nice everyone was. But, in my stomach I knew that usually all is never what it seems to be.

CHAPTER NINE

Sanchez sat at his desk shuffling through a pile of papers when one of the clerks came over to his door and knocked.

"Chief, here are those files you asked for," she said as she placed five folders on his desk along with ten pages of print-outs clipped together on top.

"These here haven't been filed yet, but they cover the dates and municipalities you indicated. So, I threw them in anyway."

"Thank you," Sanchez said as he nodded.

He opened the files and scanned each page. He held a yellow marker in his hand and highlighted various entries on the sheets in front of him. As he finished the file folders, he turned to the clipped papers which he looked through highlighting several lines. He picked up the phone and dialed a number.

"Agent Brown, this is Detective Sanchez over at Miami-Dade. Could you do me a small favor?"

"More than happy, Chief; what do you need?" Carolina said with a smile in her voice.

She liked Sanchez. During the four years since her arrival at the Miami FDLE Regional office she had become acquainted with his reputation as someone who was always open and willing to help with any case they had worked on together. So, she was not just willing to help him now, but looked forward to the next case they might work on together.

"I need you to confirm some information for me," Sanchez spoke hesitantly, stammering just a little. He never liked to be indebted to anyone, so asking a favor meant he was on the hook to Brown in his own mind. It made him uncomfortable.

But this time he knew she was the only person who would be willing to do what needed to be done to confirm what he had discovered.

"Of course. What do you need?" Carolina replied.

"Could you look for any suspicious deaths among homeless men in the South Florida area over the past several months? Try as far north as Martin County. Get me whatever case notes are available on each."

Carolina was quiet for several seconds, stunned since she knew this task would take her quite some time.

"Does this pertain to the death of that man in Sunny Isles a couple of nights ago?"

Sanchez was not one willing to spill his guts to anyone who asked, but in this case, he felt he owed it to her to tell her what was going on. He also knew this would take a great deal of her time.

"I don't know, Agent Brown. But there have been five deaths in Dade County over the past four months that seem to be similar in nature. I guess I'm just playing a hunch at this point."

"If there's something here, you'll let me in on it, won't you?" She inquired.

Sanchez chuckled and spoke with a smile Carolina could hear over the phone.

"Of course, My Dear. I'll even let you in on the bust, if it will help. Besides if this turns out to be what I think it is; well, we'll all be in on it eventually."

Even though she was always professional about everything that she did, Sanchez always seemed to make her relax and smile.

"I appreciate that, Chief. I'll get right on this. Talk to you in a couple of days."

"By the way," Sanchez replied. "I know you had a vacation planned. I want you to know how sorry I am to do this to you. But, if we're lucky, you should be able to leave town on Saturday."

"Thanks, Chief. And don't worry about me. If I miss this window, it's no big deal. I'll get the next block that comes up."

Sanchez said his good-bye and hung up the phone. He sat there for a few minutes and decided he'd better put all his notes pertaining to this case into his brief case where they wouldn't get mixed in with the big pile of files and boxes sitting on his desk.

After filling his briefcase, he placed it on the floor next to his chair. He opened the folder on the top of the pile and went to work on completing the files that had been awaiting his attention for several days.

CHAPTER TEN

The Overtown Homeless Center was in a storefront on NW Third Avenue between Fourteenth and Fifteenth Streets. The owner had renovated the building in the late nineties. But, because of the bad reputation that pervaded the Overtown and Liberty City areas, leasing any business space in the area was near impossible.

He decided to get a return on his investment by writing off the cost of the rent as a charitable donation. He allowed the large and influential Historic Baptist Church across the street to use the building. They opened a shelter where the homeless of Miami could find temporary housing and a place to get some food to eat.

An army of about fifty people volunteered to run the center and care for the people who slept there. Of course, priority was always given to women with children. Around 10:00 pm each night they allowed single men to take up the vacant beds.

The church supplied the food and the volunteers. But the bulk of the funding behind the center was a lady whose reputation for philanthropy was equal to none. She was one of the wealthiest people in Miami because her father owned Flame-Mart, the largest group of department stores in Florida.

Frankie Flambeau, the founder of the stores, single-handedly kept the famous mid-western super-stores from entering South Florida until the late nineties.

Even though a few of the other big-box stores had moved into the southern portion of Florida by the mid 1990's, Flame Mart continued to draw customers who lived in the poorer sections of the cities and in the rural areas where Flambeau had concentrated his expansion efforts.

Raised in New Jersey, Flambeau was born into an extended family of less than respectable members of the Jersey City community. He got into some trouble when he was young and had to leave the state. When he did, he left his wife and six-year-old son behind.

During the next ten years, he moved to South Florida, changed his name, and opened his first store. That's when he called his wife and asked her to join him. She did. Their sixteen-year-old son decided to stay behind with Flambeau's sister.

Two years later, Flambeau had a daughter. And it was she who became the focus of most of his attention. Twenty-one years later, his daughter Fara decided that she needed something to do after graduating from Wellesley College. So, he gave her a fifteen-million-dollar endowment and told her to find her own way.

During the past eight years, Fara's passion had become more philanthropic than economic. She was now overseeing the operations of numerous charity organizations including the homeless shelter in Overtown. She considered the charity to be her major accomplishment.

She was so smooth that she was the one who talked the owner of the building into donating the rent. But after about a year, she also convinced him that it would be in his best interest to hand over the building's deed to the church. A real coup!

As the people sat and ate their evening meal in the large open area near the back of the first floor, she moved among them like an accomplished restaurateur or maître d.

She stood about five-foot-eight with dark black hair, flashing blue eyes, and a slim yet curvy figure. When she smiled, the room would brighten like the sun shining through a sunroof, and her bright eyes seemed to sparkle in the commercial down-lights in the ceiling.

As always, she was dressed in the latest Joseph Quartana outfit consisting of a low-cut white blouse that accentuated her cleavage and a deep black skirt that stopped about four inches short of her knees. She seemed to enjoy knowing that the homeless men at the tables admired her with their eyes and in their deepest secret dreams.

Fara was a powerful presence wherever she would go, and her influence would linger in the air for weeks. She would spend a few days at each of her charities and move on to the next project on her harried yet well-organized schedule. She always found herself back at the Miami shelter at least every seven or eight days since. That was her favorite.

The charities she supported were located from Key Largo to Port Saint Lucie. She not only supported places like the homeless shelter in Overtown, she was a heavy contributor and board member for numerous high society organizations like the Miami Museum of Art, the Miami Seaquarium, Palm Beach's Society of the Four Arts, and Hospice-by-the-Sea.

But her favorite charities were the two homeless shelters she endowed and kept running. The first organization she decided to support was the Overtown shelter. Several years later, she added the Salvation Army shelter in Ft. Lauderdale to her portfolio.

Beyond her philanthropy, Fara was known more for her amazing beauty. Wherever she went, people would stop and often stare. Her father saw her potential early in her childhood. So, he paid to have her groomed to be one of the most beautiful women in the world; his efforts had succeeded.

But, she decided early not to be a "jet-setter" traveling around the world dating and being with the most beautiful people everywhere. Fara spent her life in South Florida caring for her charities, or whatever may have caught her fancy.

As she stood talking to a lady with two little children at one of the tables, she noticed a man known as "Dirty Ole Phil" walking toward her. As he passed behind her, she felt an unwelcome hand against the area just below waist.

As he walked away with a ridiculous grin on his face, she reached out with a hard, fast hand and grabbed his shoulder, wheeling him around. He found himself staring into Fara's sharp and angry eyes.

"Hello, Miss Fara. That sure felt good to me."

"Some of the richest people in the world," Fara spoke slowly with her teeth clenched, "would be willing to pay millions of dollars to be able to do what you just did."

"I'm sorry, Miss Fara. But I don't have any money."

She smiled and lifted her hand to his cheek.

"That's okay, Phil. I hope you enjoyed it because I've got a feeling that you're going pay a heavy price for that little feel."

As he looked into her eyes, his smile drifted from his face. He backed away from her and moved toward the back door. Marva Berkshire, one of the volunteers, stopped him.

"Phil, you gonna stay with us tonight?"

He glanced back at Fara before answering.

"You know, I think I won't stay here tonight, Miss Marva. I have some special places to sleep. They ain't as nice as this place, but they're fine for someone like me."

"Okay, Phil. But you stay safe, you hear?"

"I'll do that, Miss Marve. I'm always careful."

At that, Dirty Ole Phil walked out the back door and into the alley.

Around 9:30, Fara was helping to clean up in the kitchen when the evening director, a thin, slip of a man turned to Fara and spoke with a struggled smile.

"Thank you, Miss Fara. You're an angel, you are."

Fara leaned down with a smile at the ancient black man who was shriveled from osteoporosis and other diseases associated with a hard and difficult life. She kissed him on the cheek as if he were her father.

"Mr. Thomas, I'll be back tomorrow night to make sure everything is going well."

The gentle, old man looked at her as a small tear streaked down his cheek.

"God bless ya, Miss Fara," he said, "I don't know what we all would do without your help. I'll be here the same time, too."

Fara nodded in agreement and walked out the back door making sure that the lock tripped inside as she pulled against it. She walked over to her car, opened the door, and got in.

Instead of starting the car, she reached for a box of wet wipes, pulled several of them out, and wiped her arms and legs. She pulled out several more and scrubbed her face several times covering every single place on her body where her skin was exposed.

She shivered hard for a couple of seconds. She sat and took several deep breaths for about two minutes. She stared into space thinking about just why it was so important to put up with these filthy people.

Almost as if waking her from a nap, her phone buzzed several times. She pulled it out of her purse and saw that she had a text message from one of the members of the shelter in Fort Lauderdale.

She sat texting for several minutes when a fist rapped on the window causing her to jump and utter a gasp. She rolled down the darkened window a little and saw the familiar face of Dirty Ole Phil.

"Miss Fara are you alright?"

"Yes, Phil. I'm just fine. Why do you ask?"

"Well I was checking out the trash bin next door when you walked out and got into your car. Over ten minutes passed, and you didn't drive away. I was worried, so I came over here to check on you."

Taken aback at this elderly man's kindness and concern, she smiled.

"Thank you, Phil. I'll be fine."

"Okay," he said as he turned away. But he quickly turned back.

"By the way, I got to thinking about it and I'm so sorry I did that tonight at dinner. Will you forgive me? I mean, I had no right."

"Everything is fine, Phil. I've got to get going," she said as she started the engine. She pushed the up button on the power window and pulled the car out of the back alley onto Third Avenue and headed toward Miami Beach.

She needed to go somewhere and wash the dirt from her mouth for a couple of hours with her friends at The Bistro on South Beach.

Her big, black Mercedes moved though the crowded streets of downtown Miami and across the Causeway onto the Island. When she pulled up in front of one of the many nightclubs along South Beach, a young man jumped to the door and opened it for her.

"Welcome to the Bistro, Miss Flambeau," he said. "I'll take care of your car."

"Thank you, Charlie." She replied with a smile as she moved around the car and into the front lobby. Everyone around stared as the maître d opened the rope without a word to allow her to enter the foyer despite the extensive line out front.

Fifty or so people stood watching this sight and began complaining about the one woman who was allowed to just walk right into the most popular place on South Beach.

Inside the lobby, an older lady turned to one of the guards at the door. With a scowl and her chin in the air.

"Who the hell does that little tart think she is, the owner?"

Fara jolted to a stop, turned around, looked at the maître d, and pointed her long index finger at the lady.

"Throw that bitch out of my night club!"

The bouncer, smiling, looked at the woman.

"The truth is," he said. "Ms. Fara is the owner. And now I must follow her instructions."

He escorted the woman and her confused husband out the front door. Fara turned and looked at the dumb-founded and shocked people standing around the elegant lobby. She spoke slowly and deliberately.

"Does anyone else have anything else cute to say?"

A stunned silence from everyone standing there echoed through the room. With an almost instantaneous whirl, she turned back toward the elaborate entranceway and walked with a graceful swagger as she entered her nightclub.

CHAPTER ELEVEN

The night was darker than usual for this time of year in south Florida. Dirty ole Phil made his way to a special place he had carved out for himself under the 192nd Street viaduct near the Golden Shores Community Park.

Phil's bedroom was located under a thick bush that hid him from the view of joggers running along 192nd Terrace as well as from the Sunny Isles Police Patrol Cars that often cruised the area.

Despite hearing about the murders of several homeless men along A1A, Phil felt safe. His hiding place was a well-kept secret. It was pretty much invisible from all angles.

When he was ready to bed down for the evening he would check out the view to make sure that he was safe from any possible harassment. Feeling secure, Phil curled up for the night and covered himself with an old blanket he had found several months before. Despite living in Miami, some evenings could get quite cool from the breeze off the ocean.

Phil never complained. He had once lived in Cleveland and knew what cold felt like when the winter wind from northern Canada would come sweeping down across the lakes. And he knew that the cool Miami evenings during the early spring nights were nothing compared to the nights on the streets of northern Ohio.

He knew he'd never leave southern Florida since he now considered himself as "retired" to Florida. He compared himself to many of his high school classmates who graduated with him over 40 years ago from high school in Norfolk, Virginia.

In a moment of lucidity, Phil found his eyes welling up with tears wondering just how he had come to this situation: penniless and homeless. He was sleeping on the ground and begging for pennies every day to get enough money for just a few necessities. Plus, he had to rely on places like the homeless center for at least one meal a day to survive.

He had finished high school with such promise, receiving a full tuition scholarship to Virginia Tech. Graduation from there would almost guarantee a commission in the Air Force. And that meant there was little or no possibility of being sent to Vietnam, a fate which so many of his high school buddies had suffered.

With no warning, his lucid thoughts left him, and he spoke out loud.

"Burr! It's cold tonight. I hope I don't freeze. I hate Cleveland! I swear I'm going to move to Florida one of these days."

And he fell asleep holding the blanket up to his neck as his feet poked out from the other end.

At about 4:00 am, a loud crash of some kind brought Phil out of a deep sleep and to his feet in a flash. He gathered up what he could and moved out from under the overpass and onto A1A headed south.

As he walked he watched two ambulances pass him headed toward the overpass. A few seconds later he saw a fire truck pass by. He saw two Sunny Isles patrol cars pass with emergency lights flashing.

Phil walked for almost a mile when he felt tired. He decided to look for a place to sleep until the sun came up. But as he walked a little further he realized that there was a car approaching him.

Phil usually walked on the opposite side of the street from the flow of traffic. But this evening he was in such a hurry he rushed southward down the street on the west side.

He stopped and turned around. There was a black car parked about a hundred yards behind him with the lights off. Phil could feel the fear welling up inside his old and weathered body.

He wondered if this was the end for him. He ran south away from the car. He could hear the engine whirr as it approached him.

With his mind confused and unclear, Phil ran straight down the street. In the distance, he could see the police station and the possibility of safety. Without any indication of an approaching danger, he felt a strange burning sensation as he fell to the ground.

He did not feel the wheels as they ran over his body. The impact of the front end of the car had achieved its apparent purpose. It took the life from Phil before he hit the ground.

The car stopped about fifteen feet from him. It backed up and ran over his head. As the car stopped again, the driver got out, walked over and bent down and looked at Phil's broken and bruised body. The driver stood up, got back into the car and drove off leaving the poor old guy dead on the sidewalk.

Two hours later, it seemed like the entire Sunny Isles police department had gathered to investigate. DeShawn Royce was the last on the scene irritated that another vagrant had been murdered in his town. In all the years since Sunny Isles had been incorporated, there had never been this much excitement or this much criminal activity to investigate.

The residents were proud of their safe little bedroom community deep inside the greater Miami area. He couldn't help but wonder why it was that the murderer chose this little community in which to cause so much death.

And the deaths were of people who mattered to no one in particular. But Royce believed they were still human beings and worthy of his concern.

He walked over to the body. Even before he had bent down he noticed the tell-tale signs that the man's face had been run over. He knelt next to the body. He saw the tire marks embedded in the man's face.

He signaled to the crime scene investigator and asked her to take some extra close-up pictures of the man's face.

"Be sure," he said, "To send copies of those pictures to Chief Sanchez at Miami Dade and to Agent Carolina Brown at FDLE."

"I will, sir," replied the young lady with the camera.

Royce pulled out his cell phone and dialed.

"Brown here," the voice on the line said.

"Detective Brown, this is Patrolman Royce at Sunny Isles. I'm afraid we've had another vehicular homicide of a homeless man."

There was silence on the other end of the phone.

"The marks on the face," Royce continued, "Seem to indicate it may be the same killer as before. Our photographer will send you copies of the pictures in about an hour or so."

The silence continued.

"Did you want to come out to investigate?" Royce asked.

Brown took a deep breath.

"Okay. I'll be there in about twenty minutes. Don't move the body. And make sure everything remains intact until I get there." She hung up.

Royce just smiled and shook his head as he placed his cell phone back into its holster on his belt.

When the Coroner's wagon pulled up, Royce asked the deputy coroner to please leave everything as it was until FDLE had arrived and checked out the situation.

With a flourish, the deputy coroner grabbed a black body bag and threw it over the body as a light rain began to fall. A few minutes later, he had erected a tent over the body and surrounding area.

Royce walked to his patrol car to get his rain slicker. He reached in the car and called on the radio for a traffic officer right away.

He knew rush hour traffic would be underway in less than an hour. With the right lane blocked and rubberneckers slowing down, traffic was already backed up to the bottom of the overpass.

An hour later, Carolina Brown pulled up and parked on the east side of the road and crossed to the crime scene. She walked directly to where the body was still lying, not even acknowledging Royce's presence. She looked at the deputy coroner.

"What are your preliminary findings?"

He looked at her.

"It's been raining for nearly an hour. I haven't had a chance to look at the body."

"So, what are you waiting for? It ain't raining now."

A bit embarrassed, the young deputy coroner went right to work pulling the plastic from the body. He checked the liver temperature.

"It looks like he died about three and a half to four hours ago."

"Good," said Brown.

"These marks," the young man said as he pointed at the victim's face, "indicate someone rolled over his face postmortem. I can't be sure, but because of the amount of internal damage and the lack of swelling that I can feel, he was probably already dead when his face was crushed. But, I'll have a clearer understanding soon after I get him back to the morgue and the coroner does the autopsy. I'll make sure he sends you a copy of the report as soon as he's completed his work."

"Good," replied Brown. "Be sure to send me close up pictures of the entire body. Make it everything, no matter how insignificant."

"Yes, Ma'am. I'll take care of it."

Brown walked over to Royce.

"Have you interviewed everyone in the area to see if there were any witnesses?"

"I have two officers canvassing the buildings across the street talking to the residents on the front side. Unfortunately, most of the apartments look as if they're empty for the season."

"Let me know what you find out. In the meantime, I'll contact Sanchez and let him know what's happened here."

"What's your opinion?"

"I think we've got ourselves a real live serial killer, Detective Royce. And I think the homeless in Miami are not safe, particularly the males. Anyway, I'll talk to you after I see your report."

Before Royce could say a word in reply Brown was back across the street and in her car.

Royce turned to the young deputy coroner.

"That woman will either solve this case or drive me insane," said Royce. "Maybe both."

They laughed and turned back to their work.

CHAPTER TWELVE

As Sanchez walked into the rather dull building that housed Florida's premier law enforcement investigative agency, the guard took his credentials and directed him to a room on the second floor.

As he entered what appeared to be a small conference room Carolina Brown stood and shook hands with him. Within minutes, Laura Brown walked in and sat down.

"Before we begin, I wish to give a personal apology to Carolina and thank her for her dedication to this job. She was scheduled to go on vacation for two weeks this past week-end. But, when she realized how serious this case was turning out to be; well, let's just say that her commitment to law enforcement, you know. I mean, I want to say thank you to her from me and all of us for postponing your trip."

Carolina sat quietly and nodded her head. She did not smile.

"Okay," Laura continued. "Let's get started."

"Where's Othniel?" Sanchez said.

"Othniel's on his way. I think I caught him having breakfast." Laura replied.

"How do you know that?"

"Othniel and I go way back. And that man is OCD. You can rely on him like clockwork. He always does the same thing every day and at the same time."

Carolina frowned.

"That sounds dangerous," she asked.

"Dangerous?" Laura laughed. "He's been shot twice and stabbed once by people who knew just where he would be because of his habits. Yet, he still sticks to his schedule."

At that moment Othniel Frazier lumbered through the door carrying his 300 pounds of weight and his six-foot six frame quite well for a man of fifty-two. And this intimidating figure had to lower his head slightly to walk through the doorway.

"You gotta be talking about me, right, Laura?"

"Of course, we are, Odie."

"I told you never call me that. It's embarrassing."

"I know. So, sit down. We gotta talk."

Othniel sat down as he acknowledged the others in the room with a nod.

Laura turned to Carolina.

"Okay, young lady. You called this meeting."

"Right. We got us a real problem. Sanchez asked me to check on the deaths of other homeless men in the tri-county area. I found four in Broward County and one in Palm Beach which along with the five we have here in Miami-Dade, we have our work cut out for us."

"Are all the murders identical?" Othniel asked.

"The ones in Broward are, but the one in Palm Beach doesn't match exactly. Now, here's the kicker," she said as she pointed to a map on the wall with several flag pins stuck along the coastline.

"You will notice here on the map, all of these murders occurred on or adjacent to A1A. But they occurred in five different jurisdictions. So, no red flags popped up until the third occurred in Sunny Isles. A young, inexperienced detective was smart enough to see the distinct similarities between three murders in his jurisdiction. He's the one who insisted on FDLE's involvement."

"But it took a little prodding from me to get you guys involved," Sanchez chimed in.

"You're right, Chief," Carolina said, showing a little embarrassment. "But, we're in now. And I'm wondering if we shouldn't make a plea to the FBI's Behavioral Analysis Unit to help us with this one. I mean, we're dealing with several different police districts."

"I don't think that's necessary," Laura spoke up before anyone else could. "We have the resources to investigate this ourselves."

Carolina was insistent.

"We need all the help we can get. This is important."

"No FBI!" Laura and Othniel spoke at the same time.

"What is wrong with the FBI?" Carolina asked.

Othniel looked up, his eyes filled with total determination and spoke in a quiet, yet forceful voice.

"No FBI. We don't need the Feds."

At that Othniel, Carolina, and Laura talked at once, each attempting to make a point.

"Hey, guys!" Sanchez said silencing the others. "I think I've got a way to get us the professional help we're going to need for this case and not use the Feds."

At that, the room filled with an eerie silence.

"How?" Laura questioned.

"One of my best friends just retired from the NYPD as deputy chief of Police Departments for major investigations. In a word, he was chief of detectives for all of NYPD for five years He even headed up the major crimes unit. His specialties include serial rapists and murderers. And, guys, he's just retired and moved to Key West. I'm sure he'd be tickled to death to help us out with this investigation."

Silence.

"Will we have to pay him?" Laura asked.

"My office will pick up the tab, if there is one. Is that okay?" Sanchez replied.

"If he comes on board, can I then go on vacation?" Carolina added.

"No!" the others yelled and began to roar with laughter.

"I can't believe you asked that!" Laura said. "You are just too much, my dear. So, go ahead and give us the full details on these cases, Carolina."

"Each of the crimes was committed on or in sight of A1A from north of Surfside Beach to Hollywood Beach. The one in Palm Beach seems to be too far out to be connected. I'll leave that one out until we get more information and a look at the evidence. These murders cover five different jurisdictions and the total number of dead that fit our suspect's specific M.O. is nine for sure with one possible. The earliest death might have been the murderer finding his way or learning what to do."

"Ten?" Sanchez whispered. "My god, how did we miss this?"

"Chief, we have no explanation," Laura interjected. "Personally, I think it had to do with all the confusion during the re-assignments within our branch offices. Either that or we just aren't getting the information pushed to us, you know. But, we can face that problem later."

"The question we have to solve," Carolina interjected, "is what to do about this killer. And we gotta do it quick."

"You're right, Carolina," Laura said in an apologetic tone. "So, Chief, I'm going to assign Carolina to be lead agent on this case and my office will coordinate."

"That's fine with me, for the moment," Sanchez replied. "We'll see how it goes."

"How it goes is like this: you and Othniel must cooperate on this and the only way that's going to happen is for Carolina to be the one in charge. Is that clear?"

Othniel looked over at Sanchez and smiled like the Cheshire Cat.

"That's fine with me."

"Okay." Sanchez said shaking his head. "Now, can we get on with this meeting?"

CHAPTER THIRTEEN

I pulled into the entrance of a hotel located on Ocean Drive in the middle of the Deco District of Miami Beach. It was an exquisite upscale hotel with a restaurant and picturesque view of the ocean. It was exactly what I hoped it would be when I called and made the reservations.

I had decided that if I had the chance I would never sleep in another flea-bag dump again. I hated the places I had to endure whenever I was on the city's dime for a stake-out or when I went upstate to visit one of the prisons.

Although there were just four floors in the hotel, the suite I reserved had a balcony on the front facing the ocean. And since it faced slightly to the northeast, the morning sun did not shine directly through the windows.

In the afternoons I could sit out on the patio with the afternoon sun facing the backside of the building giving me a nice shady spot to sit and enjoy the view of the beach. As I stood in the room looking around at the amenities, I knew I had made it.

I was going to be so comfortable while I helped out with this case. In fact, the room reminded me of my own apartment on Central Park South except here I had a real view of the beach rather than a partial view of the park.

After settling in, I called Sanchez.

"Okay Adolph. I'm in a hotel on South Beach. Now what?"

"Great. It'll take you about an hour or so to get here. Just come to my office right away."

"Absolutely. Might be an hour, you say? Okay. I'll see you an about two."

"A visitor's pass and an escort will be waiting for you in the lobby, so you can get to my office as soon as you arrive."

"Sounds serious."

"No kidding. I'll fill you in when you get here."

I hung up and stepped into the bathroom to take a quick shower and freshen up. About forty-five minutes later I called for my car.

The traffic was so heavy that it took about an hour and twenty minutes to drive across town to the Miami-Dade Police Central Office. As soon as I walked into the front entrance, I was asked to sign in. I followed a young deputy to Sanchez's office on the second floor.

"Chief Sanchez is in a meeting with another detective," a deputy escort explained. "He asked that you wait for him here in his office."

I looked through the numerous files that had been placed on a table in the corner of the room. I could see at once that these were the files of the men who had died along A1A.

After about ten minutes Sanchez walked in.

"Notice anything special?"

"These were all done by the same person."

"How can you tell?"

"Well, they were each run down by an automobile. And these in this pile had obvious tire marks on their faces. As for the ones in this pile there is no indication on the reports of such marks, but the rest of the details seem similar. I would assume that if we checked with the investigating officers, they will indicate tire marks on the faces."

"That's what I thought, too, Perry. And since these cases seem to run across five jurisdictions, I insisted on a task force to coordinate the work of the various departments."

"I noticed that little fact as well. The murderer must have done this on purpose to prevent an immediate recognition or concentration on the case."

"So, what do you think?"

"I'm not sure just yet," I answered. "My first inclination is that the murderer is a woman, but I wouldn't swear to it. Second the person must have lots of money since the damage to the cars would need repairs without drawing attention. So, you can forget investigating repair shops."

Sanchez was taking notes on a pad as I spoke. After several more minutes, he looked at his watch.

"We need to leave. We're due in twenty minutes at FDLE for a meeting."

"Are you sure you want me to come along?"

"Yes, I'm sure."

"Why?"

"I've already told them about you and your qualifications. Everyone agreed that allowing you to help us would give us an excuse to keep the Feds out of our hair."

"Ah. Interesting take."

"Don't worry."

And with that we left the building and drove off toward the Florida Turnpike headed toward the FDLE Southern District Office.

CHAPTER FORTEEN

We walked into the FDLE building and up the main staircase to the second floor. But, before we entered the conference room, Sanchez turned to me with a smile.

"Everyone else is here. You wait in this corner of the hall. Come in when you think it's an appropriate moment. That way, we won't fool with a lot of introductions.

Carolina Brown took charge immediately. She sat at the head of a large table with eight chairs, four on each of the long sides. There was no chair at the other end of the table from Carolina. Other than Sanchez, the others around the table were Othniel Frazier, and DeShawn Royce.

Carolina began by asking Othniel what he had discovered about the murders in Broward County.

"My technicians haven't come up with anything identifiable about any of the pieces of evidence that was gathered at the scenes. There was no DNA, other than that of the victim, and nothing seemed to be out of place or that didn't already belong there."

"And did you find out why you were unaware of these murders?"

"I was not allowed to contact any of the chiefs. Sheriff Williams said he would talk to the various chiefs himself."

"And?" Carolina encouraged.

"And, nothing. And I'm not going to push the issue."

"Listen, guys," Carolina countered, "If we can't get to the bottom of the communications issue; we're dead in the water."

"It was just dumb luck that DeShawn here called me at all," Sanchez said. "Otherwise we wouldn't have known about these murders."

"We can't do our job unless we get this communication issue fixed," DeShawn chimed in. "I wasn't even sure who to call."

"It's the fault of the chief's in the two counties," Othniel offered, "No clear communication policy."

"Or it could be the same as what happened several times in New York City," I said as I entered the room. "And that's the incompetence of law enforcement officials who feel they must protect their own territory from outsiders rather than solving cases and stopping criminals."

Sanchez was on his feet.

"Ladies and gentlemen," he said, "allow me to introduce to you my friend and former colleague at NYPD, Perry Savant. He recently retired as deputy Chief of Departments for investigations."

Carolina turned to Othniel.

"He sure does know how to make an entrance," she whispered.

The others stood and shook hands with Perry, each introducing himself. As they settled back into their seats, Sanchez continued.

"Perry, please continue with what you were saying."

"I don't mean to demean anyone, but, I'm sure that Chief Taylor has experienced this first hand with local officials wanting to hold onto information for the sake of political gain or one-upmanship at the appropriate time."

Carolina smiled.

"You got that right, Chief. Our department has just recently begun gaining the respect of most chiefs and sheriffs. And that's because we're being asked more and more to help in cross-jurisdictional issues, such as this case."

"I'm sorry, guys," Sanchez said. "But please excuse me in that I do have to play this close to my chest. Sheriff Lopez is facing a re-election bid in November. His opponent is the current chief of the Hollywood Police Department. So, this case could mean a lot to him and his continuing on as Miami-Dade Sheriff."

"I'm glad that none of these murders occurred in Hollywood," Othniel added. "Chief Beasley would be sitting here himself trying to run this investigation if they were."

"Look, gentlemen, I don't care who gets the credit," Carolina spoke out. "We've got a serial killer on our hands and he's given us a distinct signature to follow that we can use to solve this case. So, instead of bitching about what's been happening, let's make something happen here and get this case finished so I can go on my vacation. Okay?"

After a moment of shock, Othniel Frazier cleared his throat.

"I for one want to see this thing resolved," he said. "So, as soon as I get back to the office, I'll put out a bulletin to the other police departments in the county requesting information on any and all deaths of homeless, especially any killed along or near A1A. That will involve at least six separate jurisdictions. I want to be sure we have all possible victims in this case."

"Me, too." Sanchez added," I'll push the other principalities with separate departments and get as much as I can as well."

"Can we meet back here day after tomorrow to put everything together that we have?" Carolina asked. "I want to make sure we know the extent of this thing."

At that we stood and agreed to meet in two days with everything we could gather.

As everyone was leaving, Laura Taylor walked up and introduced herself to me.

"Can you spare a moment? I'd like to have a word with you."

I agreed. She turned and closed the door. She spoke slowly.

"Chief, I want to be clear from the outset that I am not in favor of utilizing your help. And I can promise you no compensation for your work from FDLE. Plus, you are not official in any way with us. If Miami-Dade wants to certify you and put you on their payroll, I can't stop them."

"I understand."

"That's not all."

"Oh?"

"I'm opposed to your presence. In my opinion, you should have a police officer with you always while you are working on this case. I cannot protect you otherwise."

"I have no objection to what you've said. I'm doing this purely as a favor for an old friend. That's all. I owe Chief Sanchez. And I'm giving a helping hand to an old neighborhood friend."

She looked at me for a moment--almost too long.

"Thank you for your help," She said coldly. "All I ask is that you keep me informed of everything that you are doing so we don't step on each other's investigations."

"No problem, Captain. I'm at your beck and call."

I turned and walked to the parking lot where Sanchez was waiting.

"So, what did she have to say?"

"Nothing. She just wanted me to know that she's in charge and that in the end I answer to her."

"Pissing match?"

"Seemed like it."

Carolina exited the building walking toward us.

"Are you ready to head for the office?"

"No. I'd like to visit the most recent crime scene, if that's possible."

Carolina was so efficient she arrived just as I finished speaking.

"I'll be happy to take you out there," she said to me." I can also fill you in on the details of what's been happening. This most recent case is typical of the others we've identified as part of this killer's profile."

"Do you mind dropping me off at my hotel afterwards?"

"No problem. My car is over here," she said as she pointed to a typical unmarked black Ford police cruiser.

"Really?" I said.

"Just get in. It won't kill you."

I got in. She stepped on the gas and demonstrated that even an old car can peel rubber.

CHAPTER FIFTEEN

As we drove north on Collins Avenue, Carolina filled me in on the facts as they had them in the case.

"I called the Sunny Isles Police," she said. "They're sending the CI person who did the initial investigation of the scene to meet us. He'll be available to answer any questions we might have. He's bringing the evidence that was gathered that hasn't been processed or sent to the lab yet."

"Good. Does that mean there's a problem with getting things processed or sent to the lab in South Florida?"

"I don't think so. The problem is that we haven't been able to identify any DNA other than that belonging to the victims. And we're still working on separating items that were there before the crimes and those things that were left at the time of the crimes."

"In other words, you don't have a thing, do you?"

"Nope. That's what's so baffling. There are no clues other than a small piece of plastic from a turn signal on a Mercedes."

"What did you say?" I asked as my nerves began to tingle.

"We found a piece of plastic."

"Where? When?"

"Uh, I think it was the second murder site in Sunny Isles."

"Who has it?"

"I'm not sure. I think I bagged it and put in the evidence locker at the headquarters."

"I want to see that as soon as we finish at today's crime scene."

"Okay. We'll do it."

"That could be important in getting a handle on just what's been going on and why these murders have happened. Now, step on it. We don't have much time left."

Carolina pressed down on the gas, turned on the emergency lights behind the grill and began moving through the building traffic along Collins Avenue.

As we approached the crime scene, Carolina turned off the lights and pulled across traffic parking on the west side of Collins. A Crime Scene investigator was waiting.

She could not have been more than twenty-five. She half-jogged up to the car and bent over to stare in the driver's side window with tired eyes.

"Is there something we can help you with, Detective?"

"I'm not sure just yet. But, if you don't mind, could you please wait while we look around?"

"Of course." Then she walked back to her van.

I walked with measured steps through the area looking for something out of the ordinary. I walked over to the CI's van. She sat in the driver's seat listening to something blaring through the headphones she was wearing.

I stood near the open window of the van. Her head leaned against the wall of the van behind her. She seemed to be in another place mentally.

"Did you find any pieces of plastic or glass that would have come off a car when it hit the victim?"

She jerked up, yanked the headphones off, then pulled out a clipboard and checked the sheets that were attached. I could tell she was a bit annoyed as she shoved the clipboard in my face.

"Here's the inventory of everything that was bagged and tagged."

I looked at the list. I pointed to an item on the list. "This. Let me see this."

She looked at the paper, set the clipboard on the seat beside her and got out of the vehicle. She walked slowly to the back of her van, took out a box, and opened it. She thumbed through the items and pulled out a plastic bag with a small piece of glass in it then handed it to me.

I examined the item for several moments and looked up.

"Have this sent to the lab right away. Place a priority analysis tag on it and have the result sent immediately to Carolina Brown at FDLE."

She looked over at Carolina who nodded her head in agreement. The girl placed the bag back in the box, closed it, and placed it back into the van. She took her time to lock the back doors checking the lock several times.

I turned to Carolina and nodded.

"I think we can go now."

The van's wheels threw gravel in several directions as the CI pressed hard on the accelerator. I noticed the girl's scowled look through the side-view mirror. She was so young; and arrogant.

Carolina stood for several moments looking over at the building across the way as her eyes narrowed.

"It's hard to believe that with several thousands of people residing in those three buildings that not a single person saw something."

"Even if they were looking out a window or standing on a balcony," I said. "I doubt that they would have known what they were seeing even if they saw anything at all. Besides, at that hour of the morning, I doubt more than a dozen people were out of bed, let alone looking out a window facing this direction."

I looked up at the buildings then walked around the area one more time.

I stopped and looked intently at Carolina.

"This killer is smart and familiar with this area. There seems to have been little or no hesitation. He even took the time to pick up the glass broken on impact with the victim."

"How do you know that?"

"There is one piece of glass that was picked up and bagged as evidence. It was jagged all the way around. That indicates that there were other pieces that were broken from the same head lamp covering. And it will probably turn out to be from an expensive model of Mercedes."

"Are you ready to go back to the station and get that piece of glass?"

"No. The piece of glass I just looked at I surmise will turn out not to be glass but plastic. Anyway, it confirmed my suspicions. You can take me back to the hotel where I can get in a few laps in the pool before dinner."

We slid into Carolina's cruiser, and she drove me back to the Miami-Dade Headquarters to pick up my car. I got out and turned back to her.

"Would you be interested in meeting me for a drink later? I would love to have some company while mulling over this case."

"Sorry, Chief. Maybe some other time."

Before I could reply she moved out into traffic and disappeared.

CHAPTER SIXTEEN

At seven that evening I entered the hotel restaurant for dinner and sat at a table near a window that overlooked the beach. I thought about how fortunate I was at that moment.

I had a mystery to solve and I was living in paradise; what more could any retired cop ever want?

Of course, I loved New York. I lived there for over forty years. It made a lasting impression. But sitting here looking out at the hard bodies walking up and down the beach gave me a full insight into why so many New Yorkers move to Florida when they reach retirement age.

Two young ladies dressed in skimpy bikinis walked past the front of the hotel and crossed the street to the beach as they giggled and looked back toward me.

"Those women are far too young for an old fart like you," Adolph Sanchez said disturbing my day dream.

"Give me a break, Adolph."

"Oh, yeah, right. Sorry about that."

"Have a seat. I'm glad you dropped by."

As my friend took the chair opposite me, I signaled to the waiter to bring a service and menu for Sanchez.

"So, what brings you this far out of your way?"

"This is just a social call. The wife is at a church committee meeting at the Parish House. So, I thought I'd grab these few minutes to visit with an old friend."

"I'm glad," I said. "But, before we eat, may I bring up business?"

"Have you ever had to ask before?"

"No, I guess not."

I paused for a moment and took a deep breath.

"I think we're looking at something diabolical with these killings."

"You think there's more to this than some homeless men getting knocked off?"

"This seems to be far more insidious than either of us could ever imagine. We're dealing with a person with lots, and I mean, lots of money."

"Why do you say that?"

"This killer is committing these murders with an expensive car, or maybe even cars. Each time, some damage would certainly have occurred. The repairs had to be done fast by a small and trustworthy group of people; maybe just one. I would say that we could canvas all of the body shops within ten counties and not find any evidence of the murder vehicle being repaired."

"If that's true, we're looking at someone with a huge bank account; and lots of influence."

"I hate where this may be leading. But, not knowing much about Florida politics, I'd still figure that when we find the perp we'll have a huge fight on our hands just keeping our hands on him--"

"Or her."

"Or her in custody. And we may never get a chance to interview or question this person. The person will be surrounded by lawyers; and the highest paid among those."

"Between the two of us, we have nearly fifty years of police experience. We have an edge in this matter. We can solve this and get the evidence to convict."

"I know, my friend," I mused. "But, if this person is who or what I think, we may never be able to convict. And it won't be our investigation that's the problem. It will be because of the number of people in powerful positions that may be on someone's payroll."

"Hey, Perry. Wake up. We're the good guys here."

"Yeah. I know. But sometimes the good guys don't win."

There was a long silence as we both contemplated the depth of what we had just discussed.

"This perp is a common ordinary killer," Sanchez said. "We'll get him and watch him fry. Or, maybe he--"

"Or she!" I said with a smile.

"Or she might not survive an arrest attempt, if you get my drift."

At this point, the waiter approached and took our orders for dinner.

Several hours later, we were enjoying an after-dinner drink when Fara Flambeau entered the restaurant. She paused then walked over to the table and looked into Sanchez's eyes.

"Chief, what are you doing about these deaths of homeless men?"

Sanchez jumped to his feet.

"Miss Flambeau? Oh, uh, well, FDLE is spear-heading the investigation. I mean, they have the resources for coordinating between the five jurisdictions involved. But, I assure you that we'll catch this criminal."

"Look, chief, I've worked hard at providing these people with some sense of safety and yet--"

"I understand, Miss Flambeau. I think I know how you must feel about this whole situation. But we are doing our best to catch this man--"

"Or woman," I interjected.

"What?" Fara said with a sense of both horror and shock.

"Oh, uh, Fara Flambeau," Sanchez said. "I'd like to introduce an old friend from the City, Perry Savant."

Almost as if a switch had been turned on, Fara's face lit up with a gracious and enchanting smile.

"So nice to meet you Mr. Savant. An old friend of Chief Sanchez is someone I'm proud to know."

"We go back a long time, Adolph and me."

"And are you visiting our wonderful city? Or have you also moved down here like Sanchez did?"

"I recently retired and am living in Key West. I'm here visiting with Adolph, thank you."

"I hope you enjoy living in Florida. Key West is one of my favorite destinations. And should you need some merchandise at a good price, be sure to visit my daddy's store, Flame-Mart: Best prices guaranteed. There's a smaller version of our stores on the island. You can't miss it."

"Thank you for that invitation."

Fara turned back toward Sanchez.

"So, I expect results soon, right?"

"We're doing our best as always."

At that Fara whirled around on her heels and was out the door in a couple of seconds. Sanchez sat down hard into his chair.

I looked over at my old friend and chuckled through my smile.

"So, what or who was that?"

"A walking hurricane."

"I could see that. What I meant was your reaction."

"Oh. Well, that woman is one of those people you were talking about earlier. She not only knows she's in control of everything, she or her father also have half the judges in this county on speed dial and perhaps even on payroll. Maybe even most of my own staff."

I whistled low.

"Should we look at her as a possible suspect?"

"Whoa, partner! You don't want to wrangle with that little princess. If she had the slightest thought that we suspected her, she'd have us both so deep inside the county jail the mayor couldn't find us."

"That bad?"

"That bad."

And so, we sat in silence for several minutes thinking about what had just happened. A thought hit me, and I looked up at my friend of so many years and with a wink and a smile.

"Still--"

CHAPTER SEVENTEEN

The next morning Sanchez entered his office at the Miami-Dade Sheriff's headquarters about 7:30. The telephone was already ringing. He sighed and picked up the receiver.

"Sanchez here."

"Chief? Carolina Brown. We've got another one."

Sanchez sat hard in his chair. "Where? How? When?"

"That's irrelevant. You need to turn on your television; channel ten."

Sanchez shuffled around on his desk until he found the remote. He pushed the button and turned on the television set that was on the book shelf across the room from his desk. He clicked it to the channel. There he saw a local reporter speaking on camera to the chief of police in Sunny Isles.

"Chief, what's being done about this serial killer?"

"We don't know that there is a serial killer. I can say that we've had three killings of homeless men in the area over the past week."

"That sounds like a serial killer to me, Chief. Tell us what you're doing about this."

"We have our best people on the job. And we're coordinating with Miami-Dade Sheriff's Department and FDLE. Let me say to the people who visit or are just driving through our small town that we are here to protect everyone from harm of any kind."

"But these victims are not your normal citizens."

"And that includes the homeless as well as our full and part time residents. We will catch the person responsible for this. Now, you'll have to excuse me."

The chief quickly walked out of view of the camera.

"So, as you heard from the chief of police here in Sunny Isles there is a serial killer on the loose along A1A. We'll have a report at noon on the extent of these murders in our city. You'll be shocked when you hear how many homeless men have been killed. This is--"

Sanchez clicked off the television and set down the remote. He turned his attention back to the phone.

"This is not good."

"I know, Chief. I think we need to pay a visit to our friend in Sunny Isles."

"No kidding. How about I drop by and pick you up on the way?"

"That would be great."

"I'll be there in fifteen minutes."

Sanchez hung up the phone, walked out of the office and drove to the FDLE headquarters. There he picked up Carolina Brown and drove over to Sunny Isles.

# # #

At the crime scene, Royce was busy trying to get control of the situation. The murder took place at the north entrance to Haulover Park in a wooded area near the beach. Although the police had cordoned off the area on the east side of Collins, news trucks, reporters and people from all over the area had gathered in a parking lot on the west side. As a result, a huge traffic jam of people trying to see just what was going on backed up traffic for a mile in either direction.

The body was run over on a paved road located just inside the park area out of sight of the condos to the north and out of sight of traffic on the west. The body was evidently dragged across the pavement and pushed into some bushes.

Royce seemed frustrated as he worked to get control of the pedestrian traffic and the substantial number of news people with cameras and microphones.

Sunny Isles may be a small, quiet village with an excellent reputation for safety and community awareness, it also boasted of a highly trained and professional police force. But this type of publicity and notoriety was well beyond their experiences and expertise.

The chief had to bring in every officer on the force including reservists to get control of the north bound traffic.

When Sanchez and Brown arrived, the traffic was beginning to clear. The officers blocked off Collins and diverted traffic over to US Highway One. Sanchez and Brown moved around the road-block and drove into the park area. They walked over to Detective Royce.

"The coroner has put the time of death at about three in the morning," Royce explained. "And at that hour, there would have been little traffic. See where the victim was found? Out of sight of the road or the sidewalk."

Sanchez frowned. "This is not good, people. This killer is smart and resourceful."

"And knows the routines of these men," Carolyn said.

"What?" Sanchez said with a quizzical look on his face. "What did you just say?"

"I said the murderer knows the routines of these men. This could not have been a random act of violence."

"Why haven't I seen that before? Of course, it all makes sense now. These men were targeted by someone who knew them. And knew them well enough to know where they went at night."

"Who in the world would have known all these men?" Carolyn asked. "I mean, they're all from different areas of the country with varied backgrounds and--"

"And all of them stay in this area or at least along or near A1A."

"And the killer knew where they would be at the time of the night they were killed," Royce chimed in. "He must have known. How would he have found them so easily? Or at least how would he have known where to wait to catch them?"

"You're right, Royce," Carolyn said. "I think we need to find out just what it is that all these men had in common. You know, a meeting place? A common stopping place like a church or a restaurant?"

"Or perhaps a homeless shelter such as the one in Overtown?" DeShawn asked. "It's run by the Historic Baptist Church near tenth and first. I know the pastor there. He'll be happy to help us."

Carolina and Sanchez looked at Royce as he turned toward his car.

"You want to ride with us or meet us there?"

Royce looked back as he moved toward his police cruiser.

"I'll meet you there."

CHAPTER EIGHTEEN

The two police cars pulled up and parked on the street beside the Historic Baptist Church. The pastor, the Rev. Dr. Amos Jones, was the great-grand-son of a slave who had been freed at the age of fifteen after the Civil War and moved to Florida herding cattle for a living.

Dr. Jones was proud of his heritage as a fourth generation Floridian with strong family ties throughout the state. At one time, Dr. Jones was considered the most influential religious leader in Florida.

At 71, he still held reign on his church of 1800 members. But, the local community had taken its toll on the stately gentleman. Despite his continuing tirelessly to meet the basic needs of people in Overtown, when he stood his back was bowed slightly causing to walk with a limp.

The three detectives were buzzed into the church's office complex then ushered into a twenty by thirty-foot office with a large, antique desk Jones claimed was once owned by Robert E. Lee.

He loved to tell people he thought it fitting that the man that led the Army of The South should have provided the desk at which a Black man would help plan the integration of Black children into Southern Society.

He stood to his full height of 5'-7" as he winced with pain in his back and greeted Brown with his unique, larger-than-life smile.

"It's good to see a beautiful, young Black woman finding her way in a male dominated world. God Bless, you, Sweetheart."

He turned to Sanchez.

"I've heard many good things about your leadership at the Sheriff's office and your insistence upon equal treatment for all. I'm honored to have you in my office, Chief."

When he turned to Royce, he threw his arms around the slim, yet athletic frame of one of his many protégés from the streets of the projects. He broke the embrace only to hold both of Royce's shoulders at arm's length and wink at the other two police officers.

"I couldn't be prouder of this young man."

He walked back to his seat behind his desk which he treated like a throne from where he greeted his subjects. The twinkle in his eye gave away his delight that the police had finally come to his door for help.

"I assume you are here about the series of malicious and vile murders of God's people along A1A. I saw the news this morning; tragic."

"Yes sir," Brown interjected. "The reason we are here is to ask your permission and support in questioning the people at the Overtown Homeless shelter."

"Do you suspect someone in my congregation to be the killer?"

"No, pastor, we're simply checking out all possible leads to discovering the identity of the person or persons responsible for these deaths. And we are looking to see if the deceased men had ever visited or were regulars at the shelter."

"You think they all were here at one time or another, don't you?"

"We don't know a thing, Pastor. It was Royce who suggested we might start here since so many of the homeless people in

Miami come here to eat and sometimes sleep. Knowing if they did or did not might help lead us to another area and maybe even help us track down the perpetrator."

"I see," the old minister replied as he stroked his chin. "So, you're telling me that you don't suspect my volunteers or staff of these horrendous murders?"

"At this point, Dr. Jones," Royce said, "We don't suspect anyone at all. To be honest we have so few clues and are not sure just where to turn. But I recognized the first man killed in our area as someone who was a regular here when I was volunteering. I thought that a good person to talk to first would be you. After all, sir, you're in the forefront of helping these unfortunate men. If anyone could help, I knew you and the people who work in this ministry would be the ones."

Dr. Jones' smile creased the length of his face as he looked across his desk at Brown.

"Don't it make your heart feel good to hear a young Black man talk better than most Whites you run into?"

"Pastor," Brown said without cracking a smile. "Royce is a consummate professional, not just another poor black kid. I hope his explanation helped you to understand why it is that we're here. We're simply following a possible, if not improbable, connection to this investigation."

Dr. Jones let out a booming laugh that seemed to shake the room.

"My dear, please give an old Southern Negro the chance to gloat, okay?"

Brown had to smile as she shook her head in agreement. Royce put his face in his hands almost turning red with embarrassment.

"I'd be more than happy to escort you across the street to the homeless shelter," Jones continued." But, I'd suggest that you come back around three this afternoon instead. It just so happens that we have a staff meeting today at that time. That way you'll get a chance to meet everyone that works or volunteers for us on a regular basis. After the meeting, you'll be able to mingle among the people who'll be wandering in for dinner and perhaps for a place to sleep."

The pastor stood up; they all got the hint that they were being dismissed. So, the three stood

"We'll see you at the center at three o'clock," Sanchez said.

The pastor stood silently as the three walked out of his office.

Once they were outside and near the cars, Brown stopped the other two. She put her hand on Royce's shoulder.

"Royce, you put together a full report on the murders in your jurisdiction to this point with every possible detail, no matter how unimportant. Don't leave a thing out. Chief, you consolidate everything including any lab reports. This afternoon I'll set up a task force office at FDLE. That will help us coordinate everything. We'll keep all the clues, evidence reports, everything on these cases. Is that okay with you men?"

They both nodded in agreement.

"We'll meet at the homeless center at three," Brown said.

Royce got into his cruiser and drove to Sunny Isles Beach; Sanchez drove Brown back to her office. As he arrived at the the Miami-Dade Sheriff's department building, a deputy near the front desk attempted to get his attention through a stutter.

"Ch, Chief, the Sh, Sheriff wants ta, ta, see you A-A-ASAP."

Sanchez nodded at the deputy with an approving smile and turned toward the Sheriff's executive offices down a different hallway from his own cramped work station. The secretary announced his arrival.

"What's going on, Adolph?" The Sheriff growled through a reddish, scowling face. "I just got one terrible chewing out by the mayor this morning. And what was I able to say? Nothing! I didn't have a clue what he was talking about. Are you ready to brief me on the latest national news from Miami-Dade?"

"I'm so sorry, boss. I got the case a couple of days ago and was caught off guard by the publicity this morning just like you. I was gone most of the morning trying my best to get a handle on this mess."

The Sheriff leaned back and sighed.

"That's what I thought must have happened. So, I take it you didn't realize this may have been the work of a serial killer until today?"

"Well, sir, I had my suspicions as early as yesterday. But we got the lab results and other evidence late last evening. And just yesterday FDLE was able to put together a group of us to meet for discussions about similar murders occurring across five jurisdictions. FDLE is taking the lead on this and will set up a task force office today. I'll be meeting with the lead detective this afternoon."

"What's happening this afternoon?"

"I'll be following up on a possible tie between the victims."

"Good. So, my question now is--"

"Why am I personally involved this investigation?"

"Right."

"Well, Chief, I'm afraid I already screwed up this whole thing several days ago when Sunny Isles asked me to look at a report of a dead homeless man. I kind of, well, pushed it off to, uh, FDLE."

"You did what? Good god, man! What were you thinking?"

"I know, Boss. Please let me work this thing out for myself. I'll make sure you look good. I promise."

"You'd better make me look like the man that solved this thing, my friend."

Sanchez starred a moment. He realized the meeting had ended.

Closing the Sheriff's office door, Sanchez leaned against the wall with a huge sigh. He pulled himself away from the wall as his sweat-soaked shirt stuck to the surface. He walked quickly to his office, picked up the phone, and dialed.

"Perry? Sanchez. Let's do lunch."

CHAPTER NINETEEN

At eleven thirty, the restaurant at the hotel wasn't yet filled with diners. But, because this restaurant was so popular with the business crowd on Miami's Deco District, by twelve fifteen there wouldn't be a seat in the house.

I walked up to the front counter and handed a fifty-dollar bill to the maître d. He led me to one of the best tables next to the windows facing the ocean. I barely got seated when I heard my name from across the room.

Adolph Sanchez moved like a precision driver to get through the barriers of chairs and people to the seat across from me.

"I take it something pretty heavy happened last night or this morning.

"You're right, Perry. This thing is worse than I thought."

"I assumed that the reporter on television did not talk to you before telling everyone in Miami about a serial killer who is hunting down homeless men."

"You hit it hard, my friend. I've got to pull this one out my ass real fast or I may just lose my job. And my head won't be the only thing of mine to roll, either."

"I take it the mayor and the sheriff were after your hide today."

"No shit, Sherlock. And the problem is, I've got a total of zero evidence of any kind. Nothing points me to the murderer."

"You need to eat something and calm down."

"I'm going to be eating a great deal of crow if I don't come up with at least a teaspoon full of evidence in a couple of hours!"

"Calm down, my friend," I attempted to sooth Sanchez. "This is no different than some of the cases we handled back in Brooklyn."

"This just seems far more serious. That's all."

"I understand I'm here to help out in this. I mean, it may take us a few more days, but what we have right now is enough to begin with. We can look at some interesting and probable suspects. All we need now is to find opportunity and motive."

"Speaking of motive, here comes a motive for my murder walking across the room."

As I turned, Fara Flambeau moved like a well-aimed arrow across the room right to Sanchez talking before she got to within fifteen feet of the table.

As she approached, we both stood.

"Adolph Sanchez," she said with fire in her eyes. "I thought you were a top-notch detective. But it appears you're an S.O.B. How could you let something like this happen?"

"My dear Miss Flambeau," I said. "Will you please join us for lunch?"

Taken off guard, she stammered for a moment.

"Out of respect for you, Chief," She said with a calmer voice, "I'll be happy to join you; as long as you allow me to question your guest."

"He's all yours," I responded with a smile.

"Thanks, Friend," Sanchez spoke with a voice dripping with sarcasm.

We sat as a waiter moved to the table, put a place-setting before Fara's seat, and moved away.

"I take it that you heard the news about the murder last night?" Sanchez said.

"What else would I be referring to?"

"Please accept my deepest sympathies."

"You are disarming, aren't you?"

"Well, I believe that calm heads can prevail in any investigation of murder. I've seen it happen too often that patience, clues, and a cool head will lead to the perpetrator and a guilty verdict."

"I hope so. The homeless are beginning to abandon the shelters here and in Ft. Lauderdale. They think the murderer is following people as they leave those places; then murdering them in the night."

"I understand the fear these people must feel. But there are some things that they need to understand. First, only men from out of state have been murdered. Second, we have found several pieces of evidence that have given us a direction in which we need to look. And third--"

"What evidence?" Fara snapped.

"I'm sorry but, at this moment, I am not at liberty to discuss matters such as that. I hope you will understand my reluctance to be specific."

"I'm sorry, Chief, Go on."

"And third, we have formed a special FDLE task force to coordinate this investigation across two counties and about five police jurisdictions. So, I think we're on our way to ending these deaths."

"I'm glad to hear that," Fara paused. "As far as I'm concerned, you have two days to solve this case. After that I'll be on the warpath. And I think you know what that means."

She turned to me with what I thought was a slight smile in her eye.

"I appreciate your invitation for lunch. I cannot stay. May I take a rain check on that invitation?"

"Of course," I responded in a polite tone. "I definitely look forward to it."

Fara turned to Sanchez with a nod and walked out of the room as quickly as she had arrived.

I chuckled a bit despite myself.

"That woman is a piece of work," I said.

"A piece of something, maybe. Her problem is she believes all the gossip people spread about her. I'm convinced she comes up with most of it to put herself right in the middle of everything happening in this town."

"What about her father?"

"Oh, he's just a fine old gentleman in his late sixties who's enjoying the fruits of his labors."

"Tell me about him."

"Let's order first," as Sanchez signaled for a waiter. "I'll fill you in on the whole dysfunctional Flambeau family."

At that the waiter arrived to take our orders.

About forty-five minutes later, we sat with a cup of coffee watching the interesting people walk by.

I broke the silence.

"So, what's the story with the Flambeau's?"

"What I'm about to tell you is the result of a lot of official investigating; and, uh, not so officially."

"Got it."

"The old man, Frankie, is rumored to have moved here from The Bronx some thirty years ago. He was about thirty when he got here. So, he was no spring chicken, if you catch my drift."

"He had a history in the city?"

"History ain't the word for it. He was heavily involved with our Italian friends across the river, you know?"

"Oh."

"I got it on good authority that he may have been a hit man for one of the families. It seems he got a sweetheart deal from the attorney general when he turned against the big man in his family. He was shipped down here with a new identity and a big bank account. That's when he went into the big-box retail business."

"Legitimate?"

"Very much so. We haven't found a thing that would indicate otherwise. But, it seems he runs his business almost like a family. All the senior positions in the firm are held by cousins, aunts, and uncles, of sorts."

"I thought you said--"

"Oh yeah. Family in this case is from the wife's side."

"Who's she?"

"She's Adelaide Gramichi."

"You mean--?"

"Yep. The same. Sicily and everything."

"What the--."

"No kidding. And they ran the entire big box industry in Florida until about twenty-five years ago when that Arkansas bunch moved down here in a big way. I mean, he tried to stop them. But things were beyond his control at that point."

"What happened?"

"Not much. He hadn't kept up with the changing times. Too many people throughout Florida didn't care about him or his stores. Too many rumors, you know?"

"Right."

Sanchez took a big drink of coffee and continued. "Farah came along as a late addition to the family. The way I hear it, the old man and his wife thought they couldn't have children when she became pregnant. Interesting, huh?"

"I'll say. So, I take it she was spoiled?"

"Spoiled ain't the word. By the time she was sixteen, she did more working part time than any senior V.P. did working full time. It didn't take the old man long to realize the goldmine he had on his hands. When she graduated from Wellesley, he made her senior vice president and C.O.O. of the entire operation."

"Whoa! I'll bet that angered a bunch of people."

"Uh, right. By the time she turned twenty-four, the Board of Directors forced the old man into giving her a huge endowment and a chance to be a full-time philanthropist."

"Wait a minute. Why would he agree to that?"

"Flame Mart had gone public. It opened at fifteen. And in less than two weeks it was at a thirty-five."

"Wow. What's it worth now?"

"Shares closed yesterday at forty-eight. So, you can see why he had to agree. There were over twelve thousand share-holders involved. This was no longer a family owned and operated store. It was a major American corporation with too much at stake to be turned over to a twenty-four-year-old."

"I'll bet that didn't sit too well with that little sweetheart."

"No kidding. She invested almost a third of her endowment fund in Flame Mart shares and became a major stock holder. The Board has been able to keep her out of things to this point;

but if she continues to buy shares at the rate she has, she'll own the company in five years whether the board likes it or not. At that point, I fully expect her to fire everyone on the board and do a true hostile take-over, probably with a Tech-Nine."

I chuckled at that.

"So, she's just biding her time," I said, "By running places like the homeless shelter?"

"Right. Anyway, if she's involved in some way with this whole thing, I would be quite surprised. I don't think she would risk all she has for something as petty as killing homeless men. That's not in her nature. Besides, she has nothing to gain by being involved."

"Well, maybe we don't have to worry about that since I've seen nothing that would indicate her involvement at this point. Well, except for her OCD and control issues."

"Understood. But, knowing her and her family as I do; well, who knows what will happen?"

"So, is that everything?"

"Well, there are rumors that Flambeau had a son in New York before he moved down here. It was in the papers, you know, in the Jersey society news at the time the kid was born. Anyway, I don't know what happened to him; at least nothing's been known since before Frankie and his family moved here."

"So, did he become a part of the family organization?" I asked.

"I don't know. Probably, but I have no proof."

"That would make him in his late thirties?"

"Yes, I guess so."

"I'd have thought he'd be down here trying to get in on his old man's good side."

"Haven't had any indication of that happening. The last I heard, he was upstate doing a nickel for armed robbery about fifteen years ago. At least, that's the rumors."

I leaned back in my chair and took a deep breath. As I sat looking out the window onto the street, I thought how pleasant it was to be able to look out over a beautiful beach with numerous tanned, blond, young ladies everywhere.

A man in a black hoodie walked by in front of the restaurant looking around as if afraid or suspicious of something.

"Speaking of suspicions," I said, turning to Sanchez, "Have you gotten any word from the lab on those two plastic pieces you turned up?"

"No. But, I expect to have something on my desk this afternoon. Oh, but I did get the results on the exhaust stains on the grass. The only thing the lab guys could tell was the engine was using the highest grade of gasoline."

"There aren't that many cars on the road that burn that anymore. I know my Mercedes does."

"That's what the lab boys deduced."

Sanchez got up and placed a fifty in the check folder.

"I'll call you," he said to me. "If there is anything else."

"I appreciate that, and you don't need to pay for my lunch."

"I invited you. I'll pay. With that fifty, you can order yourself a Champaign cocktail."

We laughed. Sanchez walked out. I took another drink from my coffee cup.

"Ugh; cold."

CHAPTER TWENTY

At about five minutes to three Sanchez, Carolina, and Royce walked into the homeless shelter together. Twenty-five people were seated in the dining room. Pastor Jones stood in front of them and asked the volunteers to join him in prayer just as the three detectives sat near the back.

Sanchez noted that the group of people gathered were from all ages: one old gentleman who looked to be about eighty to a young girl who couldn't have been more than twelve. He was intrigued by the variety of ages and colors.

Although the Historic Baptist Church was a historically Black congregation. This group of volunteers was from all ethnic and racial groups leading Sanchez to realize that this ministry was a community-wide effort, not just the work of a single church.

When the pastor was finished praying he looked around the room.

"My good friends and colleagues in the work of the Lord, we face a serious dilemma. In our attempt to help bring comfort and solace to those in need, someone has decided to solve these people's needs by ending their lives. This activity can no longer be tolerated."

"Pastor, how does this involve us?" One of the volunteers said.

"Excellent question, Brother Anthony. Allow me to introduce to you three people who are here to tell us just how these horrible crimes involve your work here at the homeless shelter. I'm going to ask that the three detectives in the back of the room join me here and introduce themselves to you."

The three stood, walked to the front, and lined up next to the pastor. Sanchez spoke first.

"I'm Adolph Sanchez, chief of detectives for the Dade County Sheriff's office. Next to me is DeShawn Royce, detective with the Sunny Isles Police. And this is Carolina Brown, special agent with the Florida Department of Law Enforcement."

The audience applauded politely at the pastor's encouragement.

Carolina stepped forward. "Ladies and Gentlemen, FDLE has formed a task force to investigate the murders of several homeless men. At this point we have no reason to believe that these killings were not random. But, to be pro-active, FDLE is working with the Broward Sheriff's Office and several police departments along A1A to coordinate all information on any killings of homeless men in the county."

A gentleman on the back row stood with his hand raised as if in school.

"Okay, so you're investigating. But what are you doing to protect the homeless?"

"Yeah," said Brother Anthony. "And what's this got to do with us?"

"I wish to address those questions." Sanchez said. "They are tied to our investigation of the three most recent murders in Dade County. It appears that each of the men may have visited here either the day of or the day before they were murdered. We are not certain that their presence here was associated with their deaths. But that's the only connection we've been able to find between them so far. We're still looking at other possible connections as well."

Sanchez held up several pictures of the dead men. He asked if anyone had seen these men, and, if so, when.

"I've seen all these men at one time or another," a rather elderly woman with her hair in tight bun on the top of her head. "That white man with the light hair, he was around here just a day or so ago. Is he dead?"

"Yes, ma'am. He's dead. And do you remember what day it was you saw him?"

She thought for a moment, her eyes closed as she rubbed her chin.

"I don't recollect when I saw him last. Nope. I'm not sure."

"That's okay. We appreciate your willingness to help. What about the others?"

Several people spoke out about different pictures. A few minutes later, there was a consensus that all the men in the pictures had been in the shelter at some time or other in recent days. Carolina was taking notes as fast as she could.

"We appreciate all the help you've given us today," Sanchez said finishing up the discussion. "In the meantime, we wish to request that you keep us informed of any activity you may see that you think is suspicious or out of the ordinary. Your cooperation can allow us to identify specific men we can check up on during the night to make sure they're safe."

"So, you want us to become your snitches?" asked Brother Anthony.

"No," Royce replied. "Many of you remember me when I was a volunteer here before I went to the Police Academy."

"Wait a minute." Brother Anthony interrupted.

He walked to the front and up to Royce. He placed his hands on the policeman's face. A wide smile stretched across the old man's face.

"My, my, my! It's little DeShawn from over to the One Two Three projects. Boy, you looking real good all dressed up in that uniform. Yes, sir, mighty fine."

He laughed as he walked back to his seat while several other people in the audience commented to one another about Little DeShawn coming home.

"It's good to be back here again," Royce continued. "And please understand that this time I've come with the same heart of love for the people of this neighborhood that I had five years ago. But this time the problem is different and far worse. So, let me say that y'all need our help and we need yours. We're not asking you to be snitches, we're asking you to watch out for each other and for the people who come here for help. We need you to look out for them. You see, by calling us, you'll be helping to protect the people who come here; the people you care about."

Another person who had said nothing to this point stood up.

"How do we know these murders involve this shelter? There are several other shelters around here."

"That is true. And we don't know for sure. All we know is that we're discussing this issue with all the other shelters as well. It's just that this is the first clue of any consequence that we've gotten. We're simply trying to follow up on it. You see, we're also trying to protect the shelter as well. If the word got around that people were being murdered because they came here, well, you get my point?"

Silence filled the room for several long moments, then Brother Anthony stood and turned to the others. His face seemed strange: a darkness seemed to cover his eyes.

"Well, I for one want to help our little brother DeShawn. Him I trust. And if he says we ain't snitches. I believe him."

The crowd fell totally silent. A younger lady on the front row shifted in her seat as if nervous.

"So," Brother Anthony said to the young detective. "Will you give us a telephone number where we can reach you, Little DeShawn. We'll be happy to let you know if we see something that we think ain't just right. I'm afraid I ain't calling no police. Okay?"

With that the Pastor stepped forward. He indicated to Brother Anthony to sit. He reached over and patted the young lady on the front row on her shoulder. She smiled. He looked out at the group of volunteers.

"I want to thank these people for taking the initiative to investigate these murders and to offer their help to protect our clientele. I mean, we didn't have to protest and march to get the attention of the police on this matter. All of you know how I worked with the Miami Police to get us more patrols in this area. Now they're here. And it looks like they want to help."

"So," he said turning to Royce. "Can I give each one of our volunteers a card with your name and phone number on it? Maybe with instructions as to what to look for?"

"Yes, sir," said Royce as he handed him a packet of cards. "Here are fifty of my personal cards with a twenty-four-hour phone number on each. Also, there's a list of tips of things to look for on the back to help out as well."

The people stood up with applause. The three detectives shook the pastor's hand and walked out of the meeting.

On the street, Sanchez reached his hand out to Royce.

"I want to thank you for what you did in there. Those folks ... well, I was afraid we might have problems."

"I thought of all that and more before you did. I know how these people think, and I knew what they needed to hear. That's why I came prepared. I was hoping that would be okay. I mean, I am a rookie at this detective stuff."

"So," Brown chuckled. "What's with this 'Little' DeShawn business?"

"Hey, you gotta understand. These folks have known me since I was born. I wasn't a big kid. I mean, even now I'm still only five-foot-seven and barely weigh a hundred and sixty pounds. To folks like Brother Anthony I'll always be Little DeShawn."

Sanchez and Brown both laughed and patted Royce on the back.

"You're going to do just fine, young man." Brown said. "Just fine."

At that Royce walked toward his patrol car as the others got into their car and drove off.

As the car reached the Interstate, Sanchez looked over at Brown.

"I just hope to God this idea helps and somehow we get just a small break in this case."

"As you said, it's the only lead we've got so we have to follow it."

They both smiled as they drove back to FDLE headquarters.

CHAPTER TWENTY-ONE

The next morning Laura Taylor was busy at her desk at the FDLE Regional Headquarters. When her phone rang, she quickly grabbed it and looked at the screen. It seemed familiar; so, she pressed the answer button.

"Special Agent Taylor."

"Got a tip for you, Sweetheart."

"Who is this?"

"Oh, I'm so hurt that you don't remember me."

"Give me a hint."

"Sorry. You'll figure it out."

"Okay, so what's your tip?"

"You might want to check out that rent-a-cop from New York you got working."

"What do you know about him or this case?"

"Never mind. I'm just giving you a heads up. Ask him why he left the force. That should tell you everything you need to know."

"Okay. I'll bite. What's the real tip?"

"Look, little lady--"

"Nick Turner! You sorry little--"

"Easy, lady. I ain't finished, yet. So, check into that ex-cop. I'll bet you'll find he's involved in some deep crap. Perry Savant made big headlines in New York papers, you know, a few months ago."

"Okay, Turner. I'll check it out. But, you, you and I are finished. Okay?"

"If that's the way you want to play this--"

"It is."

"Yes. No. Well, you'll thank me for this tip." The phone went dead.

Laura immediately called Carolina.

"Agent Carolina Brown here."

"Carolina, what have you not told me about the A1A investigation?"

"Chief? I'm not sure what you mean."

"Did you thoroughly vet that NYPD cop you've got involved in this? And what were you thinking not telling me everything about his background?"

"I'm sorry, Laura. It was Sanchez that brought him in on the investigation. He's a specialist in serial killings. He retired as deputy commissioner or something like that. Sanchez vouched for him and was the one who invited him in on the case. I think he and Sanchez grew up together and even served on the NYPD together."

"So, what's he going to cost us? You know the governor has cut back on our budget."

"He's doing this as a favor to Sanchez, I think. I'll check that out to be sure, though. Believe me, Chief; this was not my idea at all. And I made my feelings clear to Sanchez when he told me."

"I trust you, Carolina."

"So, why the third-degree routine?"

"Nothing. You might want to do a deeper background check on this guy. I don't want to be blind-sided. Just keep me posted, okay?"

"I will."

As soon as she hung up, Carolina called Sanchez.

"Sanchez here."

"Is there something about this detective you brought into this case that you haven't told me?"

"Ah, Agent Brown; I don't know what you mean."

"Oh, come on. Why would my chief call me with her butt out of gear over his being involved?"

"Seriously, Carolina; I don't know what she could be referring to. He actually was Chief detective in the office of the Commissioner of Police for NYPD. He's the best in the country on serial killings, and he's also an expert on hate crimes."

"I'll have to bring it up with him when we get together tomorrow."

"Uh, there is one thing--"

"For real, Chief?"

"I know. But I can't for the life of me think why it would be an issue."

"Just tell me."

"He was outed by some two-bit ex-con. And because of the NYPD's 'don't ask; don't tell' policy, he chose to retire early rather than place the commissioner in any negative light. But, there was nothing criminal that was involved."

"That can't be it."

"What was it that could have caused Laura to go ballistic?"

"I'll have to talk to her about that. Probably one of her sources on the street. You know she's kept most of her snitches close to the chest all these years."

"I'm sure they all enjoy being close to that chest."

"Give me a break, Chief. Anyway, I'll see what she has to say about it. In the meantime, let's be careful just how we use Perry. Okay?"

"Okay; no problem. But—"

"Damn it, Sanchez. How does it get?"

"Well, there were accusations, but no proof about an alderman in The Bronx."

"What alderman?"

"Well he and I grew up in Park Slope, and one of our high school buddies later became an Alderman. Anyway, he was found shot to death in a flop house with a teenager in Brooklyn. They were both naked and in bed together; you know?"

"Okay, and what?"

"Well, it seems that some young Brooklyn detective thought that Perry was trying to cover up the whole thing because he knew the Alderman."

"Oh God, Sanchez. Why didn't you tell me about all this before—"

"Hey, Brown, he's the best there is. Plus, I know him. He didn't do what they said he did. Besides there was no proof. And the Chief of Police Departments deemed the accusations as unfounded. The whole thing was dropped. How the papers found out is anybody's guess."

"Sanchez, your credibility with me has dropped a few points."

"Fair enough. I'll call you as soon as I get that report from the lab on the plastic pieces we picked up at the crime scenes. I'm expecting it any moment."

"Okay. Talk to you then. But, Sanchez, Please—"

"I know. You'll know as soon as I know."

As Sanchez hung up the phone, there was a knock at the door. In walked Willie Abraham who had to bend over slightly to walk into the room. His 6'-11" frame often gave him problems in the police headquarters building.

But, the constant smile on his face was strangely disarming as he seemed to lumber everywhere he went.

Normally, a candidate his height would never have been accepted into the academy, but Willie Abraham was no ordinary man. Because of the department's affirmative action program, he was allowed to test out.

When he made a perfect score on both the physical and written tests, an exception was made to allow his participation. During his first five years on the force, he attended college at Florida International University and earned a B.A. in pre-law.

He entered law school at Nova-Southeastern University, attending classes at night and on the week-ends. He finished at the top of his class and immediately passed the bar exam.

But, because of his love for police work, he requested a reassignment to Internal Affairs where he worked hard to keep the Sheriff's Department free of any hint of corruption.

Sanchez was not happy to see Sergeant Abraham. This charming, tall, light-skinned Black man was one of the few men in the department who was never welcomed in any office.

As Sanchez reached out his hand to shake the large hand of his colleague, he figured that the Sheriff must be getting a great deal of heat about Savant.

Sanchez swallowed.

"Chief, the sheriff asked me to check with you on a couple of situations in your department. He's not worried, so this visit never happened ... yet. He's simply been privy to rumors about some possible irregularities."

"And to which irregularities is he referring?" Sanchez asked calmly, still not showing his building anger.

"The sheriff asked that I simply keep an eye out on what's happening with the A1A murders. That's all."

Sanchez sat silent for a few moments; then took a deep breath.

"Are you planning to follow me around on this investigation?"

"No, chief; my orders are simply to observe what's happening here. I've been asked to make sure nothing untoward occurs."

Sanchez leaned forward and placed his elbows on his desk and laid his hands down flat on top of several pieces of paper in front of him.

"Well, if that's all, I have a major investigation to oversee."

Abraham did not budge. Instead he pulled out a notebook and pencil.

"Who is the lead investigator on this case?"

Sanchez was in the process of standing up but fell back into his chair as Abraham asked his question. He realized this guy wasn't going to be manipulated. Sanchez had been with the sheriff for nearly fifteen years, yet he had never worked with Abraham. But, in less than two minutes, he realized the man was all business: a perfect fit for Internal Affairs.

Planning his words carefully, Sanchez spoke.

"I haven't assigned anyone to this case because it isn't our case. We're cooperating with FDLE. They're in charge of this investigation. Special Agent Carolina Brown has been appointed the lead agent over there on this case."

"And what is our involvement?"

"We're cooperating since several of the murders were committed in Dade County; and I have offered the resources of our lab facilities for all evidence processing. I did that to ensure the proper processing and no delay in communications. As you probably remember, the FDLE lab was cut back and merged with the Broward County lab. Also, I felt our lab was more secure than the one in Broward."

"And how did that arrangement come about?" Abraham said as he wrote down a few notes.

"I suggested it. We already had some evidence at our lab from the crime scene in Sunny Isles. Their CSI officer works directly with our lab. I thought it would be best to keep all the evidence at one place for processing. Besides, with the recent multi-million-dollar upgrade, I felt we had the best facilities available. And I wanted the sheriff to get some of the credit when the case is finally solved."

Abraham nodded his head as if agreeing and continued to write in his little book. He looked up, his eyes cold.

"And who is--" He paused and looked at his book then continued, "Perry Savant?"

"I invited Perry to look at some aspects of this case purely as a paid consultant. He's an old friend from New York."

"You recognize it's against department policy to allow unauthorized access to investigations by civilians?"

"Don't quote the regulations to me, Abraham. I developed most of 'em before you arrived."

"No offense intended, chief. You know I'm only doing my job, just like you."

"First, Perry is no civilian. He's retired NYPD and holds a PI license in Florida. And second, now that we understand each other, let me get back to my job. And you can do whatever it is that you think you need to do."

Without ceremony, Sergeant Abraham stood up, shook Sanchez's hand, and walked out into the hall.

Sanchez sighed as Abraham left. He picked up a file, opened it and began reading. A few minutes later a clerk came to his door with an interoffice envelope and handed it to him.

Sanchez immediately opened it and took out two sheets of paper, each with a title at the top: "Lab Results—Official." As soon as he read the pages, he picked up his phone.

"Carolina? Sanchez here. Both plastic pieces were from similar make and model, a Mercedes S550, one of the big ones. The paint on the one piece is the black used only by Mercedes and specifically on that model."

"Good," Carolina replied. "I'll do a quick check on the number of those in the two counties and get back to you."

"I think we may be on to something. I mean, why would a car like that be in those specific places where the murders took place?"

Laura laughed for a moment or two.

"Chief," she said. "Some of the most expensive high-rise apartments and condos are all along A1A. I don't even want to think about how many Mercedes automobiles are--"

"I knew that," Sanchez laughed. "Anyway, I'll send a copy of these reports over to Frazier in Broward and to Royce at Sunny Isles. You should be getting your copy shortly. When I'm done here, I think I'll go talk to Perry about these results and see what he thinks."

"Okay, chief. I'll talk to you tomorrow. And let's hope there's not another murder tonight."

With that little jab, Sanchez hung up and looked over at the clock. It was nearly four thirty. He picked up the phone and asked a clerk to come to his office. A young lady stuck her head in the door.

"Make copies of this and bring me one," he said. "Send a copy to Detective Chief Frazier at the Broward Sheriff's office and send another to patrolman Royce at Sunny Isles; oh, and one to Carolina Brown at FDLE."

"Yes, sir," the young lady replied and left. A couple of minutes later she returned and handed him a copy.

He picked up the phone, dialed a number, and listened to it ring.

"Perry are you eating dinner, yet?"

"It's a bit early for that, don't you think?"

"Right, so let me buy you dinner. Meet me at a little place north of your hotel on A1A called Chilly Willie's.

"I noticed that place the other day. What time?"

"I'm going to run by the house and change into something relaxing. I'll see you there about seven."

"Sounds good to me; see you then. Oh, what is this all about?"

"Evidence results," Sanchez said as he hung up the phone and folded the copy of the evidence report. He stood up, tightened his tie, and put on his suit coat. He placed the folded report into his coat pocket and walked out of the office. When he got into his car, he caught a slight glimpse of someone else getting into a car.

At first, he felt nervous but shook it off.

He turned on his engine and drove off. After he pulled into traffic, another car pulled out of the parking lot and turned in the same direction.

CHAPTER TWENTY-TWO

It was a little past seven when I walked into the restaurant. I stood waiting for the receptionist to notice me. As I looked around, I felt repulsed by the overpowering smell of beer, whiskey, and sweat. And the band!

They played so loudly that I wondered if I might lose my hearing several decibels each hour I stayed. I stood there screwing up the courage to go in. This was not the dining atmosphere I was accustomed to in Manhattan.

Against my better judgement, I entered the larger room and looked around for Sanchez. That's when I realized I was so over-dressed that I could see people looking at me pointing.

I let out a laugh as I thought about how much I needed to get used to this kind of atmosphere so common in South Florida. This part of the country is not the sort of place where you dress up. So, I took off my coat, loosened my tie, and then heard someone calling my name.

I walked toward the direction of the voice. I stared out onto the back patio which looked out over the ocean. I saw Sanchez seated at a table wearing matching shorts and shirt with a gaudy flower pattern. I shook my head knowing it was too late to bow out. So, I took a deep breath and approached Sanchez's table.

My old friend stood and yelled loud enough to be heard over the band. "Perry! Glad you could make it. Have a seat."

I made my way through what seemed to be too many people for such a small place. When I sat down I realized that we weren't going to do much talking.

"I just love this place!" Adolph said as he leaned the chair back on two legs. "It helps me take my mind off all the horrible things we have to put up with at work. Here I don't have to worry about a thing. Besides, if my beeper or cell phone rings, I won't hear it."

"I see," I said trying to be nice.

"Come on, Perry. Lighten up."

"This isn't quite my kind of place."

"I know; that's why I invited you. This is the real life-style of south Florida. I mean, look out there; the ocean, the beach, people having fun; what more could you want?"

"A little quiet?"

"You'll get used to it. Here's a menu. Everything is terrific. But I recommend the coconut fried shrimp. The sauce is to die for."

I shook my head (realizing I was doing a lot of that recently) and looked at the menu. As I did, I noticed two men sitting at a table near us whose dress was as much out of place as mine.

"So, who are your friends? They keep looking over here."

"The two suits sitting at the table looking more out of place than you? I know. I figure they're from Internal Affairs."

"What? Why would IA be interested in you?"

"They're not. They're interested in why I'm interested in you?"

"Does Dade County have some rule about detectives talking to private investigators?"

"No. The Sheriff doesn't like involving out of company people in our work. He's kinda irritated that I asked you to help out on the case."

"Hey, I know what that's all about. You want I should back off?"

"Absolutely not. I asked you to help because no one else in our department, or the United States for that matter, has as much experience as you with serial killers. Besides, I'm not going to let that little political hack interfere with a real investigation. He'll screw it up for sure."

The waiter came over. I ordered the broiled grouper with veggies on the side.

"What a wimp!" Sanchez said with a grin as he ordered the shrimp.

"You were right about those small pieces we found. They're both from the same make and model Mercedes."

"I had no idea. I just thought it was odd that we found the pieces."

"Why is that?"

"I would figure that this murderer was a bit more organized. That's all. He, or she, may have wanted us to find those pieces so we would get closer and give him a chance to show off a bit more; maybe prove he's smarter than us."

"Maybe," said Sanchez as he took a drink from the huge pineapple-shaped mug in front of him. "I've got Laura checking on the people who own that particular model Mercedes and who live in or near the area."

"That could be a long list, my friend. I would imagine that the number of Mercedes autos in this county has got to be--"

"Huge! Yes, I know. But, the paint from the smaller chip is exclusive to the newer models. So we only have to worry about two year old models of the big town car."

"I see. That could narrow it down to a manageable number which, by the way, will include me. I own a new one of those myself. Will you investigate me?"

Sanchez looked hard at me.

"What are you doing with a hundred-thousand-dollar car?"

"I just wanted one. Why?"

"You're a cop, man. That's a rich man's car."

"I know. But after twenty-five years of police work and no life outside the department and all. You see, I put away quite a bit of money in the bank. You might say, I'm pretty rich myself. Besides, I thought I deserved to pamper myself a little and buy a truly great car."

"You're full of surprises, my friend."

At that the waiter arrived with their meals.

"Whoa!" I said. "That was quick."

"Hey! Look around you. We're the only people eating. Everyone else is drinking."

I laughed loudly as we dove into our meals. The band began its own unique version of "Y.M.C.A." as the people in the place applauded and sang along. They even formed the hand and arm movements to accompany the words.

"Do you think any of these children know what that song is about?" I said leaning closer to him.

"They've come up with meanings we never thought about back in our day."

We laughed together and began singing along with the rest of the crowd.

CHAPTER TWENTY-THREE

The sound of the song "YMCA" woke me from a sound sleep. I remembered that I had programed my phone to play that song whenever Sanchez called.

"Why is he calling me this early?" I said aloud.

I felt a sinking feeling in my stomach as I pushed the talk button and answered, "What is it, Sanchez?"

"We got another one; this time, a floater. Same tire tracks on his face. But the killer rolled the body into the intra-coastal."

"Where?"

"Ninety-Sixth Street overpass right at Surfside Park."

"I'll be there in thirty minutes."

"And, Perry."

I could hear the concern in Sanchez's voice and quickly responded: "What is it?"

"Every news agency in the world got here before we did. They're calling Miami the murder capital of the world."

"That bad?"

"Worse. I just got word that homeless people are lining the streets with signs for rides out of town."

"You were afraid of this, weren't you?"

"Oh, yea; see you in a few."

I hung up the phone and got out of bed. I grab my revolver and thought that perhaps I won't need it. So, I put the trigger lock on it and placed it in the safe anchored to the hotel room floor. I finished getting dressed and left with haste.

When I approached the intersection of A1A and Ninety-Fifth Street, I turned left as the GPS instructed. Less than a block from Bay Drive, I pulled up and parked off to the side. A police road block was set up northbound.

As I walked up to the officers guarding the road, I pulled out my NYPD Retired credentials and asked if I could enter since Chief Sanchez had invited me there.

One of the officers stepped out of earshot and used his radio to call to the crime scene. He came back over and said, "Sorry about that, sir. We had to be sure."

"No problem." I leaned under the tape and walked the half-block to the park where there were about a dozen official and unmarked police and other rescue vehicles. When I heard my name called, I walked over toward the water where Chief Sanchez was standing with Laura Taylor and Carolina Brown. DeShawn Royce from Sunny Isles Police was standing a few feet away, talking to another officer.

As I moved toward them, I noticed the tire tracks leading to the water.

"What do we have?" I asked.

"Hi Perry, thanks for coming," Sanchez said. "It looks like our killer chased down and killed another homeless guy. We have yet to identify who he was. Looks like the victim got hit here with the car and the perp ran over his face as before. It also appears the killer rolled the body to the water and let it drop in."

I walked over to the edge of the water and could see where the paramedics and deputies in a police water craft from Sunny Isles were working to free the body and lift it to the shore.

"Dumb luck for the suspect, huh?" I observed.

Sanchez laughed slightly. "No kidding. When the body fell, it caught on the rocks there which wedged the body, so it couldn't float out to the ocean."

The firemen standing on the rocks lifted the body strapped to a wire basket. They raised it slowly and swung it over to the men on the shore. There, the Coroner's assistants transferred the body onto an unzipped black body bag laying on a gurney.

Sanchez and I walked over to the M.E. on duty.

"Are there any physical indications as to when this happened?" asked Sanchez.

"This one is going to be difficult because of the effect of the water on body temp," the medical examiner said bluntly. "Besides, Chief, you know better than to ask me that now. I'll be able to tell you more after we get him back to the lab."

Sanchez handed the man a card.

"Call me with the result ASAP."

"I will."

The two men from the ME's office zipped up the bag and rolled the body over to the Van.

"There doesn't seem to be much evidence here just like the others," Laura said.

"Except that there is no way the suspect's car could have avoided damage running through that fence over there," Sanchez answered.

"I'll have our people check out the repair shops in the county to alert them to report any black Mercedes brought in with front-end damage," Carolina added.

"We'll do the same," Sanchez added. We'll find that car if it's in the county."

"You know," DeShawn spoke up. "Someone who owns that kind of car might be able to have the front end fixed without anyone finding out. Either that or they could get rid of that car without anyone finding out."

"What did you say?" I asked.

"He's got an excellent point there," Carolina said.

"Adolph, you'd better have someone check out the docks," I added. "That car could end up in a container headed for Brazil if we're not careful. We'll never find it or be able to tie the car to the murder."

"This thing keeps getting more and more complicated," Laura said as she shook her head slowly. "I think we're looking at one nasty killer with a deep grudge against the homeless,"

"A grudge?" I asked.

Laura turned to me.

"Yea, these murders seem to be sort of like grudge killings, you know?"

"Look," I said, "I need to do some thinking and deeper investigating on this motivational option."

"I'm sorry, but you're not authorized to be doing any private investigating. So, I'm going to assign Carolina to go with you. She'll get you into wherever you think is necessary and authorize any questions that you need to ask."

"I'll be honored to have Detective Brown accompany me," I said.

Carolina stared hard at Laura for what seemed like a long time. She followed me to my car. As she got in and leaned back deep into the luxurious leather seat.

"Oooh! I think I could get used to this."

I started the engine, put the car into drive, and drove off. As I turned onto the street, I turned slightly toward her.

"I hope you're not too upset by your chief hanging me around your neck."

"It's not her. She's gotten a little, well; let's just say there are a few people in top positions in the county who are not happy that you're involved."

I couldn't help myself as I laughed and thought about that for several moments.

"I guess I don't blame them," I said. "I mean, Adolf is the only one around who knows me. Some people have taken his word that I'm okay."

"He's not the only one who is familiar with your work."

"Oh? And who else knows about me?" I questioned, stifling a smile.

"I've studied several of your major investigations during the past ten years. You've solved some tough cases."

"I can't take all the credit for any of those."

"I know that," she said shyly. "But, you headed up the investigations. And that means you were in charge. So, you deserve the biggest part of the credit."

"Thank you for that vote of confidence. But, I'm going to give you a little secret that most detectives discover after decades of investigations."

"What are you talking about ... observation?"

My laughter filled the interior of the car such that I almost choked. I took a deep breath and Calmed down.

"No, my dear, even as important as that is, it's not the real secret."

"So, just what is the true secret to being a good investigator?"

"Dumb luck."

"What?"

"Dumb luck: that's what every detective depends upon. You know. You watch and wait for the little event, or word, or arrest that comes your way and ends up breaking a frustrating case. Or you wait for the suspect to make that one mistake that gives away their motive or the location of a key piece of evidence."

"I see."

"Now don't get me wrong. It takes a trained and observant detective who has developed the essential skills to realize when the break happens, or the mistakes occur. It takes those unique skills to put that event or mistake together with everything else to deduce that it all fits together. And that trained eye and ear will make a case against the one person who truly is guilty. Experience and a little wisdom on the side is what real investigating is all about."

"I guess I'm just a hopeless romantic," Carolina continued. "But, I like to think that it takes more than just luck to solve cases."

"I'm not trying to take that away from you. I think that's where dedication and commitment to the job comes from. But, eventually--"

I paused and turned off A1A onto a side street leading to one of the previous murder sites. "Why don't we stop here? I think this is where the second murder occurred."

"It was the third."

I pulled up to the curb, turned off the engine, and opened the door. We got out and walked over to where some of the chalk markings could still be seen. There were also a couple of small pieces of yellow police line tape caught in one of the bushes nearby.

We walked around silently for several minutes as I looked closely at what seemed like every blade of grass and every bump in the asphalt of the street. I continued looking around and noticed how close the viaduct was that crossed the canal.

"Strange that no one saw a thing from up there or even from over there." I pointed to the south bound traffic of A1A about a block away. "How come no one from there could see what was happening?"

Carolina pointed to a nearby street light.

"That light had been either shot out or someone knocked it out with a rock. The bulb is broken. No light here."

I looked in several different directions noting the other street lights in the area.

"The murderer knew he would not be seen here. Plus, he was confident the body would not be discovered until daylight. We're dealing with a cold-blooded murderer who stalks his victims. He plans out carefully just how he's going to kill them. Yet, he's careful not to be up close and personal with the victim risking leaving evidence to tie him to the crime."

"Could our killer be a female? They're the ones who are more inclined to less personal approaches to killing."

"I've had a gut feeling all along that this murderer is either a woman or a man whose vindictiveness is not strong enough to take out their anger in a personal way."

I abruptly walked away.

"Let's go."

We crossed back over to where the car was parked and drove back to A1A. There I turned north headed for Carolina's office.

CHAPTER TWENTY-FOUR

Later that afternoon, I walked into the lobby of my hotel and turned toward the restaurant. I felt a hand on my shoulder. I turned to find Fara Flambeau looking at me almost eye-ball to eye-ball.

"Mr. Savant?"

"Ah, Miss Flambeau. Fancy meeting you here."

"No fancy; this was planned," she said with a smile. "We're having dinner together,"

"Lead the way, my dear."

As we walked into the restaurant, the maître d quickly led us to a table in the center of the large glass wall overlooking the beach. As we sat, I noticed the tables, usually almost on top of each other, were moved away from our table about five to ten feet.

This woman possesses plenty of clout, I thought admiringly. It felt odd being separated in this way from the other customers. It made me feel uncomfortable and a bit obvious; and yet: special.

The waiter immediately took our drink orders. Fara ordered a dry martini and I, a gimlet.

"Gimlet? Really?" Fara said. "I thought you to be more the scotch on the rocks type of guy."

"I plan to order their T-bone. Have you tried it? They do an excellent job with an outdoor grill in the back overlooking the swimming pool. Very sheik."

Fara smiled.

"I taught the chef here how to select steaks to perfection. He was good when I hired him. But now he's almost perfect."

"You hired him?"

"Of course. This is one of my father's places I took over after his retirement from the Flame Mart."

"Ah. Of course, you did; and five other places here in South Beach, correct?"

"Five is correct, although I closed one and tore it to the ground. I'm building a new night club just for the rich and famous."

As the waiter placed the drinks in front of us, I reached over, took a quick swallow.

"That's the vacant lot two or three blocks north?"

"That's correct. There was a big club located near there for about five years called Club New. I never could get in because I was under age. Now I'm building my own. And age will not keep people out; the lack of enough money will."

"Very interesting. You're not out to make friends, but to make lots of money."

"I don't know about that. Perhaps I'm not interested in making certain types of people my friends."

"Like the homeless?"

She sat calmly and stared at me for several seconds. I could feel the electricity in the air. But, I could see no emotional response whatsoever in this woman's eyes. She was interrupted by the waiter who asked for our orders.

Fara asked for a Sirloin medium rare. I asked for a T-bone rare. The waiter completed taking the order, thanked us, and walked away.

I spoke first.

"I'm sorry if I upset you earlier."

"I wasn't upset. I was simply wondering what you mean by that statement."

"I meant nothing by it. I was simply referring to your work with the homeless shelter in Overtown. That's all."

"Those people are not my friends. They are my charity deduction so that the IRS doesn't take more money than I think they are entitled to."

"Ah."

"Speaking of the homeless, I understand that Chief Sanchez has invited you to help with the investigation into the murders of those poor homeless men."

"That is correct."

"What have you found out?"

"Miss Flambeau --"

"Fara; Please call me Fara."

"Alright, Fara. You know, I can't discuss an ongoing investigation."

"Do you have any, what are they called, oh, yea, suspects?"

"The only thing the police have told me is they have none at this moment."

"And what about you? Who do you think did it?"

"Me?"

"Yes, darling. What about you? What do you think?"

"Fara, the police couldn't care less who I think did it. They're only interested in hard evidence."

"I know that, honey. I'm just interested in you; who you might think committed these horrendous murders."

"Well. I don't have any evidence one way or the other, but I've got a pretty good idea who did it. At least, looking at the circumstantial evidence, there is only one person in this city who would have the resources to pull off these killings."

Fara sat for several moments staring at me.

"Well, are you going to tell me who it is?"

"Why should I? I don't want to besmirch anyone's reputation by making accusations I cannot prove."

"There's no one around who can hear us. Come on. Tell me. I can keep a secret."

I tried not to, but I could not hold back my laughter. I was so loud that several people sitting at the other tables turned to look.

"Fara," I replied shaking my head. "You do have a marvelous sense of humor."

"Me?"

"Of course. You're teasing me. You know I can't talk about this. And you know I especially can't speak about my suspicions. But, I can tell you this, I'll make sure that you are the first to know when we're ready to make an arrest. How's that?"

Fara's smile was broad, yet her eyes looked hard and cold as if from a deep, emotionless anger. The waiter approached with our orders.

"I guess that will be fine. But as for now, I think our orders are ready."

At that the waiter moved the drinks to one side and placed the sizzling, expertly-prepared steaks in front of us.

As I watched the two waiters serve dinner with finesse and panache, I caught the sight of a gentleman sitting in the lobby. I remembered seeing him sitting at the same place when I first walked in. Twenty-five years in police service had helped to hone my skills of observation to the point that I noticed everything around me.

Casually, I cut my steak open and looked at the waiter.

"Perfect."

"Thank you, sir. I'll extend your compliment to the chef."

I signaled for the waiter to lean down.

"See that guy sitting in the lobby?" I whispered to him. "Whatever he's drinking, take him another on me. Okay?"

"Yes, sir," he said, but turned to Fara before moving.

She made a slight nod. The waiter walked to the bar and took a drink to the gentleman who looked up at the waiter. He looked over at me. He leaned back and took the drink.

"I was afraid your shadow might be getting thirsty."

"My," Fara blurted but stopped. She smiled and looked at me.

"That obvious?"

"I'm not faulting you in anyway. Any person in your position should probably need several bodyguards looking after her. I didn't want him to feel neglected."

We laughed together and continued to eat dinner.

Afterward, I politely excused myself and went up to my room. Somehow, I had a gut feeling I would be receiving an early morning phone call telling me of another murder. I wanted to be fresh and prepared.

As I lay down on the bed, I looked at the ceiling and had the realization that this woman hated homeless men with a passion. Yet she has spent millions to help them.

No. The thought made me sit up in the bed. She spends millions helping the women and children. Then she murders the men who are obviously mooching off the state and her. That's it. Her father would not step up and defend her as the CEO, so she's taking out her anger on these men. Those thoughts seem to put my mind at ease as I lay back down.

Again, I stared at the ceiling as my thoughts raced in about twenty different directions. Of course, the answer hit me hard and fast. *The women and children are safe.*

I lay there for several minutes thinking through the pros and cons of those thoughts. Finally, I knew I had it right. Yet, there was problem: *If Fara is the murderer; how do I prove it?*

CHAPTER TWENTY-FIVE

The alarm clock clicked on the radio. I was in a bit of a daze trying to get out of a dream in which I was in a car stopped at an accident, but when signaled to move on, my car wouldn't move.

That's when I realized I was listening to a report of an accident on I-95 on the radio. I popped up like a bolt of lightning when I realized it was seven in the morning and I hadn't received any calls.

At first, I felt disappointed that I was wrong. I had thought that Fara would do something brash after our meeting last night. My conscience got the best of me and I reminded myself I should be relieved that I was wrong. No one had been murdered by a car during the night.

I rose from the bed, took a quick shower and shaved. Looking at the clothes in the closet, I picked out a silk shirt with a weave pattern to go with my blue slacks. I picked out socks to match and a put on a pair of soft-sole shoes. I had decided that today I would spend time looking into the life and activities of Fara and the family Flambeau.

At about eight fifteen I picked up my phone and dialed Sanchez's number. When he answered, I asked if my P.I. license had been approved.

"I've got it right here in front of me, Perry. Do you want to come and pick it up here or should I deliver it to you?"

"I'll come out there in an hour or so. I'm going to get some breakfast. Then I'll be right there. Oh, and that does authorize me to carry, correct?"

"Of course; you know that."

"Can't be too sure; the laws are different state to state. By the way, can you do me a favor and do a background check on Fara Flambeau, you know, the works?"

"Are you looking for anything in particular?"

"No; I just need lots and lots of information."

"I hope you don't mind my asking why?"

"Let me discuss that with you when we're not on the phone."

"Fine. I'll see you in a couple of hours."

I hung up the phone, took one last look in the mirror, walked out into the hallway, and into the lobby. I stopped at the front desk to pick up a newspaper and entered the restaurant as my stomach grumbled.

I sat at a table near the window and noticed a black car parked across the street with a man sitting behind the wheel looking toward the hotel. I guess my detective instinct quickly kicked in because I began to plot out my next moves. So, I took my time eating and thinking through several different scenarios I could follow.

When I was done eating, I walked out to the valet and asked for my car. When the young man returned in less than three minutes, I placed a five in the man's hand and got in behind the wheel. As I drove toward the south, I could hear the other car start its motor.

So, I went about a block, made a quick U-turn, and headed back toward the north watching the rear-view mirror. The man in the car continued traveling south and turned at the next intersection.

Feeling a bit relieved, I headed out across the MacArthur Causeway and onto the Dolphin Expressway headed west to the Miami-Dade Police Station. As I approached the airport, I looked into the rear-view mirror and noticed that the car I saw outside the hotel was behind me again. Unfazed by the discovery, I drove onto the Palmetto Expressway north to NW 25th Street and exited to the west.

As I turned into the parking lot of the police station, I watched as the driver who followed me continued toward the west and turned into the shopping center across from the police headquarters.

When I walked into the office Sanchez handed me my new P.I. license and a special conceal-carry permit.

"Of course," he said. "You know we don't supply you with all the fun stuff you might want to carry."

"Yeah. I know. So, what about the information on Fara?"

Sanchez reached over and picked up an interoffice envelope and handed it to me. So, I immediately opened it and pulled out several sheaves of paper each with the name "Fara Flambeau" at the top.

"I hope this is what you were looking for," Sanchez said. "There are financials, legal documents, judicial findings, and economic analyses of your subject. Unfortunately, there isn't a lot of information out there about her. And my IT guy says that after being online for more than a minute at each search, he was shut down from the other end."

"I'm not surprised. She claims to be a private person and has the money and influence to keep her privacy intact."

"With that in mind, Perry, I would advise you to keep this close to the chest. You could make a lot of people mad by simply investigating this woman."

"Yes. I know. But, I do appreciate your thinking of me,"

I walked out and back to my car. As I got in, I threw the envelope onto the passenger seat and started the car. Looking across to the parking lot at the shopping center, I saw the same car still parked there. I pulled out and headed toward the Palmetto and downtown via the Dolphin Expressway. I parked across from the Miami City Library and went inside. I located a computer I could use.

I opened the envelope and looked through the information on the pages. As I read, I marked several passages, turned to the computer, and typed in search strings. After printing out copies of numerous web pages, I put everything into the envelope and went back to the parking lot.

As I crossed the lot, I saw the same car as before parked about a hundred feet from my car. So, I walked toward the stranger's car. As I approached, I heard the car's engine start. The man drove his car out of the parking lot.

I bolted to my car and peeled out of the lot following the other man north on Flagler Drive. Feeling my heart race, I felt my heart pound in my chest as I followed the car over the MacArthur Causeway into Miami Beach.

The guy drove under the speed limit the whole way. He finally pulled into the parking garage next to a large condominium complex. I pulled over and parked on the street and fed the parking meter. I made my way around to the side of the parking lot and found a place where I could crawl through the fence.

I made my way among the many parked cars in the lot until I spotted the car I was following. The man in the car was standing in front of the elevator doors. I paused and watched as he got onto the elevator and the doors closed.

I walked over to the car and found the windows down. I quickly looked inside and saw an envelope with a return address on it. It was the same building the man had just entered. There was no name on the envelope and nothing else in the car that would help me.

So, I walked back to my car and moved to a spot where I could see when the man returned to his car. I waited there for about twenty minutes. The man exited the elevator and got into his car. I followed as he pulled out headed north.

We traveled about ten blocks when the car turned into a parking lot in front of a low office building. I drove past the building to keep from being detected. As I passed the building I noticed that the man walked through a door with a small sign next to it. So, I pulled over and parked about a block further down and walked back to the building.

As I approached the door to the building I watched the door carefully so as to be prepared to move away. The sign on the building read "Bachelor and Cargill Detective Agency."

I walked back to my car and called Carolina. I asked if she could find out what companies employ the agency for their business.

"Perry, I'm not sure that information is available."

"Could you perhaps have one of your people check to see who it is that they get their money from?"

"Well, I could, but I'll need some sort of probable cause to ask for a warrant."

"You mean you don't have anyone who can just look that stuff up?"

Carolina had a bit of a laugh on that one.

"I'm not going to ask just where you might have learned that," she replied. "But, I'll see what I can find out."

I turned my phone off and drove back to the hotel.

CHAPTER TWENTY-SIX

The next morning, I sat in the restaurant enjoying a breakfast of eggs (over easy), bacon (well done), hash browns, biscuits, jelly, fresh squeezed orange juice and coffee. The cell phone vibrated in my pocket. With a bit of a scowl, I pulled the phone out and saw Sanchez's number on the screen.

"Good morning, Adolph," I said with a sigh. "Don't tell me there's been another murder."

"I won't. And there wasn't. But, we've got a deeper problem."

"Let me guess. Someone's been complaining."

"I need you to meet me at FDLE headquarters ASAP."

"I'll be there in about an hour. I'm going to finish my breakfast first."

"Fine; I'll see you then."

I finished eating, paid the bill, then went out to get into the car which I had arranged earlier to have waiting.

It only took me about twenty minutes to drive to FDLE's headquarters building. A rather dull reminder of the government buildings from the seventies, the FDLE building was nondescript with windows that were high enough so that no one could look in through them.

I walked in and presented my credentials at the front counter where I was assigned a visitor's badge and escorted to

Lead Agent Laura Taylor's office on the second floor. As I walked in, I acknowledged Sanchez and Carolina who were waiting. Taylor welcomed me and invited me to sit down.

"I've asked you here to address a couple of issues that have been brought to my attention," Taylor began. "First, Mr. Savant, I am impressed with your background and investigative experience. I am aware of the tremendous contribution you have made to the law enforcement efforts in New York City. And I am pleased and honored that you are willing to aid in this investigation: one which seems to lack any hard evidence."

"Thank you," I responded diplomatically.

"But, I just received calls from the Mayor of Miami Beach, the mayor of the city of Miami, and several mayors of smaller cities specifically about you, personally. Why am I inundated with calls from these power brokers in the county, Mr. Savant?"

"I have no idea, Ms. Taylor."

"Some people don't like being investigated. And when they feel pressured, they tend to place pressure on other people who then push hard on the heads of us little people. Do I make myself clear?"

"Ms. Taylor, I don't pull my punches or try to sugar coat things. So, I am going to talk directly about this case, if you don't mind."

"Just a minute," she said as she reached in her drawer. Everyone heard a click. She pulled out a small device and set it on her desk.

"Okay, go ahead."

"What's that?"

"Every conversation in this office is required to be recorded; sunshine laws. But, it seems we just had a power failure which may even have affected anyone who happened to be listening in through other devices. So, go ahead and talk to me."

I smiled and leaned forward.

"I cannot prove a thing at this point, but with what little evidence there is I have concluded that Fara Flambeau is somehow involved in this case. And the fact that from the beginning Ms. Flambeau has inserted herself into this investigation, I'm becoming even more convinced. So, my instincts tell me that she is either the murderer herself or she is behind those men's deaths in some way."

"But you have no hard evidence?"

"None, yet. I only have my twenty-five years of investigative experience in one of the largest cities in the world. And let me add that she's just arrogant enough to have done it and believe that she will never be caught."

"You can't quote me on this, but I believe every word you're saying. And I'm inclined to believe you are correct."

"As do I," Sanchez added.

"But," Taylor continued, "You've got to be extra careful in your digging. I would suggest a great deal more subtlety and less frontal assault. Do I make myself clear?"

Sanchez and I looked at each other and nodded in agreement as Laura leaned over to the drawer and turned the recorder back on then turned off the jammer on her desk. She turned to the others and said, "This has been a productive chat. I will be expecting your reports on this investigation as soon as you can get it completed."

We all stood. Sanchez and I walked out as Laura picked up the phone and dialed a number, paused, then said, "Hello, may I speak with the mayor?"

The door closed.

Out in the parking lot, Sanchez stopped me near his car.

"Why don't we meet and talk about this further at my office."

"Fine," I responded and walked to my car. Just before I opened the door, my nerves began to tingle. The old instincts were still active. I walked around the car. On the passenger side, I could see where the dirt was pushed slightly toward the underside.

I leaned down and looked under the car slowly observing everything on the under carriage. I walked my eyes toward the front. I saw what I thought had to be a bomb of some kind with a timer on it. It was attached to the bottom under the driver's side door.

I slowly stood up and calmly walked toward Sanchez's car. I went about four steps and bolted in a hard run. My brand new, beautiful Mercedes exploded and lifted off the ground about six feet. Then it crashed back to the asphalt.

People ran out of the building as car alarms went off everywhere. Several deputies bolted from the building with their pistols drawn looking in every direction.

As Laura came out of the building, she ran over to where Sanchez and I were getting up off the ground.

"My God! Are you guys alright?"

"I'm okay," I replied nearly out of breath, "purely because of those instincts I was telling you about earlier."

"I believe it. How could you tell?"

"The fact that you were so careful with the possible eavesdropping on your office, I figured perhaps I should be as careful with myself."

"I knew she was resourceful," Sanchez said. "But I never figured that she would try something like this. I guess whoever was listening in on us must have gotten angry and decided to make sure Perry could not be involved in this investigation."

"I agree," Laura said.

Within seconds, the place was surrounded by sharp-shooters and other fully equipped men and women in uniform checking out the area, looking under other cars, and searching the grounds.

After about ten minutes, Carolina Brown approached us.

"We've swept the area and found nothing."

"Thanks, Carolina. That was quick thinking on your part to clear the area immediately."

Carolina turned to Sanchez.

"Are you guys okay?"

"Other than the ringing in my ears, I think I'll be fine," Sanchez laughed.

She turned toward me, her face drawn and a frown pushing toward her chin. I had not seen that look before and broke into what I have to say was a smile of relief.

"As soon as I heard you were the target, I got scared."

"Thank you, Carolina. I appreciate your concern. But, I'm fine."

"You all know the drill." Carolina said. "I'll have a team over here in minutes to get your statements while they're still clear in your minds."

She turned to me as her eyes drooped.

"A real shame about your car," she said. "We'll get it towed after all the pictures and Crime Scene is done doing their thing. We'll have it impounded as evidence. Sorry. I know what that car must have cost you."

"Hey, I've been in this game long enough to know how things work. I guess my insurance won't cover this, huh?".

I turned to Sanchez.

"It looks like I'll need a lift."

Sanchez laughed and told me that he'd take me back to the hotel after they had finished with the investigation.

"Okay, people," Laura yelled out. "Carolina is lead investigator on this. She'll select four people to help her finish up. The rest of you get back to your jobs inside. Oh, and thank you all for your quick response to this emergency. In the meantime, I'll be studying our security here more closely."

She walked over to the building and in through the doors. Once Laura was inside, Carolina called out four names of people to help her. She dismissed everyone to go back to work. The four worked gathering what evidence there was left around the parking lot. Carolina walked over beside Sanchez and looked at the burned out and charred Mercedes.

"Interesting, Sanchez. This guy hasn't even been in town a week and he's already pissed off some powerful people."

"You are more correct than you know," Sanchez answered. He turned to an officer standing by him and dictated his statement.

With a smile, Carolina turned to the work of coordinating the cleanup.

And me? I just sat on a step looking at what was left of my car.

CHAPTER TWENTY-SEVEN

Sanchez drove toward the beach as I sat in the passenger seat. The sun was getting lower in the western sky. It shone so brightly it reflected in the rear-view mirror such that Sanchez had to shift in his seat to keep the light from blinding him.

As he drove, the low volume of the two-way radio reminded us that we were riding in a police cruiser. A domestic violence dispute resounded followed by a call for additional assets for a three-car accident on I-95.

"I think I've missed those sounds since leaving New York."

"Yeah; you kind of get used to it being there."

We rode silently for several minutes.

"So, what have you done to anger people so much that they want to kill you?"

"I can't figure this one out, unless--"

"Unless what?"

"Unless my conversation with Fara didn't have the effect I had hoped."

"What conversation? You spoke to Fara Flambeau?"

"Yep; she was at the hotel waiting for me when I got in last night. She invited me to have dinner with her."

"And you think--"

"I don't know what to think, Adolph. I never made any accusations. But, I did say I thought I knew who committed the murders."

"What? And who did you say it was?"

"I didn't."

"You what? Good God. If she thinks you suspect her--"

"I know. I thought of that last night before I went to sleep. But, I also thought she'd have gone out last night and killed another homeless man on A1A. It never dawned on me she'd try to kill me."

"Wait a minute. You don't know she was behind this bombing. I mean, this could have been done by someone you put away or hurt badly in the city before you came here. You know, like the mob or someone like that."

"Get real," I said laughing. "I can't think of anyone who would try something like that. Well, maybe a couple. But, if she's the murderer, and if she has the resources you say she does, she wants to make sure I can't prove a thing."

"I guess. Let's just hope that Laura and Carolina can discover some evidence that'll point to her or someone connected to her."

Sanchez pulled up in front of the hotel.

 In the meantime, you can tag along with me."

I opened the door and swung my legs out as Sanchez grabbed his ringing cell phone.

"Hold for a moment, Hello?"

I watched Sanchez as he listened to the person speaking on the other end of the phone. He let out a low whistle.

"Okay. We'll be right there."

Sanchez shut off his phone and placed it in his pocket.

"What's up?" I asked.

"Get back in, Perry. Your instincts were right. There was a murder last night; another homeless man. His body was just discovered in a trash bin. No one noticed it until late this afternoon."

I was silent and truly worried as I slipped back into the car.

Sanchez's knowledge of the streets was immediately apparent as he turned down a side street and moved quickly through traffic north to where he was able to get back onto A1A. He drove up into Broward County.

Continuing north, Sanchez slowed down after passing Hollywood Boulevard and turned east and into the Broward County Branch Library Parking lot.

Hollywood Police had blocked off the area and were in the middle of a major investigation when Sanchez and I got out of the car. We walked over to Detective Frazier who seemed to be overseeing the work at the crime scene.

"Did Agent Taylor call you?" The portly detective asked Sanchez as we approached.

"Yep; she said this murder is identical to the others."

"I think so, except for one thing." He walked us over to a large green garbage bin and pulled the top back.

"They found him in here."

"What makes you think this one is the same as the others?"

Othniel Frazier was not a big-city boy in the slightest and didn't care much for long explanations or even explaining himself to anyone. But, I could tell that this was an investigation he did not want to keep on his plate.

He spoke slowly and methodically.

"Well, there's the tell-tale signs such as the tire marks on the head. And the bodily injuries are consistent with being hit by a car and run over. Our M.E. said that the body was placed into the garbage bin post-mortem."

"Who's the victim?" Sanchez asked.

"His name's Nikolai Turner, I think; at least that's the best we can do now. We've sent his finger prints to the FBI to get a better read. But, the kicker is this."

He handed an evidence bag to Sanchez.

"This was in his shirt pocket."

Sanchez and I looked at the sealed plastic evidence bag. It contained an FDLE calling card with the name of "Laura Taylor, Special Agent" on it. On the back was a hand printed note that read, "Niko, Call me. L."

"Not good." I commented. "Do you think he's the one who called Laura about investigating me?"

"Nikolai's been a street informant for years. Laura developed him when she was a rookie detective at Miami PD, you know, before she deserted for FDLE. He was good and accurate ... as far as we could tell."

"Taylor should be here any minute," Frazier added.

"What worries me," Sanchez continued, "Isn't that he called Laura about something. I'm afraid someone found out about his call to her. And the fact that he had her card; that was careless on her part, and careless on his."

"Yep," Frazier added. "As much as I respect Laura, I've noticed she's gotten sloppy since joining FDLE. I mean, when she decided to be a supervisory agent rather than a detective. I hope you're wrong about her being responsible for getting poor old Niko killed."

"You hope what got poor old Niko killed?" Laura's voice cut through the air.

Frazier turned quickly and stuttered a moment.

"Good to see you, Agent Taylor."

Laura stood motionless for several seconds.

"So, give it to me straight. Did I get Niko killed?"

"I'm not sure. But, we found your less than subtle message in his pocket," Sanchez said as he handed her the evidence bag with the calling card in it.

"I can't believe he kept it. Would you believe I gave that to him nearly seven years ago? Couldn't you tell? Look, it has my old rank, address, and phone number from Miami P.D."

Sanchez looked a bit embarrassed as he handed the bag back to Frazier.

"Oh. Yes. I see."

"That fool," Laura said. "He knew better than to keep that thing on him."

"Probably thought," I offered, "he could get some favors from the other poor saps he hung around with telling them he had a friend in FDLE."

"Whatever the reason," Laura continued, "I can't help but feel some responsibility for this. I just talked to him a day or so ago. He said I should look into your past, Perry, for a clue to these murders."

"Why me?"

"I don't know. But, whatever it was he wanted to tell me got him dead."

Frazier turned toward me.

"Okay, Yankee, what's going on?"

"I have no idea what he was referring to. This guy claims I am involved in these murders, but I can prove I was in New York when the first two or three were committed. I knew nothing of what was going on here until I dropped by Sanchez's office on my way to Key West."

"And I can vouch for that," Sanchez added. "But, this guy had your name on his lips before he ended up dead. There's got to be a reason."

"And we're going to be taking this whole matter apart," Frazier added. "I can promise you that."

"Believe me, Chief; you're not alone in wanting to know why my name was drug into this investigation by street people and thugs."

At that, Sanchez suggested there was nothing more we could do there and offered to take me back to my hotel.

CHAPTER TWENTY-EIGHT

I took my time getting out of bed and eating breakfast. Around eleven a.m., I stopped by the front desk to check on any mail that had arrived. The young lady in her freshly pressed uniform smiled.

"No mail, Mr. Savant. But there's an envelope for you."

As she handed it to me, I thanked her and walked away.

I opened the envelope and pulled out a set of car keys. A typed note read: "I was truly sorry to hear about your beautiful car. So, I have arranged the blue Cadillac parked at the curb for your use until you can arrange with your insurance company to replace your Mercedes."

It was signed with a simple "F."

Not knowing just why, I laughed out loud. I threw the keys in the air and caught them in my pocket. My smile must have been noticeable to everyone in the hotel as I walked out through the front entrance.

Sitting just to the right and parked next to the curb was a brand-new Cadillac with a small card on the dashboard that read, "For Chief Savant, with compliments. F."

I pulled out into traffic and made my way toward the causeway as I dialed Carolina Brown's number. She answered on the second ring with a cheery "Hello, Chief. What up?"

"Thought I'd drop by and talk about this homeless thing."

"Are you on your way?"

"I should be there in about a half-hour."

"Great! That'll be just in time for you to take me out to lunch."

"See you then."

When I pulled into the parking lot at the FDLE office, Carolina was standing outside waiting. So, I pulled up to the front entrance and she got in.

"Nice substitute for the Mercedes."

"Not my first choice."

"Well I like it. Rental?"

"Nope. A loaner."

She sat for a couple of minutes as I pulled out and got back up onto the freeway toward town.

"Should I ask?" she asked softly.

"Nope."

"Okay. So, where are we going to eat?"

"Thought we'd go to Morton's; my treat."

"Love it!"

I drove like I'd lived in Miami all my life taking the two-and-a-half mile long Tuttle Causeway over the Intracoastal Waterway as the waters shimmered in the sunlight. It seemed you could see the bottom.

The classic view of Miami Beach stretched north to south in front of us. As the view faded into the high-rises of North Miami Beach, I maneuvered through the cavernous high-rises to the end of Fortieth Street and stopped for the Valet who greeted us with a smile.

As we walked into the restaurant, the Maître-d' showed us to a seat near the back where it was unusually quiet.

Carolina was the first to speak.

"I feel like you're going to propose to me with all this flair."

"Although that is a tempting thought, I didn't have that in mind. I asked for this table because I wanted to be sure that we were not overheard talking."

"No problem."

"So, tell me; what is going on?"

"About what?"

"About me. What was all that stuff about yesterday with that dead guy talking about me to Laura?"

"She had me doing a lot of calling after she got back from the meeting with you and all the others at the crime scene. The only thing I could come up with is some sort of connection with the accusations against you being a, I mean, you know, like maybe you might be--"

"A fag?"

"I didn't know how to put it. Perhaps someone wants to get the police to think that since you were fired over this gay thing that perhaps you were killing these men. You know, like after you were having sex with them you would kill them."

"Bull!"

"I know. I spent time looking into these murders and your trek from New York to here. There was no way you could have been involved. Plus, the ME's reports all showed no indication of sexual contact or rape of any kind."

I sat quietly for several moments as Carolina gave her drink order to the waiter. I ordered a gin and tonic. I watched the waiter walk away. I turned to Carolina.

"I appreciate your telling me about what you found. You didn't have to do that. But, that still doesn't answer the fundamental question of what's going on."

"I know. Sorry about the childish attempt at diverting the investigation away from your suspicions about Fara Flambeau's possible involvement. By the way, I wanted you to know that I agree with you on that."

"Oh?"

"Yep." She said with a wink. "I've followed that woman's career and have been less than impressed. I mean, she's one hellacious bitch, Perry. She has a temper that is most impressive; something I'll bet you've not experienced, yet."

"Nope; but that girl seems to have something boiling inside her. I get the impression she's so tightly wound she could explode all over anyone standing nearby; and she wouldn't care a whip about them."

"When she was nineteen, I was a rookie patrolman with Miami Beach. Three of us had to go into one of her dad's clubs and physically pull her out. We arrested her and booked her into the county jail."

"I'll bet daddy wasn't too happy," I had to interject.

"No kidding! In fact, we brought in fifteen people who witnessed the altercation and ultimate brawl. She was the central attraction and apparent cause. Not one person remembered a thing nor did anyone with bruises and cuts want to press charges. Her dad drove up. That was the end of each of our careers with the Miami Beach Police Department."

"The man has that much power?" I asked.

"No, the man has a lot more power."

"So, between her and her father, there is enough influence to convince anyone to do whatever they want, right?"

"Absolutely." She continued. "All I can say is that you're lucky they didn't know just when you had arrived in Miami. We all know you had nothing to do with this, but the mayors of Miami Beach and Miami both are convinced that if you had not gotten involved, these murders would not have continued."

"That's a pretty bold assertion based on nothing but the word of one person."

"Yep. But who that person is makes all the difference."

"So, what do the chiefs of police think?" I asked.

"I don't know about Miami Beach, but I do know that the Sheriff at Broward is fully supportive of you. I think the Fort Lauderdale chief is supportive as well. The catch in all this is that I've been assigned to keep you on a leash while the investigation continues. I hope you don't mind my tagging along."

"I could do worse, I guess. But, perhaps this could be a huge help. In fact, why don't we go pay a visit back to that homeless shelter after we're done here? We might bump into something important if we nose around there long enough."

"I like that idea. My badge will get us into wherever we want. But, I've got several things I have to get done back at the office this afternoon. Is tomorrow morning okay?"

"Sure," I replied. "I'll pick you up around ten."

The waiter placed two perfectly prepared grilled steaks on the table in front of each of us. With little hesitation, we both dug into the succulent meat before us.

CHAPTER TWENTY-NINE

The next day, I stopped at the FDLE headquarters to pick up Carolina who was waiting for me in the parking lot. She stood with Laura saying a quick "good-bye" as she slipped into the car.

"Let's go," she said quietly looking back at Laura standing on the sidewalk.

I stepped on the gas and shot up to the entrance to the freeway where I headed toward the homeless shelter in Overtown.

"What was that all about?"

"Oh, she was cautioning me about having you drive everywhere. She wants me to be hauling you around in that state-owned wreck of mine."

"Hey, I'm beyond those things. Twenty-five years was enough for me."

"Right. I'm up for a promotion in another year. I guess I'm hoping it will get me a better car."

I sat quietly for several moments.

"I've been thinking about how to approach this thing with Fara," I continued. "This is going to take some serious caution."

"Absolutely," Carolina said. "She'll skin us alive; or her daddy will."

"So, maybe we should treat her like any other suspect and make all our questions much less obvious."

"I like that."

"First, we never mention her name. We'll need to word our questions so people answering them will have to tell us if they are talking about Fara."

"What if they ask us if we are investigating Fara?"

"We can say something like: 'It probably means nothing, but we appreciate your honesty.' We'll just pray that no one makes the direct connection and calls Fara or her father about us."

"This is going to be hairy."

"Probably. But what part of our job isn't?"

"You got that right," Carolina laughed.

I pulled into a parking spot about a half-a-block from the front entrance to the homeless shelter. As we got out, I spotted five young men standing across the street eyeing the nice, shiny Caddy I was driving as if it could be the new pimp-mobile for their group.

So, I took the initiative and walked over to the men.

"Gentlemen, I'm visiting the homeless shelter to help out the people here. Would you do me a favor?"

"Oh, man," one of them said. "What you up to?"

I noticed that one of the men was standing in the rear with a smirk on his face. I pointed my finger and him.

"You! What's your name?"

"What's it to you?"

"Well, you look like the guy in charge."

The whole group laughed as a young scrawny Hispanic man stepped forward.

"Okay. What you want, Whitey?"

"Just a favor."

I handed him a couple of one hundred-dollar bills.

"Could you make sure that no one touches that car while my lady and I are in there helping out?"

"Whoa," the young man said as he looked at the money in his hand while the others smiled and high-fived each other.

"Man, we'll build a fence around it, if that'll help."

"Naw. Just watch it. If anyone even looks at it cross-eyed, you take care of 'em."

"Well, I don't know."

"There'll be another three hundred for you and your friends when we get done if the car is untouched. Otherwise..."

At this point, I pulled my coat back, so the man could see the Glock stuffed in a small holster attached to my belt. The man simply let out a quiet whistle.

"We cool," he said. "You got nothing to worry about your car. I guarantee it'll be fine."

"Thank you, my friend," I said.

He quickly replied in barely audible voice.

"Rawley. My name is Rawley."

"Thank you, Rawley," I said politely and walked back across the street where I joined Carolina.

As we walked into the shelter, the place was totally empty except for an elderly gentleman who was mopping the floor.

"Hey! Anybody here?" Carolina called out.

The man continued mopping the floor.

"That's a pretty stupid question, don't you think?" he asked.

"What the--?" Carolina replied, as her hand moved toward the pistol attached to her hip.

Again, without looking up or standing up straight he continued.

"Lady, who do you think I am? A nobody?"

"I'm so sorry about that. I didn't mean nothing by it."

"I know. I was just yanking your chain."

At that the man stood up and placed the mop in the bucket that sat nearby. As he stood, he revealed a clerical collar around his neck.

"I'm Calvin Horowitz," said the clergyman. "I'm one of the associate pastors at the church. And you are?"

Carolina quickly pulled out her badge and displayed it.

"I'm special agent Carolina Brown and this is Perry Savant, a police consultant working with me on the murder of the homeless along A1A."

"I'm certainly happy to meet you."

"Reverend Horowitz?" I queried.

"Yes, I know. I get a lot of looks from folks. Most people don't know that everyone named Horowitz ain't necessarily Jewish."

"I didn't mean anything by it," I said.

"You two both have some significant issues, don't you?"

"Um, uh," Carolina uttered. "Could you answer a couple of questions for us?"

"I'd be happy to, if I know the answer."

"Did you know any of the men who were murdered?" I asked, sounding a bit more settled.

"Every one of them."

"Did you ever notice any of them having a problem with others who were around here? I mean does any particular person hanging around here stand out as having any issues with the men who were killed?"

"That's a good question. I've thought about that on several occasions probably for the same reason you're asking the question. And to be honest, I can't think of anyone. No one stands out as causing any difficulties with any of those men."

"No one at all?" Carolina asked.

"No, well, unless you mean Miss Flambeau. But, she tries so hard to ignore the guys' jokes and leering at her, you know? She's a beautiful woman and most of these people rarely if ever are around anyone of her class."

"She has trouble with the men?"

"Since day one. But, these guys are not schooled in proper etiquette or manners of any kind. So, I know she understands that there's nothing insulting by their actions or words."

"Of course, she would," Carolina said as she gave an understanding nod.

I gave a slight indication to Carolina that we needed to leave.

"Well, we appreciate your time, Reverend," I said. "I hope we haven't caused you problems by coming by."

"Of course not. I'm glad you're continuing to pursue this," he said. After a brief pause, he turned his head toward Carolina.

"Just be sure that the next time you come by, bring her with you. I'm a Baptist, not a priest."

I could imagine that my smile stretched across my face.

"Absolutely I will."

"Before we leave," Carolina interjected. "Is this place always this empty before noon?"

"Well, no. But since the murders began, our clientele has, well, let's say, we don't seem to have the crowds we once had.

I'm getting worried because many of those people have no place else to go."

"We'll do our best to catch whoever is doing this."

We walked out of the shelter and onto the street into the bright sunlight and the ninety-degree heat. We walked to the car where the five guys I had spoken to earlier were standing.

As we approached, the guys separated by stepping out of the way.

"As you can see, Mister," Rawley said. "Still in perfect condition."

At that I peeled off three more one hundred-dollar bills and handed it to him.

"Just don't spend it on guns, okay?"

"Naw, man; we're gona get drunk."

And with that they piled into a beat-up old Chevy Camaro and drove off.

"That was smart," Carolina said as we got in the car.

I put the key in the ignition but stopped and turned to her.

"Here's where we find out just how smart it was."

I turned the key. The engine turned over and began to purr.

We looked at each other and burst out laughing.

We drove for several minutes as the radio personality was reporting the news at the top of the hour. Carolina reached over and turned the radio off.

"So, what do you make of what we just heard?"

"I'm not sure. What do you make of it?"

"Between you and me, I think the bitch is crazy."

That brought a big laugh.

"I think you nailed it quite succinctly," I said.

"What I meant to say was that she's got to have a serious problem hanging out at a place like that and complain because the men don't act like the men she normally hangs with."

"What makes you think the men around her treat her any differently?"

Carolina thought about that.

"Just an observation," she continued. "Unless she provoked those men."

"Now that would be sick," I observed in a whisper.

"And yet our most serious problem is we don't have one shred of evidence that she's involved in any of these murders."

I nodded my head in agreement.

I know. But, every nerve in my body and every instinct I've developed over the past twenty-five years tells me she's not only involved, but she's guilty as sin."

"Okay," Carolina answered. "We've got to prove it, or we need to move on to another suspect."

"I'm taking us to the site of the last murder. We need to look at that scene more carefully. We've got to turn up evidence. Perhaps we need to visit all of the sites."

"What do you expect us to find there?"

"Truthfully?"

"Of course."

"Well, I expect to find nothing because the people in charge of this investigation are good at what they do. I'm just hoping to find a clue that's been overlooked, something that will point us in some direction. And I don't care if it leads us away from Fara Flambeau; I'll be happy with anything that will help us find this killer."

"I'm with you on that. Oh, you missed your turn."

"No. I wanted to come into this scene from a different direction than when we came here before."

I drove down another block and pulled into the northern part of the park next to the Intracoastal Waterway. I drove into a parking space and turned off the motor. We got out of the car, put on surgical gloves, and grabbed some of the small plastic bags that I had stuffed into my briefcase.

"I'm going to walk slowly toward the crime scene from the area to the west. I want you to approach it from the east. We'll meet where the body was found."

"And what am I looking for?"

"Whatever you find."

"Whatever; uh, never mind; see you at the murder site."

We moved in opposite directions. I walked slowly, looking down and around as I trod through the under-brush and trees. I stopped next to a small sapling and picked up a match book that had been discarded and stuck it into a small plastic bag. I sealed it and placed it into my coat pocket.

At the same time, Carolina moved carefully across the open grassy area then pushed through some bushes. As she walked, she would slide her feet carefully along the ground feeling around for what might be out of place or out of the ordinary. She also found a match book that she placed into a small baggy, sealing it up.

Absently she caught sight of a small piece of black cloth tangled in a bush. She carefully used a set of tweezers and extracted the tiny cloth piece from the branch and placed it in one of the plastic bags. She continued her pacing and looking as she worked her way toward where the body had been found the day before.

I stopped just a few feet from the white spray paint that had been used to show where the body lay. I carefully looked around and moved over to where the water lapped up onto the retaining wall. I peered down and caught sight of a something shiny in the water.

I took off my coat and laid down flat on the ground. I reached down into the water but realized that the object was deeper than it first appeared. So, I kept slipping lower. My arm was submerged up to the shoulder. At that moment, I knew that my $100.00 shirt was ruined. So, I pushed a little further. I slipped off the retaining wall and fell into the water.

Keeping my cool, I turned myself upright and put my feet on the bottom and saw that the water was over my chest. So, I took a deep breath, reached down toward the shiny object, and grasped it in my hand.

As I pulled my head and arm up from the bottom, I looked up at Carolina looking at me from the shore with an amused smile.

"If we were going to go swimming," I heard her say. "We should have stopped and picked up our bathing suits."

I reached out my hand and placed the object I found into her hand.

"Tell me what that is. The water is burning my eyes."

Carolina looked at it intently for a few moments.

"It's a slim calling card case with initials engraved on the side. The case is empty."

"What initials?"

"It looks like 'F F F.' But, I'm not sure. The lettering is extremely decorative and hard to make out."

"Three F's?" I responded.

"That's what it looks like to me; but I may be seeing what I want to see."

"I understand. What's the chance that Fara Flambeau's middle name starts with an 'F'?"

"I don't know. I've never asked."

"I think we'd better find out. Now, help me out of here."

Carolina reached down and braced herself. With one hand I took hers and with the other I grabbed the wood above me and pulled myself back onto the retaining wall.

We walked back to the car where I pulled a gym bag out of the trunk and retrieved a towel to dry off. I picked up my suit coat from the ground and put it in the trunk. I dropped my pants and pulled on a pair of sweat pants from the bag.

"New Yorkers certainly are different from southerners," Carolina observed as she tried to hold back her laughter.

"How?" I replied.

"Well, a southern gentleman would have taken the sweat pants and changed in the restroom over there."

"Hey. I'm wearing boxers. Nothing's showing. So, what's the big deal?"

"My point, exactly," Carolina said.

"I think we'd better get these things to the lab," I suggested ignoring her comment.

CHAPTER THIRTY

At two AM, I sat on the side of my bed with numerous newspaper clippings and several sheets of lined paper filled with hand-written notes on them. I studied several of the sheets with a deep intensity. I jumped when the phone rang.

"Hello," I said quickly.

"You still up?"

"Yes, Carolina; I'm still up. Why are you still awake?"

"I was dead to the world when I got a call from headquarters. We've got another one. I'll be by to pick you up in about twenty minutes."

"Will this ever stop?" I said through my clenched teeth. I hung up the phone and walked into the bathroom.

At 2:45, I stood out front of the hotel as Carolina pulled up in her FDLE assigned car. I opened the passenger side door and got in. She pulled out onto A1A and headed north.

"Where're we headed?"

"Just down the road a few blocks. This one's bad; crushed against the brick wall of an old building under construction; a perfect place for a murder; no one anywhere around to see what happened. But--"

"But what? I hope to God it's a good 'but.'"

"It is. There's debris from the car."

"No!" I yelled a bit too loud. "You're kidding, right?"

"Nope; murderer left clues."

"Copy-cat?"

"Maybe. But, I don't think so. We'll see when we get there."

As we pulled up about a block from the crime scene. The place was blocked off in every direction. No one was getting in or out. So, Carolina pulled the car to the curb and parked it, leaving her red lights flashing in the back window.

We walked west on Eleventh Street, stopped at the main check point, and produced our badges. We proceeded to a vacant lot where several dozen policemen were working every possible angle. Lying next to a brick wall on the south side of the lot was a large green tarpaulin lying over a body. The coroner's wagon had not arrived at this point.

Standing near a couple of Miami Beach Police cars, a man in a uniform with three bright stars on his shoulders stood shaking a finger in the face of Laura Taylor and Adolph Sanchez.

As Carolina looked closely at the crime scene elements, I kept a close eye on the three people who were arguing with raised voices that echoed against the buildings.

After several minutes, the little meeting broke up and the man with the stars on his shoulder got back into one of the cars and left the scene. Sanchez and Laura walked over to where we were standing.

"What was that?" I said quietly.

"Don't ask," Laura said.

She walked over to where the Coroner's vehicles were just pulling up.

Sanchez glanced at the body, then at the man in uniform, then back to me.

"That was the Miami Beach Police Chief giving us a not-so-polite description of his anger over our failure to solve these murders. He's upset that the murderer has moved into his jurisdiction."

I shook my head.

"I noticed that he's not here helping out in solving this thing."

"Yeah, me too. The guy's a real ass. But I'll admit to you that I'm pretty angry that we haven't solved this thing either."

"Get a grip, Adolph. I told you who's responsible. Get on her tail and watch her every minute of every day until she screws up."

Although I thought he wanted to just slap me silly, Sanchez took a deep breath.

"You know I can't do that. Why do you think I hired you? You can do a lot more than I can. Just don't get caught. Oh, and don't take Carolina with you, either. She could get fired."

"I know. And I will. All I needed was to hear you say it."

Sanchez nodded his head. Carolina and I walked over to take a closer look at the pieces of debris that were lying around. I stopped and knelt on the ground. I raised my hand and signaled for one of the Crime Scene investigators to join me.

Vernon Mitchell had been with the Dade County Sheriff's Department for only about two years as a Crime Scene investigator after his graduation from Miami-Dade College's CSI Program. He felt good about his training, but he also knew he was still green and could use all the help he could get. He stepped over close to me.

"You need me, Sir?"

"No need to call me sir," I said with a grin. "I'm only a civilian consultant here."

Puzzled, Vernon looked over at Sanchez who pointed toward me.

"Vernon Mitchell," Sanchez said. "Meet former NYPD chief of detectives Perry Savant."

"Oh, wow. Perry Savant. I've heard a lot about your career and what you've done in helping us try to solve this thing."

"Thank you for the compliments, but I want to know why you haven't catalogued all this over here?"

"Well, I wanted to, but my chief told me that the stuff over where the body was found is what I should concentrate on."

"Right. Well, that might be okay in most cases, but in this one, we're dealing with a murderer who is both smart and devious. She'll do whatever it takes to trip us up."

"Oh, wow. You think it was a woman?"

At that Sanchez looked over at me and cleared his throat rather loudly.

I looked back at Sanchez then to Mitchell.

"Uh, I was just, well, you know. I mean she or he. That's all."

"Oh, okay. I'll tag and bag these things right away."

"This piece of glass here," I said handing him an evidence bag. "Take special note of it and run it through your data bases immediately. I want to know if this is a special piece from a particular Mercedes."

"Oh, wow," Vernon said as his voice stammered with excitement. "You think someone murdered this man using a Mercedes? That's cold."

"No, I just think that I recognize this type of glass. Just run it through the lab quickly. Call me and tell me what you find out before you tell anyone else, okay?"

"My pleasure, Chief. Happy to help."

Vernon immediately got to work placing small yellow numbered cards next to each piece of glass, plastic, and debris in the area. He took meticulous notes on each, photographed the objects, and placed each in an individually sealed plastic bag. He carefully marked each bag with an identification number and his own signature.

Sanchez walked to where the body was now being taken away. I followed him, stopped, and looked down at the ground.

"Adolph, look here."

Sanchez turned and looked down where I was pointing.

"What you got?" he asked.

"See these small pieces of debris and leaves. They seem to cover up what appears or to be or could be drag marks."

"Yes. I see what you're saying. The murderer dragged the body from over there. But what about the blood spatters on the brick wall at the spot where the body was found?"

"I'll look at those in a moment. Right now, I want to see if I can find where this began."

I walked toward the other end of the building looking carefully at the wall all along the way. I took my time and even used my latex covered hand to feel the surface.

"Adolph, what is this?"

Sanchez bent over and looked closely at the surface of the wall.

"If I didn't know any better, I'd say this looks like it was recently washed."

"Right," I said. "Why would someone wash off a filthy, crumbling wall that was under construction?"

"Vernon! Get over here to test this area for blood residue."

Sanchez turned back to me.

"This guy was hit here first, then probably hunted down in the darkness to over there where she finished him off."

"That would explain the pieces of plastic and glass from an auto in the area," I explained. "I guess she had to ram him pretty hard to get him to die."

"Hmm. An interesting conclusion. Are you saying that it had to be a woman because of the way he was killed? That's terribly sexist, don't you think?"

"I couldn't care less about being proper or politically correct or whatever you want to call it," I said. "We're after a cold-blooded killer. And if I need to offend everyone in my way, I'll do it."

I took a deep breath to calm down.

"I just want to find the truth. And if I can use a little profiling to help me, I'll do it, no matter who gets hurt."

Sanchez called to Vernon and indicated that he needed to process the area where we were standing. Vernon signaled that he would gladly take care of it.

I called Carolina to join me. She had been looking carefully at the tire marks in the dirt of the vacant lot. The Miami Beach Police blocked off the area and laid down some plywood they retrieved from the construction site to place over the ground. This protected the scene, so the investigators and coroner could get to the murdered man's body.

Carolina was working with Vernon's assistant who was an intern from Miami-Dade College. She pointed out to him which tire tracks to preserve, photograph, and maybe even to take impressions. When I called, she looked up and signaled that she would meet me back at the car. She turned her back to the young intern and pointed to a couple of other places he needed to process. Then she walked back to her car.

I had already opened the door and was waiting when Carolina walked up and got in on the drivers' side.

"So, were you able to find any kind of evidence that might get us closer to identifying our murderer?"

"No, not really," I answered.

"What was all the yelling about with the Miami Beach Chief?"

"I'm not sure."

"Didn't Sanchez tell you?" she asked.

"He told me what he wanted me to think they were talking about. Adolph Sanchez keeps information close to his chest. Allowing others to know the same things he knows is not in his nature. He knows how valuable information is and only gives away what he feels is not all that valuable to him."

"I've had that same opinion about him; but was never sure."

"Carolina," I continued. "You need to learn that lesson well. Never let others know that you know more than they think you do. That's the secret to a successful criminal investigator. Oh, and keep your head down."

"Thanks for the advice. So, where are we headed now?"

"Take me back to my hotel. I've got to get some sleep before I can do another thing."

"Right," she answered.

She drove to the hotel where I opened the door and swung my legs to get out. I paused, leaned over, and gave Carolina a big kiss on the cheek.

"What was that for?" she said pulling back.

"Carolina Brown, I like you. You make this investigation enjoyable. But, one last thing; in the morning, see if you can locate the illustrious Ms. Flambeau. Call me and let me know."

"If I find her," she said. "I'll call to let you know that I'm on my way to pick you up."

"Fine. But wait until later in the morning before searching, will you? I need my beauty sleep."

Still below the horizon, the sun had created an eerie blueish glow in the sky as I got out of the car and walked to my room. Inside, I unbuckled my belt and lay down on the bed. It was five twenty-five AM. I closed my eyes and fell fast asleep.

CHAPTER THIRTY-ONE

I jerked up from a hard sleep. As the fog cleared from my head, I heard the phone ringing. I grabbed it as if angry and about to break it into pieces. I looked at the clock to see that it was a quarter to ten.

"Why didn't you wake me earlier?

"Why should I have done that?" Came the voice of Sanchez over the line.

"Oh! Sorry, Adolph. I, you see, well, Carolina was supposed to call me and; anyway, what were you calling about?"

"The wall tested positive for the presence of blood. It was the large area right where you suggested we test. Someone was nearly cut in half from an auto which then splattered blood just about everywhere."

"Wow. She killed him there and dragged his body over to the other spot where she probably ran over his face. It looks like she tried to wash the blood from the other wall."

"Too bad she didn't know the proper use of bleach, or we'd have had a tough time proving that."

"Thanks, Adolph. I appreciate the info. Also, be sure to expedite the lab work on those pieces of glass and plastic that we found."

"Already done. The lab got began working on it this morning."

"Great. I'm going to get up and get dressed. I expect Carolina to call any minute. We're going to see if we can do some, um, surveillance work."

"Be careful, Perry."

I did my pleasantries then hung up the phone and went into the bathroom. I shaved and took a long shower. After dressing I noticed the red light flashing on the phone by the bed.

The operator relayed a message that Carolina Brown had called and would like me to call her back. I thanked the unseen voice and held down the button then released it, receiving a dial tone.

I dialed and heard Carolina's voice.

"Been sleeping?"

"Naw. In the shower when you called."

"You about ready?"

"Yep. You want me to pick you up?"

"I'm sitting out front waiting for you."

"You want I should drive? My car is more comfortable."

"I'll park in the garage," Carolina said with a smile in her voice. "And I'll be waiting for you in the lobby."

"I'll be down in about ten."

I pushed the button on the phone and called the concierge to bring the car to the front.

Finally, I looked at myself again in the mirror, took my pistol out of the safe and placed it in my holster. I put on my jacket, took one last look in the mirror and walked out of the room.

"So, where is she?" I asked as I approached Carolina.

"Her car was located at the homeless shelter."

"Ah. Good. Let's go."

We got into the Caddy and drove off headed for Overtown and the homeless shelter.

"Okay," she said as she turned to look at me. "What's the plan?"

"I don't know yet."

We drove in silence for several minutes. I exited the Causeway onto Thirteenth Street toward our destination. I started the conversation.

"Have you ever met Fara Flambeau?"

"I wouldn't know her if I saw her."

"Good. When we get there, you go in and ask if you can volunteer to help. You'll be welcomed with open arms."

"Because I'm Black?"

"No, because you're attractive."

"Oh. Right. Sorry."

"That's okay. Of course, your race does help a little," I added smiling.

"Wait a minute. What if that assistant pastor is there?"

"Oh, right. If he's there, approach him and tell him that after meeting him, you decided you'd like to help. Smile and let him know you have no ulterior motives."

"I'll think of something. So, you just want me to watch what Fara is up to, right?"

"That's it. Just come out here once you're done and we'll go from there."

Within a few minutes, I pulled up near the shelter and stopped. Carolina leaned over and gave me a kiss on the cheek and jumped out of the car.

I watched as she walked down the half-block toward the shelter. I noticed that this Nubian beauty had a perfect female shape. She turned her head to look back toward me. I laughed and thought, *she knows I'm watching her. I hope she likes it.*

Meanwhile, I called Sanchez and asked him to run the license plate on a black Mercedes parked across the street. A few minutes later, Sanchez called back.

"That car," he said, "Is owned by a holding company which is responsible for collecting and distributing funds for the Flambeau Charitable Trust."

"Great. That makes sense. Fara's at the Homeless shelter where I am right now."

"You be careful. If she gets the idea that you're on to her, we'll never hear the end of it from her attorneys."

"I know. I'm keeping a low profile."

"Right," Sanchez said with a slight chuckle, then hung up.

CHAPTER THIRTY-TWO

The Homeless shelter volunteers were busy setting up the tables in the large assembly area. Several other people were setting up cots and getting out the bed clothes for those who would be staying the night.

As soon as Carolina walked into the building, Rev. Horowitz was standing just inside and immediately recognized her.

Well, detective, to what do we owe this honor?"

She smiled a bit, embarrassed.

"May I speak to you alone?"

"Of course," he said as he led her into a side room and closed the door. He looked at her seriously.

"What is it?"

"I need your help today."

"How can I help?"

"We have no proof, as we mentioned before. But we believe now more than ever that the murderer is somehow associated with or at least has hung around here at some time. What I'm saying is that I'd like to be a volunteer so that I can simply observe what's happening. There is someone watching the outside areas also."

"Wow. That's big-time cloak and dagger isn't it?"

"No, Reverend. We're worried about finding so few clues and leads. This place is the only potential lead we have. So, we're hoping that something will happen that will help us identify who might be the one committing these murders and make this a safer place for everyone."

"How long will it take?" he asked.

"We're going to try it today and see. If we come up dry, we may try it again another day. Since we can't afford to become obvious, we definitely won't come often."

"Okay, I'll take you in and introduce you to the others. You can help serve lunch. That way, you'll be able to see pretty much everything that's going on."

"Good. Oh, and please don't tell anyone who I am. We've got to keep this between us."

"I can do that. Let's go."

The two walked out of the room and into the kitchen area. He introduced Carolina as Carole, a volunteer from a church in Miami Springs. She immediately jumped in and helped with the cooking. A little after noon, people wandered in for the free meal offered by the shelter.

Carolina watched carefully while helping to fill plates and giving aid to those people who couldn't carry their plates to the tables. She noticed that everyone who entered was either a woman with children or a couple with children. She also noticed that no single men came in for more than thirty minutes.

A half-an-hour later, she saw how much these people needed all the help they could get. She could feel her body droop and her head shake side-to-side as she thought, *If the killer had been using this facility to find her targets.*

"Or him," she said out loud.

"What?" said a lady nearby.

"I got this bad habit of talking to myself sometimes," she said.

"Honey, I know just what you mean," the other lady said with a friendly smile. "Sometimes I just talk back and forth to myself and carry on long conversations. I mean sometimes I solve some of my most difficult problems that way."

Carolina laughed with the lady. She walked away from her and noticed three men enter together. They split up and got their meals separately, constantly looking around at the other people.

She wondered if they might think the murderer was a homeless person, as well. Or perhaps they thought the killer disguised himself as homeless. She kept a close eye on the three men as she continued serving the meals.

Another ten minutes passed, Fara Flambeau entered the room with the church's senior pastor. Carolina realized who she was almost instantly. She could see that this woman had a way of virtually bringing a glow to any room she walked into.

People looked around and some of the women went up to her to thank her for her generosity in keeping the shelter open.

At that moment, each of the three men stood, walked to the trash can and deposited their food and paper implements. They gathered together near the front entrance and talked to each other as they looked toward Fara.

Carolina felt these men suspected who the killer was. She watched the men as they all stared intently at Fara, not in admiration, but with a frown in their eyes. They seemed to know something. She knew these men had to be questioned carefully to find out what they knew or at least what they had heard. Maybe this was the break they were looking.

A few minutes later, each of the three men left alone. They appeared to be acting as if not to show any sign of a problem. Fara gave the pastor and the associate pastor each a big hug and kiss on the cheek.

Both men enjoyed the gesture. With a whirl and flair, Fara Flambeau was out the door and, in her car, driving away from Overtown.

Carolina quickly turned to the lady in charge.

"I need to leave and take care of a small urgent situation at home."

The lady smiled and thanked Carolina for helping and invited her to return any time she wanted.

At that, Carolina walked quickly outside.

CHAPTER THIRTY-THREE

Carolina Brown slipped into the car next to me after I had already swung around in pursuit of Fara. I pulled out quickly and was up onto the Dolphin Expressway about a quarter of mile behind her Mercedes speeding along at eighty miles per hour.

I pushed it a bit more to catch up so as not to lose her once we exited into the traffic on the island. I looked up at the rear-view mirror and saw two Miami Police cars pulling up behind me with sirens screaming and lights flashing.

"Crap," I said out loud as I pulled over to the side of the highway. One patrol car pulled up and stopped behind my car. The other patrol car pulled over onto the shoulder beside the first.

Four policemen in the two cars quickly took up positions behind the open car doors, drawing their weapons. One of the officers took the microphone in his hand and called out, "Reach your hands out of the windows and open the doors from the outside."

We did as we were told and slipped out of the car backward. We got down on our knees beside the car.

The officers moved quickly with two men on each side. After a couple of minutes, we were handcuffed.

"I think you've made a mistake," Carolina said calmly. "I'm Special Agent Carolina Brown of FDLE. If you reach into my purse on the seat, you'll see my badge and identification."

One of the officers reached inside and pulled out the badge and ID wallet and looked at it.

"I'm sorry Agent Brown. Are you on the job?"

"Yes I am. And because you stopped us, the subject we were following got a way."

"We got an emergency report that a vehicle fitting your car and license number was harassing one of our most prestigious citizens."

"I'm not surprised. But we were not harassing her. The person we were following must have been driving close to your prestigious citizen without our realizing it."

"Did you call in your pursuit and surveillance?"

"No. That was my fault."

"For sure."

"I'm sorry about that."

"Who's your driver?" the officer asked.

"This is Perry Savant, a retired NYPD detective and Florida PI who's helping out in this case."

The officer watched as I pulled out my credentials and handed them to him.

"Okay. Sorry about interfering with your pursuit. Please be sure to let county dispatch know when, why, and who you are pursuing."

The officers released us and allowed us to get back into the car and leave. I pressed on the accelerator and moved the car eastward across the Causeway into downtown Miami Beach.

"Again, I've let that woman out-think and get out ahead of me," I commented.

"That makes two of us. I should have called in our pursuit as soon as I got into your car. Sorry about that."

"All I know is that we've got to think smarter than her. Whatever we try we must assume that she'll have already guessed it." I paused for a moment.

"She must have seen me sitting on the street near where her car was parked."

"I don't think she suspected me. And I don't think that Rev. Horowitz would have given away my presence."

"I wouldn't assume that. He probably felt that it was safe to tell the pastor. And I would imagine that the pastor would truly know in his own heart that mentioning FDLE's involvement would not be a problem. In the meantime, you can put out a BOLO for the car she was in. And while we wait for an answer on that, let's eat."

After a few more blocks, I pulled into the front entrance to the hotel.

Carolina smiled as she got out of the car and followed me into the hotel dining room. We sat next to one of the big bay windows facing the ocean. The lunch crowd had already thinned out and we seemed to have the place to ourselves.

After giving the waiter our drink orders, Carolina took out her phone and called in the request for information on the car that Fara was driving. After she hung up the phone, she looked at me.

"That bitch has got some heavy-duty contacts," Carolina said.

"We're dealing with a shrewd and intelligent woman here. She knows we know and we know she knows we know. So, we've got our work cut out for us."

"What do we do next?" Carolina asked.

"I'm not sure, but I would suspect that she'll strike again soon."

"Why do you say that?"

"Well, it's been a while since the last death. She'll be having that need to kill again."

"I think I may know who will be next. While I was helping out, three men came in together to get something to eat. But, when Fara came out of the back office, they quietly and quickly left. And they were eyeing her the whole time."

"The word's gotten around. The homeless have connected the dead men with the shelter and the presence of Fara before every death. They know, and now we know for certain."

"Yes, but we still can't prove a thing."

"Ah, that's the rub."

The waiter arrived and placed the drinks in front of us and took our food orders.

"So?" Carolina asked.

"I've got an idea. But first let me ask you what you think we ought to do?"

"Well, it appears we don't have much choice except to wait until she strikes again."

"What about the lab results on those items we picked up at the last crime scene?"

"Right," Carolina spoke quietly and hit a speed-dial number on her phone and waited.

"Carlos? Carolina. Tell me about those items we sent over from the death in Miami Beach?"

She listened for a few moments then looked at me.

"He's checking right now."

She scribbled some notes in the notebook that she carried with her everywhere.

"Thanks, Carlos. I owe you one."

Carolina put her phone down.

"The pieces definitely came from a Mercedes. But, not just any Mercedes. This was a special order with bullet-proof glass all around including the lights. It also has hardened metal in the doors for extra protection. There was only one delivered in Miami in the past two years."

"It was delivered to Fara's holding company?"

"Nope."

I was immediately shocked. I noticed the big smile on her face.

"It was a special order from her dad's company," Carolina added. "About a year ago, the Crown Prince of Syria was here to negotiate a deal with old man Flambeau. The car was ordered for his visit because he only travels in bullet-proof vehicles when not in the air."

"So," I began to think out loud. "The car has been sitting in a warehouse gathering dust until she took it out for a spin. So, did you get the address where it's being held?"

"Well, no, but Carlos is working on that for us as we speak. He promised to call as soon as he finds out from his contacts at the Flambeau Company."

At this point, the waiter conveniently brought our orders. We ate and enjoyed the few moments we had free to simply talk about other things rather than work. I realized that I was becoming more and more interested in this beautiful woman in front of me.

I thought back on my life. I had no one special to come home to; and I wondered if I might enjoy coming home to that beautiful face? My thoughts raced in several directions. I had no one. She was available. Could I be happy with someone in my life?

Besides, I found I was still angry at the rumors that were spread in the newspapers and the NYPD informal network.

Where did that anger come from other than that I was being falsely accused?

I sat across from this lovely lady as my thoughts raced to the idea of maybe asking this woman out. I wondered if perhaps the loss of a permanent job as a cop meant I now had time to think of personal things.

But, that would have to wait until after this case was over. I couldn't allow thoughts such as these to dominate my thinking. I had a murderer to catch.

"I've got an idea," Carolina said. "But I'm not sure it's wise at this juncture,"

"What is it?"

"Perhaps we could set a trap."

"A trap. I'd like to think about that. It could be way too dangerous to put one of our own in that situation."

"I know. But, maybe we could locate one of those three men and ask if we can follow him and keep an eye on him for the next several days."

"I like the way you think. In fact, I like it so much, why don't we go back to the homeless shelter and see if we can locate or at least find out who those guys are."

After finishing our meals, we walked out into the warm afternoon air of South Florida, got into the car, and drove back toward Overtown.

"Hello and welcome!" Rev. Horowitz greeted us when we entered the service center.

"Is there someplace where we can talk in private?" I said as my eyebrows narrowed.

The Reverend led us to an office off from the main meeting hall.

"Rev. Horowitz," I began. "We believe that whoever has been killing these homeless men met them here. Or at least saw them here and followed them to where he could later kill them."

"How horrible; I mean, if what you're saying is true? Oh, my God. I think I'm going to be sick."

"I understand," Carolina said. "Being here this morning and helping in the kitchen gave me a new perspective. I know why you do this for these people. They are precious and so well behaved. They truly are just regular folks down on their luck."

"I'm glad you understand the depth of my love for these people and why I have taken this on as my personal ministry through our church."

"We have a delicate question for you and fully understand that you may feel compelled not to answer. But, I think it's important."

The Reverend's eyes narrowed.

"Okay. Go ahead and ask."

"There were three men who entered the shelter together for lunch today. They left in a hurry one at a time. Do you know who they were?"

"No, because I wasn't paying attention to who was here at lunch. I was busy with our principle supporter. But, if it was who I think it was, one of the men is probably George Macomb. He's originally from Nevada. Used to be a dealer out there in Las Vegas, I think. But, he got caught cheating and spent a couple of years in prison. When he got out, he landed up here homeless and destitute."

"Do you have any idea where he might hang out at night?" Perry asked.

The Reverend let out a sigh and rubbed his bald head.

"I'm not sure, but I think he said once that he likes spending the night at a spot underneath the Causeway."

"I think he might be able to help us, but we'll see if we can find him and talk to him. Besides, he might know where the other men are. They also might be able to help. And we may need to help them."

"Wait a minute," said the Reverend. "You know, George often hangs with a man named Rupert. I don't know what his last name is, but if you think he might help out; well he usually spends his time at the North Shore Park area."

"Thank you, Rev. Horowitz. We appreciate your cooperation."

"Detectives, please find this killer. These people don't deserve this no matter what they've done or been."

"We will," Carolina said.

CHAPTER THIRTY-FOUR

We drove off toward the beach crossing the Broad Causeway. We turned on Ocean Blvd. and headed south to the North Shore Park area.

At 87th Street, I pulled into the right lane and slowed down to about thirty.

"We'll cruise along here and see if we can find this guy. Will you recognize him?"

"I think so, but I can't be sure," Carolina said hesitantly.

"That's okay."

We drove south along A1A undisturbed by the looks and the honking of people upset over our speed.

When I reached 75th Street, I turned left and left again onto Collins Drive. I moved over to the far right and drove slowly north. Once I got to 85th Street I turned right into the park.

"Let's just cruise around through here and see what we can see."

For the next fifteen or twenty minutes, I moved carefully through the park area stopping every so often to just sit and watch.

As five o'clock approached, I suggested we do another cruise on North Ocean and Collins just to be sure that maybe he might be wandering along where the restaurants are located. So, I pulled out of the park and cut across to North Ocean where I turned left headed south.

As we drove, we spotted a man that Carolina recognized as one of the men we were looking for. So, I turned left onto 80th and parked. We got out and walked up to the man who was pulling a small cart. As we got close we asked the man to stop and Carolina pulled out her badge.

The man froze with a look on his face that seemed to indicate a tremendous amount of fear.

"Sir, I'm with FDLE. We're not here to hurt or arrest you. We simply need some information, that's all."

"Um, uh, you know, uh, I don't give away information. It's like nothing's free, you hear? You hear?"

"First, tell us your name."

"Me, uh, uh, my name is, uh, uh, Rupert, Rupert, that's my name. Ask me again, I'll tell you the same. Now, I gave you information. What you gonna pay?"

"Well, sir," Carolina said. "We'll be happy to help out any way we can with cash and even food. Have you had dinner?"

"Uh, uh, you know, uh, I think I ate earlier. Can't remember, you know? You know?"

"There's a diner down the street. Let's take you there and buy you a nice meal for the evening. Then we can talk."

I opened the door to the car for the man. He took his things from the little carriage and placed them in the trunk, carefully folded the carriage, and placed it neatly next to his meager possessions. He got into the back seat of the car and sat down. Carolina closed the door and we turned around and headed south.

"I like, you know, I like this, uh, this seat. Wow. Real nice, you know?" Rupert said hesitantly, repeating it several times.

About eight blocks down, we pulled into the public parking lot across from a small diner. We entered the eatery and sat down. Rupert ordered a steak sandwich with French fries and a Coke which he devoured within just a few minutes after it was placed in front of him.

"Rupert," I said as I stared at him. "Do you know George?"

"George? George? Uh, uh, yes, uh, George is my friend. Oh no! Gotta go. Gotta meet George."

Carolina stopped him from standing by placing a hand on his arm.

"Why do you have to meet George?"

"Uh, uh, he protects me; you know. We all protect each other. If we don't, the she-devil will get us."

"What she-devil?" Carolina asked softly.

"Oh my God! Oh my God! She devours men who sleep on A1A. She's out to kill all homeless men. There's not enough food for the men and the women and children. The men got to be sacrificed for the others. I get hungry. I need food. Why do I have to sacrifice?"

"Who tells you to sacrifice?"

"The she-devil; she's the one who gives and she's the one who takes away."

"Who are you talking about?" I said to him sternly.

Rupert stiffened at my voice and said just as seriously as he could.

"She-devil," he said. "No name. Just she-devil. That's all I know."

He got up to leave as Carolina took his arm and walked with him out to the car. I quickly paid the bill.

"Where can we take you?" Carolina asked gently.

Rupert was now calmed down some and looked at her and smiled.

"I like you. You're not a she-devil. You're kind and gentle. I like that."

"Tell us, Rupert, where can we take you? You know; to meet George?"

"Yes, George, must sleep near George, sleep with the others, we protect each other; it's getting dark. Need to get to the bridge. Must get where I'll be safe."

"Can we take you there?"

"Yes. Must go south under the bridge."

"We'll take you to George."

We drove south toward the Tuttle Causeway. At 41st Street, I turned right. Rupert yelled.

"No. Not this way. The other way."

"The other way?" I asked.

"Yes, you know. The other way; the other way."

"I wonder," Carolina interjected, "if he means the MacArther Causeway?"

"Yes," Rupert said loudly. "Yes. The other way; the causeway."

CHAPTER THIRTY-FIVE

I drove across the causeway into downtown Miami where I turned into Centennial Park. I took the exit and pulled down into a large parking lot.

I drove around until I found a place where the fence was separated slightly. I could see a crevice under the viaduct. There in the darkness I could barely make out a couple of people standing around under the bridge. Rupert pulled on the car door handle.

"I gotta go. I gotta go. I can't stay here. I gotta find George to help me and protect me."

"We'll walk with you over there, so you'll be safe," Carolina said. "Is that okay with you, Rupert?"

"I'd like that," Rupert answered. "It's getting dark out. That's when she comes hunting; after dark. You can't see her coming. She strikes in the flash of a bright light. After that, it's all over."

I looked at Carolina and indicated that we should both take him under the bridge. So, we got out and Carolina helped Rupert with his carriage and other stuff. We walked past the gate and approached what appeared to be about twenty men gathered together. There was no light.

"Stop! Who are you?" someone called out.

"It's me; It's me, George. I come just like you said I should. It's me, you know, Rupert. Can I come in?"

"Who you got with you, Rupert?"

"These are my friends; my friends; my friends."

"Identify yourselves."

"My name is Perry Savant," I said. "I'm here to help you, all of you. And this is Agent Brown of the Florida Department of Law Enforcement. We heard about the She-devil and we want to help protect you."

"Bull!" George replied arrogantly. "Where have you been all this time? We've lost fifteen good men; men who never did a thing bad. They just were homeless and poor. They didn't deserve to die."

"We know," Carolina added. "We only just found out about you folks. And we want desperately to help you by catching this she-devil and putting her away for a long time."

"You can't touch her. She's invincible. You'll never get rid of her. She knows everything that happens and knows everybody who is important in this county. You can't do a thing. You hear me? So, just turn around, leave Rupert with us. We'll protect ourselves."

"We can't do that," Carolina said quietly. "Now that we know about your plight, we've got to do something about it. But, we're going to need your help to catch this person and put her away. We know who it is, but we need you to help us to catch her."

"How?"

"We just want to talk to you about what you can do. There's no catch."

"Let Rupert come first. After we see that he's alright, I'll come out to talk to you."

"Rupert," Carolina said. "You go ahead and join your friends."

After a couple of minutes, a tall, rather handsome man in his forties approached.

"I'm George Macomb."

"I'm Carolina Brown and this is a police consultant, Perry Savant."

"Yes. And you wanted me to help you?"

"We're at a loss as to how to catch this murderer you call The She-Devil. We have no clues and no clear suspects. What we were thinking was that if you would be willing, we can trap her while attempting to get to you."

"You want me to be bait?"

"Yes," I said. "I don't want to lie to you. It will be dangerous. And we cannot absolutely guarantee your safety. But if this works, we'll be able to pin the other murders on her."

"Mister, you're asking me to be the sacrificial lamb for these other guys?"

"I'm afraid so, Mr. Macomb." Carolina said.

"I, I want to, but I'm scared," George said as he looked at her. "I mean, I spent three years in the pen in Carson City. I know the tough life. But, this person; I mean, she's pure evil."

"So, will you help us?"

"I'll let you know."

I pulled out a cell phone and handed it to him.

"My number is programmed into this phone. You call me with your decision. I'll explain what you need to do next. Okay?"

Macomb took the phone and quickly put it in his pocket. He turned and walked back to where the others were hiding. Carolina and I watched him disappear into the darkness. I sighed as we walked back to the car and drove off.

CHAPTER THIRTY-SIX

The morning sun shone like a spotlight on my face as I sat in the restaurant having breakfast. The phone rang as if an alarm going off. Recognizing the number as the burn phone I gave Macomb last night, I answered quickly.

"I'll help you," the male voice on the other end said. "Meet me tonight, nine-thirty, at the corner of Seventy-ninth and Harding."

The phone went dead.

I sat a bit stunned at the brevity and conciseness of the call. So, I immediately dialed Carolina and told her what had just happened.

"I'm expecting several reports in from the lab today," She answered. "I'll be by around two to pick you up, if that's okay."

"Sounds good. I've got some research to do on my own. So, I'll be in my room most of the day."

I turned back to my breakfast with a fresh understanding and a plan for the day's work. It felt good to be busy: the only life I'd ever known. I mentally added up the total number of days I worked and realized that I had taken only five days off and no sick days in my twenty-five years with the NYPD.

I lost most of those days because the department only allowed a five-year accumulation. But the check I received for the past five years was such that I had enough money for a down payment on a house in Key West. Once my flat sells, I'll be able to pay off any mortgage I would have on a house.

My thoughts and planning carried me through breakfast. I headed up to my room and changed into shorts and a pull-over hooded top. I put my I.D., a twenty-dollar bill, and my room key in my pocket and went downstairs and through the lobby.

I took off at a jogging pace north on Collins for about two miles and then reversed the route and returned to the hotel a little over an hour later.

After taking a shower, I walked out onto the patio and sat down with the computer in my lap. I typed for a while. At about noon, I went down for lunch. Right at two o'clock sharp, Carolina pulled up in front of the hotel. I opened the passenger door and joined her in the unmarked cruiser.

"Here's the print out on a special edition Mercedes limo that belongs to the Flambeau Company," said Carolina said. "Note that it was sent to the Westside Auto Repair Agency the day after the murder."

"It's missing, isn't it?" I asked quizzically. Carolina nodded agreement as I continued. "That's got to be an amazing coincidence."

"I agree with that," Carolina offered. "Perhaps we should go out there and ask around; see what happened to that car."

"I like a good treasure hunt."

Carolina hit the gas pedal and we pulled out and headed to the Westside Auto Repair Agency.

As we approached the repair shop, we saw a four-acre yard full of junk cars hiding behind a privacy fence. She pulled up into a parking spot on the street.

We got out and decided to walk around the yard before approaching the shop office. As we moved between the many types of vehicles crushed and stacked, we also noticed a rather rustic, hard-looking gentleman in jeans and a soiled T-shirt stepped out from among the cars.

"Can I help you people?"

Carolina pulled out her badge.

"We're looking for a high-end Mercedes limousine that was brought in here for repair a days ago."

"What'd you want with that?" the man retorted.

"We're investigating a murder and we suspect that it may have been involved."

"I don't know nothing about no murder, so just get the hell off my property unless you got a search warrant."

"That will be fine," Carolina said politely. "I'll simply call in the Miami-Dade Police cars waiting down the block to close this place down until the search warrant arrives which could take at least all day."

"Look, Lady. You think you can fool me. There ain't no cop cars down the street."

Carolina reached on her belt and pulled up a small two-way radio receiver, pushed the button on the side and spoke into the phone, "Okay, bring in the reinforcements, Sergeant."

I leaned over to the man.

"It's not wise to ever call the bluff of a woman detective. She's got too much to prove."

In what seemed like only seconds, four Miami-Dade patrol cars pulled up with lights flashing blocking the entrance to the yard. The man simply turned away and walked over to his car and drove off.

We stood at the street and watched the man drive away into the distance.

About an hour later an FDLE car pulled into the yard. The driver jumped out and handed a paper to Carolina who turned to me.

"Here's the search warrant," she said and led four sheriff's deputies into the building to search for the Mercedes limo. After a search of the entire property which took well over two hours, we came up empty handed.,

"I should have figured she'd never leave that limo here after the repairs were made," Carolina said.

"That car is probably on its way to a crushing bin by now."

"But, Perry, why did he leave like that? He knew we wouldn't find the car."

"He's only inconvenienced by us. But, he's terrified of her. That man is headed north out of the state and hopes she doesn't send someone after him."

"I don't think the same way you do, Perry."

"I know. But working for the NYPD for twenty-five years; well, you realize that some people are just pure evil. That seems to describe Fara."

Carolina sighed deeply.

"We'd better wrap this up and get on over to the park. We're supposed to meet up with Macomb in about three hours."

We finished the investigation and made sure that the place was pad locked and marked with police tape. We watched as the officers left. We got into Carolina's car and drove away toward North Miami Beach as the deputies locked down the property.

The traffic was terrible as usual. A major accident on I-95 shut down the north bound side such that traffic was being diverted off at NW 103rd Street. Carolina got a little frustrated and began cussing at the drivers cutting in and out and driving everywhere, especially on the shoulder.

Her anger grew so that she turned on the red emergency light on her car, pulled over onto the shoulder, and put a stop to the dozens in too big of a hurry for a traffic jam.

After about ten minutes of driving five miles an hour, Carolina moved quickly with the emergency light and pulled off. She cut over to North Miami Drive and headed north to the beach. She turned south on Harding and into a parking space a half-block south of Seventy-Ninth Street. After turning off the engine, she rolled down the windows.

"Okay, I guess we just sit and wait for Macomb to show up."

"There's a sandwich shop right down there. You want something?" I asked.

"That's a great idea. I'll take a tuna roll and a diet Coke."

"Be back in a few minutes," I said as I got out of the car and walked the hundred yards or so to a little sandwich shop where I put in the order and waited patiently for the food.

While I was getting the food, Carolina briefed a couple of Miami-Dade detectives who had arrived. She gave them the instructions as to what to expect and who to be looking for. The two went back to their cars to wait and watch.

I returned a little past nine. I got into the car and handed Carolina her food.

"I would have expected him to be a little early," I said.

"He's homeless, Perry. He might not even own a watch."

"Oh, he owns a good one. I saw it on his arm while we were talking last night. This guy may be homeless, but I get the impression he has the money to afford whatever he wants."

"Why would he be living on the streets?"

"I have no idea. He said he'd meet us at nine-thirty. Let's see if he keeps that promise."

We sat in the car waiting. The radio crackled slightly.

"Any sign of our pigeon?"

Carolina looked at me.

"Tim's a bit of an ass, but he's a good detective."

She took the microphone in her hand.

"No sign, yet. We'll wait another hour then I'll make the call."

"Ten-four. Out," Tim said.

It was a little past nine-thirty when Carolina's cell phone rang.

"This is Agent Brown."

"I thought you might want to know," said a high-pitched voice. "The Surfside Police have just responded to the reported death of a homeless man in the alley off seventy-seventh between Collins and Harding. You and Perry might want to get there quickly."

"Who is this? Who are you with?" The phone went dead.

"What?" I asked.

"I, uh, some woman just said we need to investigate a murdered homeless man two blocks from here."

"Who was it?"

"Hell, if I know. I've never heard her voice."

"A woman?"

"Yeah."

"Fara. She found out what Macomb was up to and showed us who's in charge of this investigation."

"Let's get over there," said Carolina.

She called the other detectives and told them what had happened and asked them to stay and keep a watch. She pressed on the accelerator making the tires of her cruiser squeal against the pavement.

Carolina pulled across three lanes to make a left onto Seventy-Eighth St., turned quickly into the alley on the right. As she did, a Miami Beach Police officer was there to stop her. She showed her badge and the officer directed her to park on the left out of the way. Carolina and I were out of the car even before the engine had died.

We walked down the alley to where there was a black sheet covering what was apparently a body lying in the middle of the alley. Several officers and detectives from both Miami Beach and Surfside Police Departments were working the scene. As we approached, Vernon Mitchell saw us and met us as a Surfside detective stopped us.

"Detective," he said. "These people are with me."

The detective didn't argue but simply stepped out of the way.

"What do you have?" Carolina asked.

"The dead man had this in his pocket," Vernon said as he handed her the cell phone that Perry had given to Macomb.

"Oh, no," I said as I stepped over to the body and lifted the edge of the tarpaulin. "It's Macomb. We were supposed to meet him tonight about three blocks from here."

Vernon signaled another detective over to where we were standing.

"This is Detective Sergeant Kevin Black of the Surfside Police Department," Vernon said. "Kevin, this is Special Agent Carolina Brown of FDLE. She's the lead detective on the investigation into the numerous murders of homeless men along A1A."

Kevin smiled as he reached out to shake hands with Carolina.

"I'm sure glad you've arrived," Kevin said. "I mean, I'm happy to drop this case in your lap. I'm no expert on mass murderers."

"Well, Detective, neither am I. But I'm learning fast. This is retired NYPD chief of detectives Perry Savant," she said pointing at me.

"He's helping us out on this case as a consultant. And he's a real live expert on mass murderers."

"Sure, glad to meet you, Sir. Vernon told me about you both. So, you know this man?"

"No. We only met yesterday," said Carolina. "He was supposed to meet with us this evening but never showed up."

"I guess he was busy, huh?"

"Yeah. Seems like it."

Two other detectives walked toward us and stood a few paces off.

"They're with us," she told Vernon. "So, what did you find?"

"Not much. There are tire scorches on the pavement on Seventy-seventh headed toward the alley here. It looks to me as if someone chased Mr. Macomb here into the alley and ran him down."

"Man, that's cold," I whispered to Carolina.

"This is what killed him," Vernon said as he pulled the cover back and indicated the bullet hole in the man's chest. "Went right through his heart. I doubt he felt a thing."

Carolina looked at me, her eye brows high and her eyes wide. She noted the furrowed eye brows on my face.

"Where are you sending the body?" she asked.

"Where do you want me to send it?"

"Send it to the county morgue. I'll call and make sure Doc Estavez sends me the results. I'm particularly interested in the bullet."

"That could be a problem," Vernon said.

He lifted the body and pointed to the man's back.

"See here? The bullet went through and through. There's no telling where it is."

Carolina turned to Kevin.

"Do you have a team searching the area for that bullet?"

"I told you I'm not a murder detective."

"Get the rest of your team up here immediately," Carolina said to Vernon. "I'll call Miami-Dade and have them send a team out to help. We've got to find that bullet."

She leaned toward me.

"Her first mistake."

"I can't believe, I mean, she's either getting sloppy, or-"

"Or, she didn't do this?"

"Right. But, let's assume she's feeling the pressure and needed to take care of this situation with more speed. She must have wanted to be sure he was dead."

Carolina handed her card to Kevin and asked him to call her as soon as they found anything at the crime scene that she needed to hear about. She walked over to the extra detectives who were helping with the stake-out and told them to head on back to headquarters.

She and I looked at each other, let out a big sigh, walked back to the car and drove off toward South Beach.

As Carolina pulled up in front of the hotel, I turned to her and asked, "Do you have any plans tonight?"

"Oh, Perry, Please. I'm tired and need some sleep. This case is worrying me terribly."

Uh, perhaps you misunderstood me. I thought you and I might go out together and check out Fara's favorite night spot."

"That's not such a bad reason for asking me out. I'll be back in about two hours. I think the club doesn't get going until around midnight."

"Good. I'll shower and change into my suit and meet you back in the lobby at eleven-thirty. And, uh, I can't wait to see you dressed up for the evening."

"Hey, I clean up good."

Carolina's phone rang. She answered it listening intently to the person on the other end of the line for several minutes. I sat still watching her face with the intensity of a researcher in a library full of old manuscripts.

Carolina hung up the phone and turned to me, her eyes fluttering.

"You are not going to believe this; but that car she drove the other night and took in for repair? Well, it seems it went to the dock and was shipped out this evening headed for Johannesburg."

"South Africa?"

"South Africa. And the ship isn't due to dock there for two weeks."

"I have a contact in the Johannesburg Police. I'll see if he can meet that ship and impound the vehicle."

"Good. I'll be back in ninety minutes," she replied.

"I thought you said it would take you two hours."

"Yeah, I did. But we've got to get this bitch before she kills anyone else."

"I agree with that," I said as I slipped out of the car. I turned back to her.

"See you then," I said as I turned the phone off and walked into the hotel.

CHAPTER THIRTY-SEVEN

The Club Mystique was one of the big-name hot spots on South Beach. Fara Flambeau bought the building and converted it into a high-end night club where some of the biggest names in entertainment performed every week-end.

People were lined up down the block and around the corner waiting to get in.

As I pulled up in the Cadillac sedan, a valet rushed over to open the door on my side as another pulled open the door for Carolina. I handed the keys to the young man who instantly handed me a numbered check card.

As we approached the bouncer out front, Carolina opened her purse and asked the man to look in. As he did, he could see her FDLE badge and immediately pulled the rope back and allowed us to enter. As we passed through the front door, the bouncer pulled a small microphone from his coat sleeve and said something into it.

As we approached a second man standing at another door with a strong gate. Entering briskly, I noticed three cameras focused on the lobby and heard the self-locking door behind us shut tight. I leaned down toward Carolina.

"This place has more security than a bank."

"And harder to get into than a bank," she replied as we approached a young man dressed in a tuxedo. He immediately pulled open the gate and handed a small card to another man in a tux who escorted us to a table near the front of the audience within five feet of the edge of the stage.

"I can't believe she figured we'd be here tonight," I mused as the young man held back a chair for Carolina.

"Perry," she said smiling, "She's anticipated our every move. So why not this one?"

When the waiter arrived, he introduced himself, "My name is Armond, and I'll be your lead waiter tonight. I have been instructed to tell you that you're welcome to order whatever you wish this evening. Your tab has already been taken care of as extra special V.I.P.'s."

I shook my head as I felt my eyes roll back.

"Okay, I'll have a Seven and Seven."

The waiter turned to Carolina.

"And the lady?"

"The lady will have a Tom Collins," I said. As the waiter walked away, I looked at Carolina with a slight grin.

"You're not on the clock tonight."

She smiled, shook her head.

"So, what's the plan?"

"We just watch and listen."

The entertainment began and the two of us enjoyed what was going on. After the first show ended, Carolina heard a familiar voice behind her. It was the same voice she had heard on the telephone giving her the tip that a murder had taken place.

"Welcome to my club."

I immediately stood up and turned toward Fara and indicated Carolina.

"Miss Fara Flambeau, may I present to you Special Agent Carolina Brown--"

"Of the Florida Department of Law Enforcement, of course," Fara broke in. "Happy to meet you."

"Please don't feel compelled to pay our tab. I can do that," I said.

Fara swung around and quickly sat across from Carolina and crossed her legs seductively pointing them toward my face.

"It is one of the few pleasures I find in life. Besides, I feel that since you accepted my invitation to come tonight, I'm obligated to pick up the tab."

"Well," Carolina drawled. "The invitation was difficult to turn down, to say the least."

"Of course, darling. I always get what I want. And this evening I wanted you both here with me. I feel I owe you for helping me to be far more successful than I could possibly be otherwise."

I glanced down at my cell phone as I spoke.

"So, where do we go from here?"

"Oh, darling, I'm sure you'll figure that out all by yourself. You've done so well thus far. I always use lots of hints, you know, like every woman should. But unfortunately, not everyone is smart enough to figure them out, let alone recognize them. That's why I find myself enthralled with you."

She reached over and stroked the inside of my leg passionately.

"I'm glad I intrigue you," I answered as I lifted her hand and placed it carefully into her own lap. "But, I fear you may not be so interested once I pull it all together and arrest you for murder."

"Murder? I haven't the slightest idea what you're talking about. Perhaps you're not as sharp as I thought you were. Didn't get this one at all, did you?"

"Oh, I got it. And I'll get more every day that passes."

"I wish you all the luck in the world, Perry Savant."

Then Fara was on her feet and half-way across the floor and backstage as both of us followed her every move.

"Do we need to follow her?" Carolina asked.

"I don't think so. She's got something planned for us here tonight. She wanted us, no, expected us to show up. We've got to stay until we find the clue or the information she intends for us to get."

"So," Carolina answered coyly. "I guess we should simply have a little fun together." She leaned over and pressed her nose gently against my cheek as she reached down and gently massaged the inside of my thigh.

"Well, I won't need to work out my legs tonight," I said. "They seem to have been worked on pretty well."

We laughed together as the waiter set the drinks down on the table. We each picked up a glass and clicked them together both wondering just what would happen this evening.

CHAPTER THIRTY-EIGHT

Six-thirty the next morning, my phone rang waking me from a sound, hard sleep. As I rolled over to get my phone I immediately became cautious, remembering that I was not alone in the bed.

I looked at the phone and saw that it was Sanchez calling from his cell phone. I moved quietly into the bathroom and closed the door.

"Adolph? What's happened?"

"We got another floater."

"Homeless man?"

"Yep. And this one is bad. His legs are broken. Looks like he was hit at forty or fifty miles per hour and literally knocked into the water. I can hardly believe the car didn't go over as well."

"Sounds like our killer is getting more brazen, as well as bold. We'll be there in thirty minutes."

"We?"

I immediately realized what I had just said and fumbled for a moment. "I'll be there, Adolph. I was up late last night. I'm not even awake, yet."

"Okay," replied Sanchez as he hung up the phone with a little chuckle.

Standing in the bathroom, I looked in the mirror. I was wearing nothing at all. So, I turned on the faucet and threw some water on my face.

"What the hell?" Carolina said out loud as she bolted upright in the bed. She pulled the sheet back and looked down.

"I'm naked."

"That's what normally happens when you go to bed with someone," came my quiet reply from the bathroom.

"Oh, hell, Perry. What do we do now?"

"How about savor the experience?" I said as I stepped into the bedroom. "It wasn't bad was it?"

"Well, no. But I don't remember much."

"Me neither," I said as I reached down for my clothes that were strewn around the room. "Which is something strange. I've been known to drink my share and more and have never gotten so drunk that I don't remember what happened afterword."

"Me neither."

My face went pale as I stumbled over my words.

"Oh, no. Fara."

"What?"

"Fara drugged our drinks to put us out of commission while she committed another murder."

"Oh, come on, Perry. That's absurd."

"Why is it? She's been one step ahead of us and still is. Let's get dressed and go to the crime scene."

"I only have the dress from last night. That's a bit much for work. I'm going back to my place and change. I'll meet you later."

"Sounds good to me."

I explained to her just where to meet me. I walked up to her, gently touched her cheek, and kissed her.

"Just remember that it was the drugs. And, uh, I'm reminding myself of that, too. And yet, I find myself not regretting whatever happened."

"If anything happened," Carolina reminded me with a sweet smile.

I stepped back and stared at this attractive woman in front of me; I found myself realizing that for the first time in my life I might be falling in love.

So, I leaned over and gave her another kiss. She walked back into the bathroom to finish getting ready for the day. I watched through the mirror as Carolina lifted her slender, well-formed body from the bed and squeeze into the dress from the night before.

She walked to the bathroom door.

"I'll meet you at the park in about an hour."

I turned and nodded with a face covered in shaving cream.

"How about a kiss good-bye?"

She smiled.

"I'll take a rain check on that kiss," she said as she placed a finger on my cheek, took a little shave cream, and rub it on my chest. She twirled on her heels and was out the door in an instant. I stood there mesmerized for several moments then returned to shaving and showering, smiling all the time.

About a half-hour later, I guided the Cadillac north on Collins and took a right through the entrance of Haulover Park. I bypassed the two parking lots and drove toward the inlet itself but was directed to park in a parking lot to the left by a sheriff's deputy. I showed my ID and walked over to where I could see the body lying on the ground wrapped in a black body bag.

I walked over to Sanchez who was looking at the body in the bag. He looked up at me as I got closer.

"I thought," Sanchez said faintly. "You weren't supposed to be investigating without Carolina holding onto your leash."

"She's on her way. What happened?"

He pointed to where the driveway neared the edge of the water of the inlet.

"You can see the tire marks from the braking tires. This guy was floating in the water just over there, caught in the roots of those banyan trees."

"This was not as well planned as most of the other murders," I said. "It looks like it was a quick decision, kind of like Macomb's death."

"Yeah. So, what do you think? Are we talking about two different people?"

"No, I think we're talking about one murderer who is either getting sloppy or subconsciously wants to get caught."

Sanchez chuckled a little.

"I ain't holding my breath on that theory."

"Yeah, I know. But, I'm still convinced this is the work of Fara Flambeau."

"Come on, Perry. Keep quiet about that. Keep it between us. We could find ourselves in court fighting for our lives if that ever got out publicly."

"I don't like it that we have to be so careful about that bitch. She's going to keep on killing until we stop her. It's time we got bolder about our investigation."

"I know. And I agree with you. But for the moment, we have nothing. Did you hear me, Perry? Get me some real evidence of her involvement and I'll personally arrest her."

I shook my head and walked over toward the water to look more closely at the paucity of evidence available. As I stood there for several minutes, I felt someone standing next to me. Without giving any indication.

"What took you so long?" I spoke quietly.

Carolina smiled.

"I drove the speed limit."

I smiled.

"So, what do we have?" Carolina continued.

"Another poor bastard dead at the hands of Super-bitch."

"And what evidence do we have to make that accusation?"

"My gut."

"Too bad your gut can't testify in court."

"Are you going to start on me, too?"

"Naw. But, I'll rib you a little until we come up with some real evidence. Speaking of evidence, have you called your friend in South Africa?"

I looked at my watch.

"It's a little after five there. I'll give my friend a call."

As I dialed the phone number into my cell phone, I looked at Carolina and winked.

"If that car is there, we got her."

"I wouldn't put any money on it being there."

The voice on the other end of the phone had a gravely and rustic sound.

"Good day!"

"Hello, my friend," I said.

"Perry Savant. How the hell are you?" the voice on the other end answered immediately.

"Not much. I'm retired, now, and working as a private dick in Miami."

"Some people have all the luck. When you're ready for a partner, give me a call."

"Partner? Of course. But right now, I need information."

"Shock. Why else would you call?"

"Yeah. I know. I need more than information. I need a big favor."

"Anything, Perry. Just ask."

I took a small notebook from Carolina's hand as she pulled it from her pocket and handed it to me. I read the shipping details aloud.

"Can you find that shipping container and tell me what's in it?"

"Of course, Perry. When's it due?"

"It should be at the port on the thirtieth or so. Not sure. Let me know what you find."

"Will do."

As I clicked the phone off, I looked over at Carolina.

"Two weeks before we know what's going on with the container, if it arrives at all."

"Perry, we need to realize we've lost a valuable piece of evidence and that she's getting the best of us."

"And more homeless men are going to die."

"So, let's stop her."

"You've got an idea?"

"I'm not sure. But I'd like to run it past Laura first."

"Follow me to the hotel and let's go talk to her together."

"I'm going to do this on my own because I want her to think that this is my idea alone. If you come--"

"I got it. No problem."

Carolina leaned over and kissed me on the cheek, walked back to her car, and drove off.

As she was walking to her car, Sanchez strolled up to me, stopped a few steps away, and stood quietly, his eyes fixed on me.

"What?" I said as I turned to him.

"Did she just kiss you?"

"What of it?"

"Nothing, man. I've just never known you to be interested in, well, you know, women. That's all."

"Are you saying I'm queer?"

"No. I'm just saying what I said. That's all."

"Look, Adolph, I've never had time to think about anyone other than myself and my job. You know that. So, I never thought about anybody else before. Carolina is a beautiful woman and, well, I've got little to occupy my time these days and--"

"And you found out you might be interested in someone else?"

"Right. So, anyway, she's got some ideas on how we might be able to catch our killer. So, she's going to talk to Laura to get her okay. We'll contact you as soon as we have the plans in place."

"Good. I am so ready to get this solved."

"I know. I'll let you know as soon as I know."

I walked around the crime scene one more time to make sure I hadn't missed anything. I drove back to the hotel where I went into the restaurant to have some lunch and to wait for Carolina's call.

Around two, Carolina entered the restaurant. I think my heart rate rose. I felt my face go flush as she approached the table. I stood and pulled the chair out for her. We both sat down.

She pulled a notebook out of her purse and looked at me. I thought she was going to say something, but she didn't. She stared at me for several moments.

"What?" I replied looking back at her.

"Are you blushing?"

"What? No, yes, I'm just--what do you have?"

"Okay; Laura gave me the go-ahead for several of my ideas. The first thing is to spend the next several days shadowing Fara. I want to just get a feel for her routine, especially in the evenings."

"I think you're on to something; old-fashioned police work."

"Everything old school isn't bad or outdated."

"You realize this is going to be a boring several days, don't you?"

"I've done surveillance before. But, I'm convinced we'll find out something she doesn't want us to know."

"I hope you're right."

I paid the tab and we both went out to Carolina's car and climbed in.

"I figure she'll never think this old thing is following her."

"I don't know. She's been more observant than I would have guessed. But, we'll find out."

I sat back as she pulled out into traffic and headed toward the large palatial high-rise where Fara's office was located. Finding a rare parking spot on the street, Carolina pulled in quickly and put the car in park. She rolled down the windows as a cool breeze swept through the car.

"We've had Fara under constant surveillance for the past three days, despite the protests from some of the big wigs at city hall. But Laura's kept them at bay so far. The last report put Fara in her office about two hours ago where she's been in meetings."

"When's she due out?"

"We're not sure. She has no commitments on her calendar after two-thirty. We'll see what she does after that."

"How do you know so much?"

"We have someone inside her office; a paid informant."

"Good," I said, followed by a long silence as we both watched the building.

At two-thirty a large black Mercedes limousine pulled up in front of the building. Less than a minute later, Fara and two neatly dressed men exited the building and got into the car.

Carolina had to do a U-turn to follow the long sleek auto north on Brickell Avenue. It moved with efficiency through the mid-afternoon traffic. As we followed the car up onto the Interstate we were traveling near seventy-five miles per hour north toward Fort Lauderdale.

Carolina worked hard at the wheel attempting not to appear like she was following the larger car. After about ten miles, she quit bothering with the touch-n-go routine and simply settled in at about fifty yards behind.

After about forty minutes, the limo exited at Broward Boulevard and went east pulling up in front a large building near the intersection of Andrews Boulevard. Fara and the two men got out and walked in.

Carolina pulled past them and parked in a parking lot about a half-block east stopping in such a way as to see the front entrance of the building. The limousine waited out front instead of parking in the garage.

Carolina called in our position and requested information on the building. After several minutes a voice over the radio relaying it to us.

"The only occupant of the building is a large exporting business owned by a subsidiary of RLF Industries. That's the holding company for Flame-Mart and numerous other companies owned by the Flambeaus."

"Thank you. Out."

"How extensive is their business influence?" I asked.

"I can't think in those numbers. But, I assume they handle all of their own exports and imports as well as most all of the manufacturing and marketing. They're located in or have influence with the leaders of nearly twenty different nations."

"Oh," is all that I could say. I continued to stare toward the limousine parked in front of the building partially blocking the busy Broward Boulevard. I watched as cars would come to a stop trying to avoid the big, expensive car that sat blocking the right lane marked as a no parking zone.

About ten minutes later, a Fort Lauderdale Police car pulled up behind the limo turning on its emergency lights. The officer got out and walked over to the driver's side and leaned down for a few seconds. He casually walked back to his car and got in.

I was amused when I noticed that the officer was not writing a ticket but was simply sitting there with his emergency lights flashing. Another ten minutes passed when Fara exited the building alone and got into the car. As the limo drove off, the police car turned off its lights and did a U-turn headed back toward downtown.

Carolina pulled out behind the limo and followed four or five car lengths behind as the black Mercedes turned onto Federal Highway headed south. When we approached the tunnel, the limo swerved at the exit to Las Olas and turned off on a side street. Not wanting to be spotted, Carolina drove past the turn, made a U-turn, and went back to fourth and turned right. She could see the limo several blocks ahead parked in front of a large, palatial estate at the end of the street.

Carolina turned left and pulled into a parking lot where she backed into a spot. From there we could watch the entrance to the house. Again, Carolina picked up the microphone and called in the address.

The voice on the radio said: "That address belongs to Senator Jose Salazar."

"THE Senator Salazar? The same man who owns half of Fort Lauderdale?"

"Oh no, Carolina. What have we stepped into?" I asked.

"I don't know. But I'll bet it smells bad."

As we continued sitting and observing the Salazar residence, a Ft. Lauderdale Police cruiser pulled up and stopped in front of us with emergency lights flashing. The officer stepped out of the car and walked to Carolina's window.

"May I ask what you are doing here?"

Carolina reached around and pulled out her badge and showed it to the officer. At that point, Fara's car pulled out of the gate and drove out passing us as we sat blocked in by the patrol car.

The officer looked at the badge and pressed the microphone switch on his radio.

"Base, this is eighty-two, the unknown vehicle just reported is a couple of FDLE agents."

The radio squawked.

A voice sounded: "Hold one."

After a couple of seconds, the voice came back on.

"What are their names?"

"Sir, I need your ID," the officer said as he peeked into the car.

I handed my PI license over to him. Carolina looked at the officer.

"This man is working as a consultant on a case."

The officer took the ID's back to the car.

"She's devious to the max," Carolina said. "I never thought she'd pull something as crappy as this."

The officer walked back and handed both ID's to Carolina.

"Agent Brown, I apologize. We had a report of a suspicious vehicle in a parking lot that was supposed to be vacant. Just doing my job, you know."

"No problem, officer. I understand."

At that the officer went back to his car and drove off.

"It looks like we're going to have to be a lot more discreet in the future. She's much more observant, or should I say suspicious, than I had figured."

"Might I suggest we go back and get my car? Then let's see if we can find her again. She might not suspect someone in a Cadillac as following her."

"Maybe she might think you were stalking her."

"Yeah. Right."

We both laughed as Carolina pulled out of the space and out into the street heading back south toward Miami Beach.

CHAPTER THIRTY-NINE

Two weeks passed without a murder. I found myself able to sleep better. So, when the phone rang at six that morning, I was barely awake. The familiar voice of Manfred Maughan, my contact in INTERPOL, came on the line and shocked me out of my stupor.

"Awaken, my friend. I have news on that shipping container you asked about."

"It's six in the morning, Manfred. Why couldn't you wait a couple of hours before calling me?"

"Is it six already? Bloody inconsiderate of me, Chief. I'll remember that next time."

"Okay, okay. What did you find out?"

"We confiscated the container with the numbers and lading order you sent me. We opened it and found it empty."

"What? Empty?"

"Correct. And since there were nearly five hundred containers on that ship, the police superintendent would not allow his men to go through all of them. So, we looked for any containers with a one-number difference but turned up nothing."

"Okay, Manfred. You did well. I appreciate your rapid response to our request."

"Next time you're in Johannesburg, be sure to call me."

"I absolutely promise to do that. Cheerio, my friend."

And with that I hung up the phone, laid back down on the bed, looked up at the ceiling, and whispered a sigh.

After a few minutes, I got up, took a shower, and went down to the restaurant for breakfast. At around eight, Carolina walked in and joined me.

"So, my boss is ready to take me off the case because we have several drug-related issues that need our attention."

"She knew she would have to back off after that little fiasco in Ft. Lauderdale."

"I'm sure she did," Carolina sighed.

"And I'll bet she knew that if she waited at least two weeks, that the police agencies would assume that the killing had stopped."

"No, she's much smarter than that. She planned this out carefully knowing we would find out about the container today or tomorrow."

"What are you going to do?"

"What do you think I should do?" I asked.

"Well, if you stay on the case as a private detective, then we can keep in touch. Maybe you can think of me as your client. That way I'll be able to watch your back and we'll be protected by detective-client confidentiality."

"I like the way you think," I said in a soft voice as I reached over and touched her hand.

She smiled back and placed her right hand on mine.

"I'm not quite ready to give up this case."

Our eyes met and locked for several moments until Carolina's phone broke the spell with its ring. She answered.

"Brown here."

She listened for several moments with a couple of "uh-huh's."

"I'll get right on it." After putting her phone away, she looked at me.

"She may have screwed up this time. There's been another death of a homeless man and Laura said that as of this morning, FDLE has taken complete control of the investigation and has ordered me to take charge permanently."

"I'll be--" I uttered with a smile. "I hope this one is hers and not a copy-cat. If that's the case, we're screwed rather than her."

"Yeah, I know. But, let's proceed as if it is her and see what happens."

I paid the bill. We walked out of the hotel. A handsome young man pulled up with my new Mercedes. I opened the door for Carolina then walked around handing the valet a twenty-dollar bill.

Pulling out, I stopped abruptly before entering traffic.

"Where am I going?"

Carolina smiled as she reached over to touch my shoulder in a loving caress.

"You are so funny. We're headed back to Sunny Isle. This murderer has a thing for that little community. Anyway, our contact at the crime scene is DeShawn Royce, remember him?"

"Okay, let's go."

I maneuvered through the streets north to Sunny Isle arriving at a construction site on Collins near 195th Street. The police tape surrounded the entire vacant lot. We could see that construction had only begun a few days earlier. The ground prep was still far from ready for the foundation to be poured.

This murder scene showed one set of tire tracks onto and off the lot. The officers that responded first immediately blocked off the area and kept the scene pristine. Even though

Carolina and I were several hours later than the first responders, we found the scene still intact and the body still in place.

It was covered by a large piece of black plastic. Several pieces of plywood had been laid down on which people could traverse the scene without disturbing any possible evidence.

We walked out to where Detective Royce oversaw his department's work on the scene. He even had kept the coroner at bay as he waited for us to arrive. As we approached Royce's face betrayed his excitement when he saw Carolina.

"Well, agent Brown, it's nice to see you again. I was told that you are now in charge of the investigation of all these homeless murders."

"Nice to see you as well. So, tell me what we've got."

He reached down and uncovered the body. We peered down at the badly mangled body of a man in his mid-thirties dressed in obviously worn and dirty clothes. The stench that filled the air was that of someone who had not bathed for weeks rather than that of a rotting corpse.

Carolina quickly snapped on a pair of gloves and placed a handkerchief over her face as she knelt down to look at the wounds. His legs were broken near the thighs. Plus, there were tell-tale tire marks over the face, arms and mid-torso.

"This looks like the work of someone who was angry with the victim, not that of the sort we've seen in the past."

"She wanted to mangle this guy," I said quietly.

"No kidding," Royce said as he gave out a nervous laughter.

"I wasn't being humorous."

At that Royce stopped, his face glowing with embarrassment.

"Just trying to bring a little levity into the situation. Sorry."

Carolina pointed to something in the man's hand.

"What's this?"

As she pried each finger away, she removed a small piece of paper from the man's hand. She carefully opened it, noticing it was a calling card. The name on the card was a surprise for all three of them. It read, Fara Flambeau, CEO, The Flambeau Foundation."

"What the--" Royce caught himself.

"Either she made one hell of a mistake or she was not the one who killed this man," I added.

Carolina sealed up the card in an evidence bag and put it in her pocket. She and I continued going over the body with great care pulling threads and pieces of hair from the victim's clothing.

"I don't think any of this will help us," she said sealing up another evidence bag.

"What about this?" Royce called out as he pointed at a high-heeled shoe half-buried in the dirt lying alongside of the tire tracks.

"Bag and tag it. We'll look at it later," Carolina answered.

I continued to scour the area between where the body was found and the place where the wheel tracks left the pavement. As I finished I looked around in a wider pattern. I called over to Carolina.

"This whole scene seems so familiar. Virtually no clues at all."

"I know but keep looking anyway. I'm in charge now. No half-ass scene coverage under my watch."

I looked over at Royce with a slight smile. He smiled back when a slight glint caught his eye. Buried partially in the sand and dirt was a large piece of yellow reflector glass just like that which I had found earlier. That piece which had turned out to be a body part from a Mercedes Limousine.

"Carolina, I think this is important," I said as I placed it in an evidence bag.

She walked over to where I stood, took the bag from my hand, and looked at it more closely.

"This is just like that other piece we found several months ago. I wonder--"

"Do you think it could be from the same vehicle?"

"But, that vehicle was shipped off to South Africa."

"Well, now, that's not true."

"What?"

"I got a call this morning from my contact in INTERPOL who told me that when they opened that cargo container, they found it empty. The car never left our shores."

"And when were you planning to tell me that important piece of information?" she said as she stared at me with her piercing detective eyes.

"Um, I'm telling you now?" I said knowing it was a stupid thing to say.

"I'll get this to the lab right away," Royce chimed in just in time to calm the air. "We should soon find out what kind of match we have."

Carolina walked over to Detective Royce.

"I think we have everything we need here. It's all yours."

"I'd appreciate it if you'd keep me informed."

"Will do."

Carolina walked back to the car where she joined me. I did not hesitate to get seated and waiting for her. I started the car and pulled out into traffic.

"So, after we drop this off at the lab, where do you want to go?"

"I think it would be smart to drop in on the good reverend at the shelter. I'd love to hear what's going on there."

"Sounds good to me."

CHAPTER FORTY

The sun beat down hot against the open concrete in Overtown that afternoon. Most of the trees had been knocked down by the several hurricanes that had ravaged South Florida over the past ten years.

Unlike the numerous neighborhoods throughout the Suburban Miami area that were pretty much back to normal, trees and destroyed buildings in Overtown were rarely replaced.

Many of the buildings that had been burned down during the riots of the late eighties were never rebuilt. The area was pock-marked with vacant lots that the city had taken over and kept cut.

Driving through the area one might think he was in a small southwestern town that had lost many of the residents because the loss of factories or the dreams of those factories moving in that never materialized. Carolina glanced over at me then back at the road.

"Kind of depressing, isn't it?" She said.

"There are parts of Brooklyn and The Bronx that look like this. Seems like the local government attitude is the same down here as it is up there."

"What? Don't give a care?"

"Right. There's not much money down here as it is. It would seem to me that the county and city would find it advantageous to get people interested in this property and come in to develop it."

"You would think."

"The street's a bit deserted. Not like the last couple of times we've been down here."

"That's why," Carolina said as she nodded toward the store on the corner that had been bustling with people several weeks before.

"Looks like a pretty bad fire took out everything."

"Yeah. Common down here. Sometimes when rival gangs get into turf wars, this kind of thing happens as a way of saying 'If you want this area, you can have it--without any amenities.'"

"That is so sad. But, I guess we don't have to worry about your car getting jacked."

I pulled up next to the entrance to the old storefront that was the homeless meal and sleeping center for the church. We got out and walked to the building. As I pulled on the handle, it opened immediately. We walked in.

"Hello! Anyone here?" Carolina shouted.

There was no sound at all; just a slight echo from the empty rooms. We walked into the dining area and into the kitchen. We noticed that the back door stood ajar. I held Carolina's arm back then pulled out my pistol. I walked out into the alley behind the building. Seeing nothing, I stepped back into the kitchen.

"Where could everyone be?"

"While you were outside I thought I heard someone walking around upstairs."

We walked toward the front to another room off to the side where a set of stairs led to the upper portion of the building. As we slowly made our way up the stairs, I could hear some moving and shuffling. I cautioned for Carolina to keep her pistol holstered as I put mine away.

"Hello! Is anyone up here?"

There was no answer. Carolina pulled out her pistol and tugged on my arm to allow her to go ahead. I knew what she was doing and pulled back out of her way. She stepped up slowly and stood beside an open doorway from which we both could hear shuffling.

She signaled to me that she was going in. She turned around with her pistol held outward and found herself immediately confronting a surprised and confused Rev. David Horowitz.

Stepping back, Horowitz pulled the headphones from his ears.

"My God, you almost gave me a heart attack."

"Why didn't you answer when we called out?"

He held up the ear phones and MP3 player.

"I like listening to some of the pastor's old sermons while I'm cleaning up. I'm sorry if I caused you concern."

"That's quite alright," Carolina said. "Remember? I'm detective Carolina Brown and this gentleman is a police consultant and private detective named Perry Savant."

"Yes. I remember you both. Wait a minute. Were you with NYPD several years ago?"

"Retired chief of detectives," I said.

"I remember that big case you solved, big drug bust and the killing of two police officers?"

"That was fifteen years ago."

"Did they execute the dude?"

"I'm afraid not. He got twenty-five to life."

"He'll probably get paroled on some technicality."

"God, I hope not," I said. "He'd come after me as soon as he got out."

"So, what do you guys need on this beautiful sunny afternoon?"

"We have a few questions to ask," Carolina answered, "about the involvement of your volunteers."

He nodded his willingness to hear her questions.

"Have any of your volunteers had harsh words with any of your clients?"

"If any did, they would be requested to leave the premises immediately and never come back. We do not tolerate any untoward actions when it comes to our clientele."

"I understand. Let me reword the question. Has anyone who is related in any way to the mission had harsh words or sarcastic words with any of your clients?"

Rev. Horowitz looked at me with a frown revealing that he might suspect what we were up to.

"I think I've answered enough of your questions," he said calmly. "I have a lot of work to do before the evening meal. So, if you don't mind, I'd appreciate it if you'd excuse me."

Carolina reached over and lightly took my arm. She turned away and headed for the stairs. I paused for a moment or two then followed her out.

"What was that all about?" she said as we reached the car.

"I'm not sure," I replied. "But, I got a feeling he knows what we're up to in our investigation. Expect a call from Fara's attorneys or someone like that on her behalf before the day is out."

"Wow. Do you think he knows what she's up to?"

"No. I believe that if he suspected something, he might not call the police first. I think he's for real. The Senior Pastor, on the other hand, has a lot more to lose if Fara Flambeau no longer becomes available to support his work."

"He's still protecting her?"

"Right," I replied. "Because he doesn't suspect a thing ... yet. I got the impression that my question may have jogged something in his memory that he was not ready to admit to. He may have even just now put two and two together and got four. He'll call her, and she'll reassure him that everything is fine and not to worry about it."

"I'm angry. We're fighting a long, hard, uphill battle, aren't we?" Carolina said.

"Yes, we are. But, I believe that we can stop her and put her where she belongs."

"And where's that?"

I almost blurted out something like jail but stopped and just smiled. For once in my life, I was contemplating that her death in a violent shoot-out would be better than a lifetime sitting on death row as her attorneys bombarded the court system with appeals, motions, judgments and the like.

So, I got into the car and sat quietly as Carolina drove back to the hotel where she pulled under the front entrance portico. I opened the door and left her car stopping momentarily to look back as Carolina pulled out and headed back to her place.

I just stood there for several moments looking as the car drove out of sight.

CHAPTER FORTY-ONE

Several days later, I was sitting out by the pool doing some personal work on my laptop computer. Dressed in shorts and a T-shirt, I felt comfortable and at ease with the world.

As I scanned several pages on the computer my concentration was interrupted by someone calling my name.

"Perry Savant?"

I was surprised to hear my name with such a strong and official sounding voice. I calmly looked up to see a pair of dark sunglasses on the face of Willie Abraham. He flashed a Miami-Dade Police badge.

"Yes, may I help you?" I answered.

"May I sit down?" Willie asked politely with a bit less authority.

"Of course. I take it this is an official visit?"

"No, Chief. I just want to chat for a few moments about your involvement with the Miami-Dade Police Department."

"Ah. Of course." I folded the laptop and placed it back in my briefcase. I took a long drink of a glass of iced tea mostly watered down from the ice that used to be present.

"So, what can this old, retired detective do for you?"

"The Sheriff received several calls from some important people in the area warning him of your involvement with our department. So, he asked me to investigate the matter. You

·

know how important perception is, especially with elected offices."

"I understand."

"I have done some reading and I've talked to some people in New York. I'd just like to hear your side of things before I give my report to the sheriff."

"Number one, I have never practiced or been an active homosexual."

I decided to just blurt it all out at once and get it over with.

"But, that's what I was accused of by someone who had a grudge against me. The problem, as best I can recreate, was that since this guy had known me from high school and lived in the neighborhood where I grew up, the newspapers seemed to put a lot of trust in him. You know? He had the creds to be believed."

"I see," he said with a slow drawl. "So, what happened?"

"You can imagine what happened. I had been appointed Deputy Chief of Departments for investigations -- third in line from the Commissioner himself. I oversaw all detective work throughout the NYPD. This guy simply could not handle my success, I guess. By accusing me of being openly gay and saying that my activities were embarrassing to the NYPD, well, the Commissioner simply couldn't afford the adverse publicity. When the press asked about alleged illegal activities ... well, you can imagine."

"I can."

"About a week before I left, an alderman from Queens, where I grew up, was found shot to death in a rather compromising position in a flop house. The seventeen-year-old boy he was in bed with was also shot. They were both naked."

"Good heavens."

"Yea. Well, the old school mate I mentioned called the newspapers and told them that I was trying to cover up for the alderman because I was gay as well. So, you can imagine what a terrible predicament I found myself in. I mean, how do you prove a negative? So, I simply agreed with the commissioner's suggestion that I retire immediately, admit to nothing, and leave town."

"I appreciate your honesty. The NYPD commissioner himself told me the same story and said that he fought with the mayor over asking you to leave."

"I was not aware of that," I said knowing the surprise on my face was evident.

"Yes. He also said that your being allowed to retire early was a compromise."

"I appreciate your telling me that. I mean, I suspected it. But I wasn't sure. I left town immediately."

"Well, I think you've helped me out. I can give my report to the sheriff."

"Do you mind telling me what your recommendation will be?"

"Hey, we're more lenient on this issue down here in South Florida." The big detective leaned over closer to me.

"Besides," he continued. "I'm gay."

I sat speechless.

"So, I'm going to recommend that the sheriff hire you on full-time as a senior detective."

"Don't do that."

"Why?"

"Simple. I like my freedom. I've decided to establish myself in Key West. I think the commute would be hell."

Willie Abraham laughed so loudly that people all around the pool area looked over toward him.

"You are good," He replied. "And I'd live in Key West, too, if I could afford it."

Willie stood as I did. I stretched out my hand for him to shake. After we grasped hands, Willie walked away, without noticing a group of scantily clad young women sunning themselves by the pool. He disappeared into the lobby.

"That was Miami-Dade I.A. What did he want?" Carolina asked as she walked up from behind me.

"Hello to you, too, Carolina," I said as I leaned over and kissed her on the cheek.

We sat down.

"I think he said his name was Willie Abraham. He didn't say he was with I.A. But, I'm not surprised."

"So, what was he asking about?"

"I'll tell you some time. It wasn't important at all. And, it had nothing to do with this case. He was just checking out some rumors for the sheriff. Nothing for you to worry yourself about."

"Okay. But, you gotta know I get the creeps when I see I.A. around."

"I know. I've been there. So, what've you got today?"

"Why do you think I have something for you?"

"Uh, I haven't seen you in three days. Today you show up about the same time that I.A. comes knocking."

"Okay. You got me. I got a call from one of our informants about a big black Mercedes finding its way into a low-rent warehouse district. You know, not a normal place for something like that to be driving around. Seems it's been seen many times over the past several months. Beginning to catch attention."

"Did you get an address?"

"Why?"

"We're going out there to investigate, aren't we?"

"Not without a search warrant."

"Okay. You stay here. I'll go. I'm not official police. I don't need one."

"Good. I'd better come with you just in case."

We walked to my room where I changed into more appropriate clothing for breaking and entering. As I walked out of the hotel, Carolina reminded me that she was in charge.

"So," she said. "If we happen to see the Mercedes in one of the warehouses, we are not to act until I can get a search warrant delivered. I want this to stand up in court."

"Gotcha! I'm all yours."

When the valet drove up with Carolina's plain white three-year-old Ford Crown Vic, we got in and drove across the causeway toward the warehouse district west of the airport. Carolina weaved her way off the Expressway and onto Twenty-Fifth Street. She made a quick right into a long row of warehouses.

She pulled across and down from a building that did not have either an address or a sign announcing what company it was. Yet, there were indications that there had been plenty of activity in the area recently. So, she put the car in park and turned off the engine. She turned to me with a smile.

"We'll just sit and watch," she said. "Don't want to be in too big of a hurry and tip our hand."

"I know the drill," I said with a slight smile.

We sat there for nearly an hour. At last, a large overhead door rolled open near what appeared to be the main entrance.

"Here we go," said Carolina as we both slipped down in the seat so as not to give away our presence. Barely over the top of the dashboard, I saw a large Mercedes that seemed to be several years older than mine pull up to the opening and turn to head into the building.

Carolina sounded a low whistle.

"I've never seen a limousine like that before," she whispered.

The windows were tinted so dark that we were unable to tell who was driving the car as it passed by.

After it disappeared into the building, I pulled on the door handle just as Carolina grabbed my arm and shook her head from side to side. I closed the door and continued watching.

Only a couple of minutes later a red Audi pulled out onto the street and headed back toward Twenty-fifth while the large overhead door slid smoothly closed behind it. The Audi also had tinted windows such that neither of us could make out who was driving.

Carolina clicked on the speaker on her phone and dialed. She gave Laura the address where we were located. She also asked her to get a search warrant out there right away.

"I think we've found the car that's been involved in the murders."

"Good for you, Carolina. I'll dispatch two additional units for backup. I'll be there in ten to fifteen minutes. Watch over the place to be sure that nothing disappears in the meantime. But remember, Carolina, don't you or Perry enter that building before I get there. Understood?"

Carolina turned off her phone.

"Let's go check and make sure that the car is still in there," she said. "I'll look through the front. You go around to the other side to be sure someone didn't slip the car out the back while we were out here. And, Perry? Do not enter that building."

At that we were out of the car and moving at a fast pace. Carolina sneaked her way to a window and attempted to look inside. The panes were filthy and made of reinforced glass that distorted any image visible inside. She was unable to make out any vehicle resembling an automobile inside.

At that moment I felt almost like I used to be when I was a young detective running up the stairs of the old tenement high-rises in the Bronx. It made me feel young again to be in the action. When I got to the corner of the building, I checked to see if anyone was on the other side. I moved to a window that appeared to be clear enough to see through. What I saw surprised me. The room was empty other than a large shipping container in the center. But no Mercedes.

Two large SUV's pulled up in front of the warehouse with red and blue lights flashing followed by four Miami-Dade Police cruisers, one of which pulled around where I was standing. So, I went around to the front entrance to see what was going on.

The FDLE and sheriff's deputies surrounded the building and prepared to cover as the SWAT unit arrived and prepared to enter the building. A couple of minutes later, Laura Taylor pulled up, got out of her car, and walked over to where Carolina and I were waiting.

"We've been able to ascertain that there is no one in the building and that the Mercedes must be enclosed in a cargo container inside."

"Okay, Carolina, here's your search warrant. At least I got the wording to include any attached buildings or any containers inside the building. I just hope that the car is in there and that you're right about it being involved in these murders."

Just out the corner of my eye, I caught movement at the end of the road. It was a red Audi speeding away.

"Oh, no!"

"What?" Carolina said as she whirled around.

"I think she stopped and waited to see what was going to happen."

"Who?" asked Laura.

"Whoever was in that red Audi. Probably the person that drove the Mercedes into the warehouse. That same Audi just slipped away down the street. We'd better be ready for a battalion of lawyers to meet us before we can get an impound wrecker here."

Carolina grabbed the search warrant out of Laura's hand and called out to the other officers.

"Open that damn door!"

She stormed over to the door and followed the armed men as they swept into the building with guns at the ready. Simultaneously, Laura dialed a number on her phone and ordered a wrecker at top speed to get to her location.

"Yesterday!" she exclaimed into the phone.

Inside, three FDLE agents and two Miami-Dade deputies cleared the building as Carolina ran over to the container with bolt cutters in hand and snapped the large lock that held the doors closed. She swung the heavy steel doors opened with a clang as they hit the sides of the container. She looked inside. It was the Mercedes they had been looking for.

Immediately, Carolina entered the container and looked closely at the left front headlight assembly noticing that there was a piece of the outer plastic broken. She called me over and pointed out the place she had found and pointed to a dent in the front grill work.

"And that spot there, I believe, will end up being blood."

She stepped out of the container and called over to Laura.

"Call the Crime Scene people to get out here. We need to do an immediate analysis of this thing."

"They're on the way," Laura responded.

She turned to one of the FDLE agents standing near her.

"Seal this place tight. Only authorized Miami-Dade or FDLE get in or out. No matter what happens, you don't let anyone near this container other than our own people. You hear me?"

The man indicated he understood and called the others over to where he was standing and gave instructions about what to do. He assigned men with assault weapons at the ready at each door and one at the front of the container.

A matter of minutes later, a large Cadillac Limousine and an SUV with darkened windows pulled up. Four men exited the SUV and stood in front of the Cadillac. A man stepped out of the limousine.

"You people are trespassing on private property," he said. "As the official representative of the Flambeau organizations, I order all of you to leave at once."

Laura stepped in front of the gentleman.

"I am Laura Taylor, lead agent for the Southern District of the Florida Department of Law Enforcement. I hold a duly authorized search warrant for this property. I would advise you and your men to leave the premises immediately or be arrested for obstruction of justice."

The gentleman took the search warrant, looked at it and handed it back to her. With a smile on his face he handed her a legal document he had in his coat pocket. She opened to see a Federal District Court order expunging the search warrant.

With a blank stare on her face, she looked at the smiling man.

"I'll have the attorney general look at this and tell me whether or not I must obey it before my people and I will move from this spot."

She pulled out her phone and dialed a number.

"Charlene, is your boss in?" She paused for a moment and looked up at the gentleman who was still smiling.

"Kevin, I've got a problem. Can you send someone out to my location right away to help with a messy legal problem I've gotten myself into?"

Pausing again, she listened for a moment.

"Okay. At least you know where we are. I'll wait for your call."

"He's already been contacted and told what to do," the gentleman said, his smile growing bigger.

"You might as well wash that silly grin off your face. Ursula Burbank of the DA's office got your message and a copy of the search warrant. She just told me that her assistant just handed the Federal Judge you must have in your pocket with the evidence that ties this car to the murders. He's waiting right now for a reversal of your squash order."

The man's smile began to drop. The back door of the limousine opened. Xavier Flambeau got out and stood in front of Laura Taylor.

Although Laura was five feet eight inches herself. She had to look up the man who stood before her. His jet-black hair was slicked against his head almost as if held down by machine oil. And the large mustache on his face appeared as black as the hair on the top of his head. At nearly two hundred and twenty pounds and over six foot in height, he presented an imposing presence.

"Dear lady, my name is Xavier Flambeau. I own this building. This is where I keep a special vehicle I bought several years ago for special occasions. It is bullet-proof all around and extremely valuable. That is why I keep it in a locked container inside a locked warehouse."

Laura did not bat an eye-lash.

"Thank you for confirming ownership of the suspected vehicle. We won't have to prove that part of our case. In the meantime, I would suggest that you send your lawyers and armed goons away from here. They're costing you a fortune standing here doing nothing. And your feeble attempt at subverting the law will not work. No matter how much you paid that judge, he'll back down once he sees the note from the AG.

While she was talking, one of the lawyers got a phone call and stepped away to answer it. Flambeau's eyes darted to the lawyer then back at Laura.

"We'll see," he said with a smug assurance.

The lawyer who had taken the call reached over and whispered in Flambeau's ear.

"Okay, Ms. Taylor. You may have the car; for the moment. We'll be talking again soon."

Flambeau and his lawyers disappeared into their cars and drove away.

"What just happened?" Carolina said quietly.

"I think that Kevin got the squash order squashed."

"I wonder if Mr. Flambeau will get his money back."

With a laugh, Laura shook her head and walked back into the warehouse. As Flambeau's limousine left, the Crime Scene investigators drove up in their large van and began their detailed analysis of everything in the building.

CHAPTER FORTY-TWO

The next day, Laura Taylor got the phone call she had been expecting. The voice on the other end had a strong Cuban accent yet was exacting and clear such as one would expect of a seasoned politician and community leader.

"Good morning, Agent Taylor. My name is Carlos Barbosa."

"Senator Barbosa! What a privilege to hear from you."

"Thank you. I have followed your career closely. A mixed-race woman from the south, well, you've come a long way. Senior Supervisory Agent for the southern district of Florida."

"I appreciate the compliment. But, I've worked hard to get where I am."

"I'm sure you have, my dear. But you've also made a few mistakes along the way, I surmise," he said in a questioning tone.

"Of course, Senator; I'm only human. But, I've learned from my mistakes and have turned them to my advantage."

"It seems that a few people in Tallahassee and Miami are wondering if you made a huge mistake yesterday."

"Oh?"

"Mr. Flambeau is an influential member of our community, as you know. Although he no longer runs the big box stores that have his name, he gives a lot of money to local charities and supports local politicians in a big way. And it seems imprudent to upset him."

"Our intention was never to try and upset Mr. Flambeau."

"I'm sure that you are correct in your statement. But--"

"The only but here is that if he decides to be upset that his daughter is killing people, that should not be my problem."

"I see. And what proof do you have that she has committed a crime?"

"Let me preface my statement by saying, Senator, that I am not at liberty to discuss an ongoing investigation by my department. But, I will say this. Mr. Flambeau attempted to interfere with our investigation. He tried to stop us from executing a search warrant on one of his properties, a property that housed a vehicle suspected in several murders."

"I understand that your search warrant was issued on flimsy evidence."

"Well, you have a right to your opinion. But, a sitting state judge found that we had probable cause that we might find pertinent evidence in and on that vehicle. If you had been the judge, you could have turned down the request. Other than that--"

"Yes, I know what you're saying. I'm just asking that you tread lightly if you should investigate Mr. Flambeau in any way."

"Senator, we tread lightly in all our investigations to make sure we do not tread on anyone's rights, no matter how many businesses they own, or don't own. But, we will execute legal warrants in whatever way we deem necessary. Is that all you wanted to talk to me about?"

"I think you get my message, correct?"

"Yes, sir, I do get your message. And I would respectfully request that you never attempt to interfere in any of my other investigations in the future. Understood?"

There was silence on the other end of the line for what seemed to be several minutes.

"Are you there, senator?"

"Yes I am, Agent Taylor. We may be talking again in the near future."

"Anytime, senator, as long as it is to report a crime that you have witnessed rather than to speak of a crime that you are not involved in. Do I make myself clear?"

With that the senator hung up the phone. Immediately Laura dialed Chief Sanchez's number.

"Chief Sanchez speaking."

"Chief, Laura. You'll never guess who just called me."

"Oh, let me guess, Senator Barbosa."

"Yeah. How did you know?"

"He called me earlier. Got my butt reamed pretty good, and in Spanish."

"What did you tell him?"

"Nothing other than a nice thank you for his opinion. That's all."

"Flambeau seems to be playing hardball to protect his daughter."

"No kidding. She's all he's got other than a billion dollars. He's got to help her in some way."

"He could do us all a favor and lock her up himself. I think the taxpayers would save a couple of million dollars in legal costs."

"That ain't going to happen and you know it. Especially after what happened to his older son some twenty years ago.

"I didn't know he had another child."

"Sad story of a life gone wrong. He was arrested when he was only eighteen. Some said he was killed by inmates who hated his father. At least that was the official story. Others think he was ordered executed by a gang of drug rustlers who wanted to use his contacts to transport their drugs. Anyway, that's all I know about him. So, in the meantime, keep the investigation going."

"Have you gotten an answer back from the lab, yet?"

"Nothing new, yet," Sanchez answered. "I put high priority on the evidence, so I'm sure we'll know more by tomorrow."

"Okay, Chief. Just keep me informed."

"Will do, Laura. Oh, and I got a call from Palm Beach County. It seems they had a similar murder late last night along A1A near Delray Beach."

"Are they sure it's the same murderer?"

"No, but they'd like you to send someone up and look at what happened and help them out with it."

"I'll send Carolina and maybe even Perry."

"Good idea. He's the one on top of everything we have."

"Take care chief."

With those last words, Laura reached over and clicked the phone and dialed Carolina's number.

CHAPTER FORTY-THREE

Interstate Ninety-five through Miami is almost always wall to wall traffic most anytime during a week-day. So, I felt a bit relieved as I crossed into Broward County and the traffic thinned out.

I sped up to seventy-five miles-per-hour in the high capacity lane. That move cut about ten minutes off our drive time.

For comfort, I volunteered to take my car. Laura sat in the passenger seat navigating.

"Take the Atlantic Avenue exit east toward the ocean," she said.

With a minimum of effort, I guided the Black Mercedes over to the right lane and onto the exit ramp.

The drive toward the east was uncluttered since it just turned eleven o'clock. When we reached the stop light at A1A, I turned to the right. I pulled to a stop where five police cars had parked along the side of the road.

An officer directed traffic around the north bound lane. The Coroner's van sat next to the large CSI truck. A large military-type tent covered the body.

A young police officer stopped me as I pulled up. I rolled down the window. Carolina leaned over toward the open window and flipped open her badge.

"I'm agent Carolina Brown from FDLE."

With that the officer pulled the barricade out of the way and allowed us to slip into a spot still some distance from the crime scene. I placed a flashing red light on the roof as we exited the car.

As we walked away from the car, I heard the young officer turn to another policeman speak.

"I've just got to get a transfer to FDLE if that's what they get to ride in."

The other officer laughed.

"Man, the guy she's with is probably a Rent-a-cop, you know, PI. That's how they get to ride in style."

A captain with the Palm Beach County Sheriff's office walked over to where we stood and stretched out his hand.

"You must be the folks from FDLE."

"I'm Carolina Brown, lead agent on the A1A murders in Dade and Broward. This is Perry Savant, a private consultant and expert on serial killers."

The captain shook hands with each of us.

"We weren't sure if this murder was connected," the captain said. "But we thought we'd better let you know about it."

"Let's take a look," Carolina said.

We walked over as one of the Coroner's aids who pulled back the plastic cover over the body. Carolina and I bent down to scan the body, looking for the signs we had come to know.

"Is this where the body was found?" Carolina asked.

"No. We moved it to here so that we could get to it more easily."

"Show us exactly where you found it."

"This way," the captain said and led us about twenty-five feet down a narrow path in the sand with sea grape on either side. As he stopped, he pointed to a spot where the sea grape had been disturbed.

"The body was jammed up inside the sea grape."

"Jammed?" I asked.

"Yeah, it looks like someone had stuffed the body into the bushes to hide it from pedestrians and passing traffic."

I turned and scanned the pathway carefully.

The Captain looked back at Carolina.

"What's he looking for?"

"Tire tracks."

"Tire tracks? You can't get a car up in here."

I stopped and walked back over to where the body was being placed onto a gurney. I stopped the men for a moment and looked closely at the man's face. I noted the bruises around the man's mouth and nose. I also noticed that the man had swelling around one eye.

I picked up the man's left hand and saw bruising on the knuckles and backs of the hand. I pulled the man's shirt back and viewed bruises around the mid-section. I could feel that at least one rib had been broken severely.

I straightened up.

"Let's go, Carolina. This is a local murder."

I turned to the Captain.

"You can turn this thing over to the Delray Police. With the contusions on the body and the scars on the man's hands, I think this guy was killed by a couple of other thugs who threw his body in there to hide it."

"This isn't the work of your murderer?"

"Nope," Carolina said. "We've kept several vital details from the press and from our reports to the other counties. But, if you had read our first release, you'd have known this wasn't ours."

The captain scratched his head.

"I guess I need to pay more attention to those circulars. Sorry about making you drive all the way out here."

"No problem at all," Carolina added. "It was a nice break to get away from the hectic atmosphere in Miami. Oh, and can you recommend a suitable place to eat while we're here?"

"That's easy. Go back toward Atlantic and you'll see several places on your left. I like Boston's. The food's good even if it is crowded."

"Thanks," Carolina said.

She and I walked back to the car and drove toward the restaurant where we stopped and had lunch together.

We took the opportunity to talk a bit about the case.

"Remember our attempt at trying to follow Fara?" I asked as I waived the waiter over for the check.

"How could I forget that fiasco?"

"I know. But, perhaps if we put on a little pressure by following her again she might slip up and do something stupid. We'd be in a position to jump in and catch her."

"I don't know. I could get fired this time."

"If you get fired, I'll hire you. We could get some work done."

"That's such a sweet thought, Perry. Thank you."

"Hey, for the first time in my life, I think I've found a partner that I could get along with and maybe even like."

"Had problems in the past with partners?"

"You've pegged me. I think maybe I've always been a loner. At least I was able to work better alone than I could with the partners I was paired with as a junior grade detective."

"You must have done something right to get promoted to the chief position."

"Maybe. But, I've always done my best work by myself--until now."

"I think we'd better get back to Miami," Carolina said after a brief pause.

"What about putting on some pressure?"

"I need to get some sort of clearance for that this time."

"Okay. We can talk more about it in the car. I think this could be an important strategy. We've got to do something to get this case resolved. It's been dragging on far too long."

"We'll see."

We stood up from the table, walked out of the restaurant, got into the car, and drove toward I-95 where I headed south. The traffic was already heavy. I dropped Carolina off at the FDLE headquarters a little after four.

"I think this has been a productive trip," she said as she opened the door.

"How do you mean?"

"Deciding we need to be more aggressive is important."

"Yeah, maybe." She responded. "All I know is that it's been nearly two months and we're no closer to catching her than the day we first met."

"I agree. That's why I think this trip was worthwhile."

"Is that the only reason?"

"Well, I learned something new."

"Good," I answered and watched Carolina as she shut the door and walked into the main entrance and disappeared.

I noticed something different about myself as I drove out of the compound and onto the entrance ramp to the Dolphin Expressway. I felt, sort of, well, happy inside: a feeling that is totally alien to me.

CHAPTER FORTY-FOUR

The next morning around ten, my cell vibrated as I sat at an outdoor table next to the pool enjoying a late breakfast. I felt my heart leap as I heard Carolina's voice.

"Perry, got good news and bad news for you."

I couldn't help but laugh at her statement.

"Okay, give me the bad news first."

"There's been another murder. Same M.O. and same everything except--"

"It didn't take place on or near A1A."

"Right. But, it's got to be the same killer."

"She had to go hunting elsewhere because the homeless don't want to be anywhere close to A1A, right?"

"That's what it looks like to me."

"So, what's the good news?"

"Right after I got the word and talked to Sanchez to get all the relevant details, I called Laura. She telephoned the Sheriff and the Miami and Miami Beach Police Chiefs. They concur that you and I need to get more aggressive in capturing this killer. Oh, and the Sheriff said, and I quote, 'Burn the Bitch!'"

"He said that?"

"He did. So, when can you be ready for me to pick you up?"

"How about you meet me here around twelve-thirty. We'll get a good lunch and begin with a full stomach."

"Sounds good to me."

"That'll give me a chance to call a few people and see if I can locate our target. Maybe we'll get a bead on just where she might be heading out for today."

"See you then."

I hung up the phone and turned back to my meal. After a few minutes, I realized that someone was standing near me. I put down my fork and put my hand into the inner pocket of my coat where I kept a small .22 caliber pistol for emergencies such as this. I stopped my hand movement when I heard a familiar voice.

"You won't need that pop gun in your coat pocket. I'm not going to hurt you."

"Fara Flambeau," I said as I pulled my hand out and picked up the fork again to continue eating.

"Care for breakfast?" I asked without looking up or even looking around at her.

She strolled to the other side of the table and sat down.

"No thank you. And since you have a guest coming for lunch, I won't stay too long."

"What can I do for you?"

"It's not what you can do for me, it's what I can do for you."

"Okay. So, what is it you can do for me?" I said as I took the last bite on the plate and looked Fara straight in the eye.

"I want to let you know that the police didn't find one thing on my father's car that was relevant to the murders of homeless men along A1A."

"And you know this how?"

"I have a lot of good friends in high places around here; a lot more friends than you have."

"Okay. I believe that. So?"

"So, following me around or continuing to delve into my records and past activities will not get you what you want."

"And how do you know?"

"Because, there's nothing there. You understand?"

"I think so. But, I've dealt with much smarter and more devious criminals in my years."

"Smarter and more devious than?"

I kept my mouth shut and stared at her.

"Aw. That hurts. I thought we could be friends. I mean, you do remind me of my father."

"Flattery will get you nowhere in this matter. Neither will threats. So, don't even go there."

"I wasn't. I've learned that you don't take too kindly to threats."

"You got that right."

"Okay. So, how about this. Let's say I'm innocent of these murders. And let's say maybe someone is trying to frame me. Would that convince you?"

"Convince me of what?"

"Convince you that I haven't had a thing to do with any of these murders."

My eyes were riveted to hers for several moments.

"You, my dear," I said calmly. "Are going to be arrested within the week for a minimum of ten counts of first-degree murder."

I continued to stare at her but could see no sign of emotion.

"Oh my! Look at the time," Fara said as she stood up and threw her purse strap around her shoulder. "We'll have to continue this conversation later."

"I assure you that this conversation will continue," I said, my eyes never leaving hers. "In an interrogation room at Police headquarters."

Fara whirled around, walked out past the pool, and into the lobby of the hotel. I smiled knowing I had just gotten to her far worse than I had imagined I could.

I reached over to the briefcase that was sitting on the ground next to me and pulled out a thin laptop computer and began typing. Every so often I would look at the screen and write down items in a small notebook.

I worked through the morning until nearly one o'clock when I heard the smiling voice of Carolina Brown as she walked over toward my table.

"Perry, here you are. You're usually inside where it's much cooler."

"Sweetheart, it's forty degrees in New York. I'm thoroughly enjoying this seventy-eight-degree weather down here in Florida."

Carolina sat across from me and smiled as she continued her report.

"Just before I left, I got a call from Laura who said that several local politicians have been calling the sheriff all morning telling us to back off investigating Flambeau's daughter. We need absolute proof that she's involved in these crimes."

"She was just here a couple of hours ago."

"No way."

"And she let me know that she cared so much for me that she wanted me to know people were not happy about me investigating her."

"Nice of her to get them to complain about you specifically."

"Right. At least she wasn't lying to me."

"She had her people busy all morning. So, what did you learn?"

"She's a cold-blooded murderer."

"How could you tell that?"

"Easy. She's not had much sleep lately. I think this schedule she's set for herself trolling the night life for victims has taken its toll on her. I honestly think she was begging me to stop her. At least, that's what I intend to do whether she wants me to or not."

"And you learned all this from one conversation this morning?"

"I think so," I mused. "At least this conversation solidified a lot of things in my mind."

"Good. Where do you want to begin this afternoon?"

"I haven't a clue since she showed up here."

"It's nearly one. Let me try something." She dialed a number on her phone and paused as she waited for the answer.

"Carson, what've you got?" She listened as the person on the other end spoke; she continued: "I appreciate it. Call me if there's any change."

Almost immediately, a waiter stopped at the table and took our orders for lunch.

"Who was that?" I asked after the waiter left.

"Agent Carson. He's on surveillance at the Homeless shelter. I was checking to see if maybe Fara had shown up there."

"My guess is that she'll stay away from that place, especially after that last conversation we had with the young minister."

"Yeah. I agree. But, I didn't want to take any chances."

"So, what else have you done?"

"I have agents posted at Fara's two apartments, her main office building. We also discovered a little hide-away she scoots off to when she wants total privacy."

"Why am I not surprised about that little piece of information?"

"We also have two agents posted in the front and back of the night club. If she shows up at any of the usual places, we'll know it."

"Good," I said as I leaned back with a smile that stretched the width of my face.

"What?" Carolina said.

"Oh, I was just thinking how much I wish I had had you as one of my detectives about ten years ago."

"Why?"

"Because, I might have ended up staying in New York instead of running away down here."

"What the hell does that mean?"

"I don't know. Maybe I've become quite fond of you and of spending time with you. That's all."

"You flatter me."

"I know. I mean, I've got to be fifteen years older than you."

"It's more like twenty."

"Sorry. I'm not good at guessing people's ages."

"That's okay. I'm flattered that you would find me interesting. You're almost a legend in the police arena."

"I appreciate that, I think," I admitted. "Anyway, you're the first girl in thirty years that has attracted my attention."

"Perry, are you attracted to me?"

"What kind of a question is that?

"No. I mean it. Are you attracted to me?"

I stared at her for what seemed to be several minutes but was more like two seconds.

"I think I am."

"Well, when this investigation is over, and we're no longer working together, we can talk about this in more detail."

"I'd like that."

"In the meantime, we need to keep our focus on finding this killer and make sure she gets personally acquainted with 'old sparky.'"

"Old what?"

"'Old Sparky' the nickname the executioners have given our electric chair."

"Oh."

Lunch arrived, and we ate with an unusual simultaneous air of comfort and discomfort. And yet, I found myself thinking that perhaps I'd finally found the one I'd been looking for all these years.

CHAPTER FORTY-FIVE

Carolina and I arrived in a dark SUV and parked behind the plain-looking, three-year old Ford parked across the street and down the block from Fara Flambeau's apartment building. The single man in the Ford got out and walked back to our SUV, opened the back door and got in. It was Agent Williams of FDLE.

Sitting behind the wheel, Carolina turned to Williams.

"They let you have one of the new SUV's?" Williams said. "You're moving up in the world."

"I think the director wanted to show us he was interested in this case. So, what's happening?"

"She got here less than an hour ago. She has three cars parked in the garage, so you'll need to watch for all three. She has a red Audi convertible, a blue BMW convertible, and a Mercedes S550."

"She has a Mercedes here?" I asked quickly.

"Yes. But the valet says she rarely drives it."

"Thanks, Williams," Carolina said. "We'll take it from here."

"You want I should move down the street and back you up?"

"That'll be great. It'll be up to you to keep up. She's a difficult one to follow."

"No problem. I'll be behind you."

Williams left and drove further down the street. He parked in a parking lot where he could easily follow whatever direction the we went.

"He seems to be a good man with a great attitude about his job," I said.

"He's just like almost every person we have at FDLE. They are all consummate professionals."

A large black Mercedes pulled out into traffic and turned away from where we were sitting. Carolina guided the big new SUV out into traffic and followed the Mercedes. Carolina looked in her rear-view mirror to assure herself that Williams pulled out to follow us.

The big auto weaved its way through traffic toward the ocean finally pulling into the parking garage behind the night club Fara owned. We pulled up where we could see the Garage exit opening onto Ocean Drive. Williams took up a position on Collins where he could see the exit on the backside into an alley. We all sat and waited.

After about an hour, the phone rang. It was Collins.

"She just walked out the back door and got into a cab," Williams said. "I'm behind them headed north on Collins."

"We're on our way," Carolina answered as she pulled out into traffic.

"I hope he doesn't spook her," I said.

"Hey. He's good. He'll keep with her."

For the next several minutes we drove north. When the phone rang, she grabbed it and answered.

"What've you got?"

"She's turned west over the Tuttle Causeway," Williams reported.

"Has she spotted you, yet?"

"I don't think so."

"Make sure she doesn't." Carolina explained. "This may be our only chance to catch her."

"I got her covered."

"You don't need to be a micro-manager, you know," I said as she turned off the phone.

"Old habits die hard."

"I understand. But--"

"Yeah. I know."

We moved quickly through traffic and finally caught up with Williams. Carolina carefully pulled up next to him and gave a signal. He slowly backed off as she followed from a different lane.

The taxi moved into a warehouse district a long way from the one where they confiscated the other car.

"How many cars does this broad have?" I blurted out.

"Broad? Are you kidding me?"

I smiled as I turned to her. That's when I saw the big grin on her face. I answered.

"Thanks for the grammar lesson."

"You're welcome," she replied coyly.

The taxi driver slowed his speed along the front of an isolated unit at the end of a long row of warehouses. He put on his brake and stopped in front of the center unit entrance. Fara stepped out of the Taxi and took a moment to scan the road in both directions. She walked to the door, unlocked it, and went inside.

At the same moment the taxi driver put on his brakes, Carolina hit her brake pedal sharply and swerved hard to the left into an alley to avoid being seen. I looked at her a bit shocked at the maneuver. She pointed to her nose and to mine.

I reached up to feel the blood flowing just above my lips. I pulled out a handkerchief and dabbed at my wounded nose.

"Are you okay?" Carolina asked as she stopped the car in a driveway about six hundred feet down the row of warehouses.

I held my handkerchief over my nose.

"I'll be fine, I think. That was quite a maneuver you made."

"Well, when I realized the taxi driver had nowhere else to go, I knew he would be stopping pretty soon. That's why--"

"Why you threw me against the dash?"

"It wasn't intentional. I didn't do it to hurt you."

"I know. I was quite impressed. That was quick thinking. Next time I won't take my seat belt off so soon."

"Thank you."

We got out of the car and walked back to the corner of the building. As Carolina peeked around she saw the door closing to the warehouse. She saw the taxi turn around. Carolina pulled back and called Williams.

"Where are you?"

"I'm back at the main entrance to the warehouse area. Are you still with her?"

"Yeah. We're watching a building she entered a moment ago. You stay there in case she has another way out."

"Will do," he said.

Carolina looked over at me, her eyes narrowing.

"I think we can slip over to that window and see what she's up to."

"See that large door there? If she came barreling out through there, she'll make us for sure."

"You're right."

I moved to watch around the corner as Carolina went back to the SUV, turned it around and pulled up behind me, leaving the motor running.

I continued watching for several more minutes. Carolina's phone rang.

"What?" she said quickly.

"A black Mercedes is approaching me. I see a woman wearing sun glasses at the wheel. I think it's our girl."

"She's trying to give us the slip," Carolina shouted through the open window. "Perry, get in before we lose her."

CHAPTER FORTY-SIX

The Mercedes moved quickly through traffic never getting more than five miles over the speed limit. Weaving onto Interstate 95 it headed north. As we followed, we swapped places several times.

At one point, Williams passed the Mercedes and exited the highway only to move quickly through the light and back up onto the highway about a mile behind.

"That was a smooth move he just made."

"I told you he was good."

"Where could she be going? Wasn't that the Broward County line back there?"

"Yep."

"Wait, she's taking this exit up here," I said as she pulled off at the Hollywood Boulevard exit heading east. I quickly pulled out my cell phone and dialed Williams' number and told him which exit to take.

"I'm right behind you," Williams replied, and the chase picked up quickly as the Mercedes picked up speed headed toward the ocean.

After reaching A1A, the Mercedes turned north and drove straight hitting every green light. The car went past the Dania Beach Boulevard intersection continuing north.

"What the hell?" Carolina said under her breath.

"What?" I asked.

"This road dead ends just up the way at the Ft. Lauderdale Inlet."

"What's she up to?"

"Beat's me."

We continued to follow the car to where the road ended in a parking lot. The two FDLE vehicles quickly pulled up behind the Mercedes. Carolina, Williams and I all popped out and ordered the driver to exit the vehicle.

The door opened slowly. Two slender legs swiveled out and a tall young lady got out of the car. She was dressed in a bathing suit, sun glasses, and a large brimmed hat.

"Who are you?" I asked.

"Who are you?" the woman replied, her angry eyes piercing mine.

"I'm agent Carolina Brown. This is agent Williams. We're with FDLE. And this is special consultant Savant. Now, you tell us who you are."

The woman opened the purse she had slung over her shoulder and pulled out her driver's license.

"My name is Melody Parker."

"Is this your car?"

"No, it is not."

"And do you know the owner?"

"Of course. It's Miss Fara. We're friends and I'm doing her a favor."

"What favor is that?"

"She asked me to drive the car here and wait for her to arrive."

"When is she supposed to arrive?"

"I don't know. She said that I was to leave the car here no matter what. If she didn't show up, I was to take a cab home."

"Where's Fara Flambeau?"

"She didn't tell me where she would be just that she might meet me here. Otherwise, I was to simply enjoy the beach at the park."

Williams leaned over and whispered in Carolina's ear.

"Boss, she just pulled a fast one on us, didn't she?"

Carolina nodded.

"I'm so sorry to have bothered you," Carolina said with a smile. "Enjoy your time at the beach. It's a lovely day for it, although you don't have much sunlight left."

The three of us huddled together next to Carolina's SUV as we watched the lady pick up her things and walk toward the beach.

"We've been snookered," I said.

"Yep," Carolina answered.

"What do we do now, wait to see if she shows up?" Williams chimed in.

Carolina laughed out loud. "Go home, Williams. I'll see you at the office in the morning."

Williams shook hands with me and Carolina, got into his car, and drove off.

"So?" I asked.

"I guess we troll A1A back into Dade County and see what happens. If we don't discover something by seven, I'll buy you dinner."

"Sounds good to me."

We got into the car and drove toward the park entrance.

"Pull over into that parking lot facing traffic exiting the park," I blurted out. "Trust me."

About an hour later, the Mercedes moved out from under the Dania Beach Boulevard overpass. I pointed at it.

"There. There she comes."

Carolina easily moved the big SUV out into traffic three or four cars behind the big black Mercedes despite the onset of darkness.

As would be expected, the Mercedes kept right to the speed limit down into Sunny Isles past Ninety-Sixth Street where Collins Drive separates and becomes Harding Drive, one-way southbound lanes of A1A. The Black Mercedes continued south.

We followed about four cars back.

The Mercedes reached Eighty-third where it made a quick turn east and disappeared.

Carolina pushed the accelerator and moved from the left to the right lane and turned right onto Eighty-third. The Mercedes was nowhere to be seen. She slowed as we both looked down the alley on either side of the street. We followed the left only curve and drove about a hundred feet when I reached over and touched her arm.

"Turn around. I think I saw something back there."

She made a quick U-turn and drove to where the curve back to the right began.

"Stop," I said.

"What now?" Carolina asked.

"Not sure. But, if it were me, I'd have pull into that public parking lot and wait to see if I were being followed."

"That makes sense. Want to pull in there?" Carolina said as her eagerness showed in her smile.

"If we do and no one is there, she'll--" I said.

"Yeah. I know. What do you say?"

"Let's do it."

"Which way?"

"Right straight into the lot. It looks about a hundred yard deep. I'd be sitting at the end with my lights off." I suggested.

Carolina pulled out of the parking space and drove the hundred feet or so and turned into the parking lot. There was one street light illuminating an area just as we turned in.

"Oh, this is bad. Let's light up our entrance," I suggested.

A ping sounded against the windshield as a bullet ricocheted off the bullet-proof glass. I threw open the door as Carolina hit the brake. She put the car into reverse. The wheels squealed.

I dove from the SUV rolling over toward a concrete barrier that blocked the parking lot from the apartment house next door.

Several more shots rang out with the tell-tale pop of a nine-millimeter Glock. Carolina's SUV stopped short of the entrance to the lot. I heard the loud bangs of the forty-five that I knew Carolina carried: a big punch for a nice young lady.

I carefully looked up over the barrier and was immediately hit by chips of concrete knocked off by a bullet that whizzed by my ear. I fell back and moved to the right side of the barrier. I reached around with my right hand and steadied the pistol. I fired three quick rounds.

I rolled back to the other side and shoved the pistol into my left hand and reached around firing another three shots.

I heard tires squealing on the pavement. I popped my head up just enough to make out the Mercedes heading for the entrance to the parking lot and freedom. I took a deep breath and ran quickly toward the SUV and jumped in.

"Hit it!" I yelled out.

There was no response. I turned my head toward the driver's side. Carolina was not in the car. The driver's seat was covered with glass pieces. I noticed the entire inside of the front was covered in small shards of safety glass.

I carefully stepped out of the car, watching for any signs of movement. With my pistol drawn, I slowly moved around the back of the car. I stopped in stunned silence.

There on the ground on the driver's side was Carolina lying motionless. I looked around to be sure that the Mercedes was gone. I holstered my weapon, bent down, and placed two fingers on her neck. After a couple of seconds, I moved my hand up, and held her cheek for several seconds.

For the first time in my life, I felt a tear slowly slide down my cheek. I sat back onto the ground, leaned against the car, and wept like a baby.

After what seemed several minutes, I calmed down, pulled out my cell phone, and dialed nine-one-one.

CHAPTER FORTY-SEVEN

About thirty minutes later, I sat in the back seat of a sheriff's patrol car. Units from FDLE, Miami Beach Police, and Sunny Isles Police were helping in the investigation of the shooting in the alley. Shooting a cop gets everybody's attention. Even the Mayor of Miami Beach was present.

When Laura Taylor arrived, she spoke to a police officer from Miami Beach who pointed toward the patrol car that I was sitting in. She walked over, leaned down, looked in at me.

"I'm so sorry, Perry," she said. "I know you two had been working hard on this case. I expected a lot of things to happen, but never this."

"It was a lucky shot, Laura. It looked to me like she was hit when one of the bullets finally shattered the glass. I think that's when she was hit in the shoulder. But, when she tried to dive out while firing her revolver; well, I think you know what I mean."

"I know. I am broken hearted. She was the hardest working detective I've ever known."

We paused for several minutes. Laura continued.

"Did you see who it was in the car?"

"I know who it was. It was Fara Flambeau."

"Perry, this is important. Did you actually see her face at any time?"

I sat for a moment quietly reflecting. When I saw the car pass by outside the park, I had not noticed the face in the windshield but rather that the black luxury car was the same one we had followed. Or so I thought.

"No. I just assumed; I mean, it had to be her. Who else could it have been?"

"I know, Perry, I know. But, your assumptions won't even come close to getting us a search warrant for any of her vehicles."

"Well, how about the license number?"

"You got the license number on the car?"

"Of course. I'm not simply a private eye, I'm a retired street cop. I know what to do."

"Hey, no criticism here."

I handed her a small sheet of paper I had torn from my note book.

"Here are the details. If you find that car there will be numerous bullet marks on it."

"You mean bullet holes?"

"No. That car was a tank: fully armored. It even had glass that our weapons could not penetrate."

"You were in a reinforced SUV. At the least, it should have protected you."

"Not from jacketed rounds. It only took two rounds against the windshield to cause it to shatter into a thousand pieces."

"Okay, Perry. We'll get a BOLO out on this license and see what happens." She reached in and placed her hand on my shoulder. She walked over to where several men were talking to the mayor.

I sat with all kinds of wild thoughts going through my head.

What could I do now? Would I be allowed to remain on the case? Would people blame me for Carolina's death? Why didn't I tell her how I felt about her?

My thoughts flashed back to the present when I heard the voice of my longtime friend, Adolph Sanchez.

"Hey, P.D."

Wow! I thought. I haven't heard that name in over thirty years.

P.D. was my nickname in high school. I had insisted that everyone call me that because I wanted to get into the Police Department when I graduated. Besides, I didn't want to be called a sissy name like Perry.

Later at the Police Academy I realized that no one said a word or even snickered in the slightest when my name was called. That's when I decided that it was okay to be Perry.

"I am so sorry, Man," Sanchez continued. He reached down, opened the door to the patrol car, and said, "Come on. I'll take you back to your hotel. Everyone here is done with questioning you."

"Why? I thought they'd want to take me downtown, you know."

"Yeah. I convinced them that you had nothing to do with this other and that you happened to be a passenger in Carolina's newly issued SUV. I think finding those armor-piercing rounds convinced the Miami Beach Chief that there was nothing you could have done."

"I can't believe she was using cop killers. God! She's serious about not being caught."

"I know. Let's get out of here."

We walked over to Sanchez's car and left the scene. I couldn't help myself as I looked back to see Carolina's body still lying on the ground covered by a large tent the police had erected. It covered the SUV to keep the evidence from any chance of rain or dew.

Also, they had put up a plastic barrier around her body while the Crime Scene and Coroner's crew completed their investigations.

We drove for several blocks before Sanchez broke the silence.

"You're taking this pretty hard."

"Yeah. I know."

"Why?"

"I don't know, Adolph. I swear. That Bitch is going to pay."

"I get it, man. But, you've got to stay clear-headed from now on. You still have no evidence of her involvement. And with this shooting, you know; I mean killing a cop. That's serious, now."

"We've got to bear down on the case and find the evidence we need. Hopefully the stuff they pulled from the scene back there will help us tie all this to her."

"Right. That's the way we need to be thinking."

"Also, I'm going to spend every waking hour watching everything that woman does. I want to know when she goes to work, when she brushes her hair, when she goes to the bathroom. I mean, I'm going to find out everything there is to know about her, and even more."

"Good. But--"

"But what?"

"You cannot become so obsessed with proving it's her that you fail to see any evidence that it might be someone else."

I knew my friend was right, but I wasn't about to admit it. I was determined to make sure I proved it was her. She wasn't going to get away with murdering the most important woman in my life since my mother died five years ago. I might have even ended up wanting to marry Carolina. But now? Well I will never know.

As we pulled up in front of the hotel, it was still dark. I opened the door.

"Are you hungry?" Sanchez asked. "I'm buying."

I thought for a moment.

"Okay."

Sanchez put the car in park and took his keys leaving the police cruiser sitting under the overhang at the front of the hotel.

We walked into the restaurant. We were the only customers in the place. Five-thirty in the morning was a bit early for most South Floridians in the Deco District. And the tourists wouldn't be stirring until at least eight.

After being seated and having coffee served, Sanchez looked at me thoughtfully.

"What?" I asked.

"Nothing. I'm just worried about you; that's all."

"I'll feel a lot better once we get this murderer behind bars for good."

"I understand. I want that, too."

"Good, because I've got a plan for what kind of action to take next."

"That's just it, Perry. There are no more plans for you."

"What?"

I sat there staring at my friend who was not looking at me.

"What is it, Adolph? Tell me."

"You're the problem, Perry. The chief here and the sheriff both want you off the case, permanently, now."

I sat stunned followed by an uncomfortable pause.

"Okay." I said. "You can tell me that I am no longer involved as a consultant to the police and sheriff's office. But, if I decide to investigate these murders as a licensed private investigator, you cannot stop me."

"I know that, my friend. But, please understand that if you get in our way, you may find your license to investigate no longer exists."

Saddened at the words from my old friend, I simply took a deep breath.

"Okay," I finally said. "If that's the way it's got to be; then that's the way it's got to be."

CHAPTER FORTY-EIGHT

Two days later, I sat in my car parked near the parking garage at a condo high rise on the ocean front. It was six am. From my location, I could see both the front entrance and the exit to the garage.

I knew it was likely I might sit there for hours waiting for Fara Flambeau to come out for the day. But I was willing to take the time. That was all I had, now.

I had pondered just what I would do next. I knew I couldn't live if I was unable to do investigative work. That license was more than a source of income. It was a continuation of the only life I had ever known.

As a young boy, I was enamored of my father's courage, how he could put on that NYPD uniform day after day and go to the station house not knowing whether or not he would come home to his family. It was hard enough having to get up every day and not put on a uniform, but at least I could investigate crimes.

About an hour before dawn, I sat on the side of my bed looking down at the pistol. It was the one I had carried as a drop gun for so many years never having to use it. Now I had it legally. Now I saw a way to face the future. If I were dead, they would bury me in my uniform. I would wear it for eternity.

Looking at the Glock in my hand, I realized that using it for a way out was not an answer; it was an excuse. I was better than that. I had talents the police could use. Okay, so Carolina and I made a bad choice by not arranging for a back-up to cover our stake out.

I was still an excellent investigator. My talent for seeing past the evidence was invaluable. And my ability to turn over the right rocks and find evidence was an incalculable asset.

No, I decided, the only way to honor her and our relationship was to find her killer and make her pay. Only then, perhaps, I could repair the hole dug deep in my soul.

I would make Fara pay for taking away the only woman in the world I had cared about; maybe even loved. If I were making a mistake striking out on my own, so be it. I would not be denied.

Around ten in the morning, my phone rang. When I answered I recognized almost immediately the voice of DeShawn Royce of the Sunny Isles Police Department.

"Chief Savant, I was wondering if we could talk."

"Sure. Where would you like to meet?"

"Where are you now? I can come to you, if that's convenient."

"Sure. I'm doing a little surveillance work down on the ocean front." I gave him the address and a description of the car I was sitting in.

Ten minutes later, an unmarked patrol car pulled up and parked about a half a block behind my location. I could see Royce in the rear-view mirror. I watched him as he got out and walked to the passenger side door and got in my car.

"Well, Detective Royce, what can I do for you?"

"I heard about Carolina. Man, I'm so sorry about what happened. I know she was more than a colleague. She was more of a friend. I wanted you to know that I've been asked to be a pallbearer at the funeral."

"I think she'd have appreciated that. I think she liked you."

"Yeah, well, I also heard that you were not working on the case, at least not with the official sanction of the sheriff or the Miami Beach Police."

"You heard right."

"Well, I was wondering if perhaps you might still be investigating the string of murders or at least Carolina's death. I mean, this is the building where Fara Flambeau has a large apartment."

"And your point is?" I teased.

"I was wondering if you'd mind working with me. I've got my chief's permission; even his blessing. He said I might learn a few things from you. He can't pay you, but he would appreciate your help in the matter. What do you say?"

"Sounds good. Will I be official in what I'm doing?"

"The only thing the chief asks is that I let him know everything we're up to all the time."

"I have no problem with that. You can check in with him all you want. But, we'll need to be ready to move at a moment's notice, like right now."

"What?"

"Fara's pulling out of the parking lot in her red Porsche right there."

Immediately I started the engine and pulled into traffic to follow her. As we drove, Royce dialed a number into his phone and instructed the person on the other end to send a couple of officers to pick up his car and take it back to the station. He asked to be transferred to the chief and explained that we were following a possible suspect in the murders.

We drove for several minutes as the Porsche made its way through the traffic without speeding. Near the south beach area, the car pulled into a parking lot next door to a restaurant.

I pulled up to where we could again see the front of the building as well as the exit to the lot.

After several minutes, we could see Fara Flambeau seated at a table in front of the windows that looked out over the ocean.

"Wait here," I said. "I'm going to go in and talk to our little darling."

Royce nodded his assent.

I got out of the car and walked into the restaurant and up to the table where Fara was seated.

"May I join you?"

"I was hoping you would," she said. "I saw you watching my building."

"That obvious?"

"No. You're good. I'm better."

I pulled out the chair opposite Fara and sat down.

"I take it that you aren't expecting anyone else?"

"No. This little excursion was for your sake only."

A waiter walked up to take my drink order. "Coffee."

I waited a moment for the waiter to leave. I turned to Fara.

"The only thing I can't figure out is why."

"Really?" she asked.

"No. I've thought it through and have been unable to fully grasp what's going on. I mean, you have everything. You're beautiful, rich, educated."

"And?"

"You, um, your father runs everything at the company."

"Right."

"What do you run?"

"Nothing. Nada. Zilch. Zero."

"Ah. So simple, and I missed it."

"You're an intelligent and insightful man. When I heard what had happened to you, I did some research into your past. And immediately, I knew you were a man worth my attention. So, we shall see which one of us is the best."

"No."

"What? No sporting spirit?"

"No. I'm unwilling to allow anyone else to die."

"What are you talking about?"

"I was sworn to uphold the laws of this country. And one of these laws is the freedom to pursue happiness. If a person prevents another from pursuing their happiness by killing them, well then, it's my job to see they are punished. It's as simple as that."

"Oh, please. There are plenty of people who don't deserve to pursue happiness or prophet."

"And what gives you the right to choose for other people what they deserve?"

"Because, like you, I'm smarter than most people. They need someone to tell them what to do, not to merely show them."

"Isn't that what some people would call arrogant?"

At that Fara simply smiled at me.

"Well, it's been nice talking to you."

"I've got one more thing to say. Be aware that I'll do everything in my power to apprehend, charge and convict you of murder."

"I know that, silly. That's why I admire you."

And as quick as a blinking eye, she was up and out of the restaurant. I stood up, took out a ten-dollar bill and dropped it on the table as I walked out.

When I got into the car, I quickly put the keys in the ignition and started the engine. I pulled out into traffic.

"What happened?" Royce asked.

"Nothing. And this did me no good."

I pulled out a micro tape recorder from my pocket and threw it onto the seat. Royce picked it up, rewound the tape and listened on a small headset. After several minutes he turned it off.

"You're right. She never says anything actionable."

"She's smart; that one. It's going to take more than a simple investigation to catch this girl."

"What do you want to do?"

"I think we should set a trap for her."

"How?"

"I don't know, just yet. But, give me time to work things out and I'll get back to you."

"Okay."

Almost immediately, I pulled into the parking lot of the Sunny Isles Police Department Headquarters where Royce got out of the car.

"Be sure to call me before you act," he said, turning back to me. "Please."

"I will. And you call me, too."

"Will do, Chief. When should I pick you up?"

"How about I pick you up here tonight around ten?"

"I'll be here."

"Oh, and Royce? Dress down. We might be out most of the night."

Royce smiled and waved at me as I drove away headed back to South Beach.

CHAPTER FORTY-NINE

About eleven-thirty, Royce and I sat in my car on Collins Avenue near Seventy-Ninth Street. Royce was not as chatty as Carolina on these stake-outs. I found it refreshing. As we sat there, I kept an eye out toward Seventy-ninth as Royce watched behind us for any activity.

I saw two men walking toward the park entrance from west on Seventy-ninth. One was pushing a shopping cart filled with what must have been personal items. They both appeared to be homeless and somewhat disheveled. I indicated to Royce to look at them.

"I know one of those men," Royce whispered. "He's a regular at the homeless shelter."

"What about the other?"

"Him I don't recognize, but I would guess he's been there before as well. You want me to talk to them?"

"No. Just let them go about their business. Take the two-way with you and follow them. Keep me apprised of everything out of the ordinary."

"Will do," he said.

He waited for the men to cross the street and walk into the parking lot at the south end of the park. He got out of the car and walked toward the direction in which the two men had gone.

I sat there for nearly a half-an-hour when I caught a glimpse of something familiar in the rear-view mirror. I slipped down in my seat and watched as a black Mercedes passed my car and turned into the parking area of the park.

Officially, the park was closed to the public at sundown. But tonight, the park officials had agreed to keep the barrier raised for the evening at the request of the Sunny Isles Police Chief. I started the car and pulled in after the Mercedes.

I drove through the parking lot but could not see no sign of the large black auto. My headlights lit up what seemed to be fresh tire tracks in the dirt leading onto one of the asphalt walkways that crisscrossed the park area between the beach and the street.

I steered my vehicle north onto the walkway and drove slowly along the path. At each intersection where the dirt road crossed the asphalt pathway, I stopped to see if there were any indications as to the Mercedes' direction. I continued straight for nearly two blocks when the two-way radio crackled quietly with Royce's voice.

"Perry. DeShawn. Over."

"Go ahead," I replied.

"I'm about fifty feet from where the two men settled down for the night under a large Banyan tree. But, I just spotted some movement along a walkway near me. It looks like an auto of some kind."

"I'm right behind that car not too far."

"I'm located about a hundred feet due east of the car's current location. The two homeless are well hidden north of me."

"Keep an eye on them."

"Wilco."

"Out," I said.

I set the radio on the seat beside me. I continued driving northward at a snail's pace hoping not to be detected by the driver of the Mercedes. I moved another fifty or sixty feet when I was able to see the rear of the big car ahead of me.

I stopped and turned off the engine. I sat and watched to see just what would happen. Could this be Fara looking for another victim? Could it simply be one of those people who pose to be wealthy but, his only asset is the car he's driving.

He supported himself with the contributions of elderly ladies needing a nice-looking gentleman on their arm. Or, perhaps it was just a couple of young people finding a quiet place where they could get it on in the back seat without being noticed by the police.

The door to the Mercedes opened to allow the interior light to flicker revealing the distinct figure of someone dressed all in black emerging from the car. The door closed quickly. The light couldn't have been on more than five seconds. I watched as the figure disappeared into the woods ahead of the car.

I quickly called Royce.

"She's on the way. Be alert."

"Wilco," came Royce's reply.

I exited my car and followed as best I could into the wooded area ahead of me. I could not see very well but did not want to give away my position by using a flashlight. Every couple of minutes, I caught a slight movement through the moonlight reflecting through the leaves of the trees.

Gradually, I noticed the flicker of a fire up ahead. The two men had built a small campfire perhaps to help them keep warm and maybe even cook on. I could now see the striking figure of the person ahead of me about fifteen feet. Silently I stood in place waiting for her to make the first move. What she did, I was not expecting.

I almost panicked when I realized that she had turned around and was headed back toward me. I had screwed up royally by following her even though I knew she would eventually go back to the car. I froze in place pulled tightly against a nearby tree. I watched as the dark figure dressed in black walked right past me.

As she continued walking toward her car, I let out a soft breath. I walked with as much stealth as I could back to my own car. I was full of anticipation wondering just what she might do when she got to her car. Would she see my car sitting not fifty feet behind hers? Or would she take her car and go blazing through the trees into their campsite attempting to kill them both at the same time?

I was angry with myself. *Have I screwed up this stake-out?* I thought.

I heard something behind me. With instincts honed over twenty years of police work, I walked a little slower and timed myself. I moved my left arm, reached out, and grabbed the person behind me by the neck. I had my pistol out jamming it into a man's face. It was Royce.

I immediately let go and placed my hand over Royce's mouth. I signaled silence with my finger over his lips. We moved silently toward the car. In an instant I also saw movement I assumed was the car we were following. It was barreling in the direction of the two homeless men. We jumped into my car and fell in behind the larger Mercedes.

We were able to see the big black car move down a path. It swerved directly at the two men who miraculously stood up a couple of seconds before. This gave them the momentum to dodge the Mercedes as it shot into their camp upsetting the grocery cart and rolling over the fire.

In the darkness there was a moment of pandemonium as the two homeless men tried to get away from the charging car which had swerved in what appeared to be an attempt to crush one of the escaping men. The black car was rear-ended. The driver became stunned by the shock of a second car's interference.

The big Mercedes leaped forward between two Palmetto trees and headed for a nearby walkway exit out to Collins Avenue. The car's tires squealed as the driver saw the three large pylons that prevented cars and trucks from entering the park area from that direction.

The Mercedes swerved and plowed through the sand and scrub pine on the south side of the pylons reaching the street with only a few scratches.

The drive guided the Mercedes across Collins and onto Eighty-Fifth Street. Royce and I were right behind and moved quickly to pursue as Royce pushed the talk button on the two-way radio.

"Large Black Mercedes Benz, four door sedan, License Foxtrot-Foxtrot-4-Foxtrot, west on Eighty-Fifth now turning south on Harding. All units pursue."

As he was talking a patrol car pulled out of a side alley off Eighty-fifth and joined the pursuit with lights flashing.

Realizing what was happening, the driver of the black vehicle turned quickly west and back north as several other patrol cars joined the chase.

I could no longer see the Mercedes. It had somehow alluded the dragnet we had prepared.

"Where's the damn car?" I said aloud to no one in particular.

"It just disappeared. I don't understand," Royce replied.

We followed the route we thought the car had taken, driving slowly along the streets, looking carefully down each break and alley. After several minutes, we looked at each other with that look of total frustration people get when they faced utter defeat.

Several reports come in that the Mercedes had disappeared into nowhere. No one had any contact. I swung a right onto Eighty-fourth and a right again onto Byron.

Arriving back at Eighty-fifth, I turned to the left and stopped at a bridge just ahead of us. Royce talked into the radio.

"Seal off Biscayne Point entirely."

As soon as he said that, the report came back that two units of the Sunny Isles Police had sealed off the Seventy-Seventh Street Bridge, the only escape route to the south of the Biscayne Point Island Paradise.

"If they didn't get across that bridge before our units blocked it," Royce shouted. "Then we got him. There's no way off this island but here or there."

I had a sinking feeling in my stomach, hoping I had made the right decision about Fara's escape route. I got out of the car and looked back to the east where two units of Sunny Isles and three units of Miami-Dade Police were just arriving.

Royce walked over and instructed the two Miami-Dade patrols to seal off the bridge. He told two of the units of Sunny Isles to do a slow rolling search of the streets around the area just in case. The other unit he told to fill in the blockade after the sergeant followed them across the bridge.

Royce called on the two-way and instructed, "No one crosses the bridge. No one!"

He requested the shift commander to send two patrol cars to begin a slow rolling search of the island from the bridge northward while he and I searched from the north southward.

Royce turned to me.

"You want a piece of this?"

"Of course; I haven't come this far to step out of the way."

"After you, my friend," Royce said as we got into the car and crossed the bridge into one of the most exclusive neighborhoods in Dade County.

I drove slowly along the street headed west. After several blocks, I stopped the car.

"Royce, get hold of your dispatcher and have someone check to see if Fara, or Flambeau or Flame Mart owns a house in this neighborhood."

Royce immediately called in the request on the two-way. About two minutes later, we heard the voice of the dispatcher call with an address on Daytonia Road on the south end of the island. Royce called all units to converge on that address.

When we arrived, the other units had already pulled up and blocked off the house, sending a couple of officers around to the back of the property. The house was huge, probably in the eight to ten thousand square foot range. One of the officers in the back reported that there were two docks, but no boats were tied to either one.

Royce walked up to the garage and looked through a small window in the door. When he shined his light through the glass he could easily see a large black auto inside. The distinctive hood ornament told him exactly what type of car it was. He walked back out to the front as he called on the two-way for a search warrant.

I turned to Royce.

"Smart move calling for a search warrant even at this hour."

"If that car is the one we're looking for, I don't want any legal issue standing in the way of our using it against her."

"I get you. But, I'll assure you if she ditched that car here, she was almost immediately on a boat headed to who knows where after turning off the ignition."

"I agree, but it doesn't stop us from getting as much evidence as we can while things are still fresh. She's probably not going anywhere other than home. Daddy Dearest is still her refuge."

I smiled realizing that this young man was not as inexperienced as I had thought when we first met.

Twenty minutes later, a car pulled up and Adolph Sanchez stepped out followed by a lady in her forties.

Adolph introduced Ursula Burbank of the DA's office.

"You may enter the premises," she said. "I just hope you know what you're doing and that the car in that garage is the one you're looking for."

We walked around to the side door and broke the window so that Royce could put his arm in and unlock the bolt. He opened the door and walked into the interior. Royce turned on the light as I put my hand on the front hood and said, "Still warm."

Other police and Crime Scene officials entered after I pressed the button opening the overhead door. They entered the other part of the house and began their search and analysis of the property.

An hour later, I walked outside and sat down on the edge of the ornate porch at the front of the expensive mansion. I was truly dejected. We had not found even a single finger-print in the place. Someone had so completely cleaned the premises there was not a single piece of evidence to point to the person or persons who had recently used it.

The car in the garage was the one we had chased out of the park. But it did not have a single piece of evidence inside. The crime scene investigators couldn't even find a hair follicle to use to tie it to anyone who had recently driven it.

I was on the verge of admitting that I had met my match. I was chasing a murderer who had committed the perfect crime and continued to commit perfect crimes right in front of my eyes. I kept wondering just how I was going to prove that Fara Flambeau was the A1A killer.

Sanchez came out of the house and sat down beside me. He was quiet for several seconds.

"You realize, my friend, that you cannot win every case, don't you?"

"No," I answered. "And I'm not convinced that this case is finished, yet."

"This woman is just too smart, too devious, too rich for us to stop."

"She'll screw up. All we need to do is to keep the pressure on. Maybe we should even tighten the screws."

"I know. Do you have any ideas I can use since you're no longer on the case?"

"This girl is bleeding me dry of ideas. But, I've just got my brain back in the detective mode. Give me a couple of days to ponder this some more. I'm sure one of us will come up with something."

Royce's voice came from behind us. "Come up with what?"

"Have a seat and join the beaten bunch." I said not even turning around.

"It ain't that bad, is it, Chief?" Royce asked as he sat down next to me.

"She snookered us again and left not one shred of evidence anywhere in this place. Yeah, maybe it is that bad."

"Dammit, I thought we had her this time."

"Yeah, me too."

"Royce," Sanchez interjected, "I consider you a pair of fresh eyes, what do you see in this?"

"Chief Sanchez, I'm not sure what to make of all this. I'm totally confused. Maybe after I've had time to analyze what's happened and put everything together in front of me, I might be able to come up with something."

"Let me know if you do. In the meantime, I think the two of you working together is a good idea. Perry, you understand that I can't pay you anymore. But, if you want to be a private consultant or aid to Royce here, well, that's a different police jurisdiction, you know."

"I gotcha, Chief. No problem."

Everyone in the investigation finally met out front and Sanchez made the decision to end the investigation and close everything up as the tow truck finally arrived to impound the Mercedes as evidence in an attempted murder case.

Sanchez had even arranged for a glass company to come out and replace the small pane of glass in the garage door so that when the last officer drove away, no one would be able to tell what had been happening at this residence.

When I turned onto A1A, my thoughts strayed to all those precious human beings who were simply down on their luck economically. And they had had their lives cut short simply because some spoiled little rich girl thought it would be fun to kill people no one would miss.

"Are you okay?" Royce broke the silence of the last ten minutes.

"What?" I said as my mind flashed back into the present. "Sorry about that. I was just thinking that we've let down all those men who have lost their lives on this, one of the most beautiful drives in the United States. How come they had to be sacrificed? Can you answer that?"

"No, I can't, Chief. I don't understand this whole case. I mean why them? Why murder? Why only homeless? Aren't there just as many homeless around as there were several months ago?"

"I know what you mean. These few deaths haven't put a dent in the problem of homelessness. And now Miami-Dade is getting a bad rap in the news. It's like what happened during that stretch of terrible car-jacking and murders of visitors to the city several years ago."

"I was in high school at the time. And I was scared to death to drive around the city in a rental car. I understand why people were scared to come here for a visit. Even my uncle who lives up in Delray Beach told us that if we wanted to visit with him, we'd have to come up there 'cause he wasn't about to come down here."

I smiled at that and continued driving quietly for several minutes. Then a thought hit me like a bolt out of nowhere.

"The boat," I said.

"What?"

"The boat, Royce."

"The boat? Oh! No! The boat."

"First thing after we get some rest, you check on what boats the Flambeau's own and see if you can locate all of them. If she made her escape on one of their boats, there'll be evidence on it. At least we might find something."

"Right. I just knew working with you would be a university education for free."

"Hey. Don't think you're getting out of this without it costing you dearly. I always cash in my chips."

We were still laughing as I pulled into the parking lot of the Sunny Isles Police station and Royce got out.

"See you later this morning," Royce said as he shut the door and walked over to his own car.

As I drove south toward the hotel, all I could think was that it was four in the morning and I needed to be up and working this case no later than nine. I reached over and turned up the music on the satellite radio as I drove back to the hotel. Less than thirty minutes later, I dropped off into a dead sleep.

CHAPTER FIFTY

A folder with the facts surrounding the incident the night before and a list of the three boats owned by the Flambeau family and corporations lay on the judge's desk as he rifled through the pages.

Ursula Burbank was easily able to get a search warrant covering all properties associated in anyway with all the boats and their moorings.

"I sure hope you know what you are doing, Ms. Burbank," the judge said. Ursula smiled and left the courthouse with the warrant in her hands.

I stopped at the police station and picked up Royce. Since he had already talked to Ursula, we drove right over to the DA's office, picked up the warrant, and drove to the nearest location on the list: a private dock next to the Epic Tower Building in Downtown Miami.

To be safe, Royce called Sanchez and told him where they were headed and why. He asked if he could dispatch a couple of patrol cars to assist in the investigation. Sanchez was more than happy to oblige, and the units were sitting out front waiting for us when we arrived.

Sanchez asked about the other two boats. Royce informed him that one was at their estate in the Bahamas and the other was located in Key West. Royce handed the warrant to the dock manager.

The manager looked at the warrant after which he indicated for us to follow him as he led us to the boat.

"This could spell the end of a lucrative relationship with Mr. Flambeau," The manager said.

I looked at him with a sly smile.

"After this," I said. "You may be glad you're no longer connected in any way with the Flambeau family."

When we arrived where the Flambeau's fifty-three-foot yacht was moored, we stepped on board. Royce opened the door to the cabin and stepped in, finding items strewn around. Lying on the floor was a stack of clothes, all of which were the same rich black of the interior of the boat.

I looked at the pile.

"Only someone as picky as Fara would have made sure that the blacks in her outfit would match exactly."

Once we had determined the boat was secure of anyone on board, Royce signaled for the crime scene unit to begin the work of processing the entire ship. This was quite an undertaking since this particular yacht had four levels of staterooms and an engine compartment that was as large as the main living quarters. The CSI unit was able to investigate every possible nook and cranny on the boat in just under three hours.

In the engine room, under the housing for the starboard engine turbine, a CSI technician discovered a pistol wrapped carefully in an oilcloth rag and stuffed snuggly into an area near the stern section of the housing. It was a nine-millimeter Glock and fully loaded.

When the techs brought it to the deck, I watched as one of them released the magazine and showed me the bullets. I looked at them.

"That woman never ceases to amaze me. I'll bet that pistol is the one used to kill Carolina." I said as I pointed at the bullets in the magazine.

"The bullets in evidence were jacketed just like these."

I shook my head side to side as I walked over to talk to Chief Sanchez who had just boarded the ship.

"It shouldn't take our people long to get everything processed," Sanchez told me. "It doesn't look like all that much to go over. Besides, I got a feeling this pistol is going to cap things for our Miss Flambeau."

I didn't smile.

"What's wrong, Perry?"

"I know this looks bad, but this girl is way too smart to simply have left evidence that would point directly to her."

"I don't know," Sanchez said. "But it seems to me that you guys frightened her so much last night that--"

"No. That's not it, my friend. She had this well planned. All the murders have been located close enough to the house on Biscayne Point that she always had an escape route."

"This fifty-three-foot yacht wasn't anchored off Biscayne Point. The docks around there are not equipped for a ship like this."

I pointed to a fifteen-foot runabout tied to the rear of the yacht.

"No, but that could have been."

Sanchez turned to one of the CSI techs with a scowl.

"Did you process the dingy on the stern?"

"Yes, sir. We picked up finger prints and other items we could not immediately identify. But, it's clear now."

"And that thing hasn't been out of the water all that long, either," Sanchez added.

I stuck out my hand to Sanchez.

"Call me as quickly as you get something, will you?" I asked.

"Will do," Sanchez replied. "What are you going to do this afternoon?"

"I don't know right now. I'll give Royce a ride back to the station, and maybe I'll go sit by the pool and unwind."

We all shook hands, Royce and I walked back to the car and drove over to Miami Beach, stopping in front of the police station.

"Well," Royce said getting out of the car. "I guess I won't be seeing you anymore."

"Why?"

"Well, we've got her dead to rights, don't we? I mean, the pistol and all."

"No, Royce. We don't have her dead to rights. Even if her DNA is all over the clothes and her finger prints are all over the boat, that doesn't place her anywhere near any of the crime scenes nor the murders themselves. As for the pistol, we'll know more after it's processed. We've got a lot more work to do before we'll be ready to close in."

"I guess you're right."

"Why don't we take a day or two off from this case?" I suggested. "You get some other work done and I'll get some relaxation done on the beach. Call me tomorrow evening and let me know where things stand. We'll talk about what to do next."

"Sounds good to me," Royce replied and walked into the station.

I paused for a moment, drove out of the parking lot, and headed south toward my hotel wondering whether or not things could get any worse.

CHAPTER FIFTY-ONE

I was in the bathroom preparing for the day ahead. The television was on in the other room when I heard something that grabbed my attention.

A national news network was reporting on the killing of homeless men in Miami. I quickly stepped into the other room to hear the report.

A young lady in a blue suit and holding a microphone was in the middle of a report.

"The latest statement from the police," she said. "Is that several suspects had been cleared and the police were back to square one. But rumors persist among the homeless who believe there is a conspiracy to get rid of them because the city was so proud of the new baseball stadium downtown. The homeless believe that the city administrators want to drive the homeless out of the area. We'll be watching this story from Miami. This is Tanya Peters."

I grabbed the phone and dialed Sanchez's number.

"Good heavens, Adolph," I yelled into the phone. "What's going on?"

"What are you talking about?"

"The report on the television just now."

"Oh, that. I haven't a clue. I mean, I have no idea who they've been talking to."

"Who's this reporter Tanya Peters?"

"I've never heard of her. I don't think she's local."

"You want me to look into it for you? You know, privately?"

"The only thing I can say is if you wanted to look into it on your own, well, I can't stop you. I mean you are a legally authorized private detective."

"Gotcha. Thanks for the advice, Adolph."

"Just be careful."

"I will."

I hung up the phone and finished getting dressed. After eating a quick breakfast in the restaurant, I headed out for downtown Miami to see if I could track down this reporter.

As I drove across the MacArthur Causeway I noticed a couple of news trucks sitting in the Centennial Park area. I recognized one of the trucks as the one that was seen behind the reporter when she was on the air. So, I took the exit and pulled around to where the trucks were lined up.

The news people had discovered the large group of homeless residing under the causeway. They were gathered to get interviews with these destitute people. I pulled my car into a parking space and walked over to where the trucks were parked.

I approached a man who was sitting beside the truck I had identified from the video.

"Could you tell me where I could find Tanya Peters?"

"I'm not sure," he replied. "But I think she's over by the viaduct talking to the group of homeless gathered under there."

"Thank you," I said.

I walked over to where I saw a smaller group of people gathered.

Sure enough, Tanya Peters was the center of attention as the homeless seemed to be reveling in their newly-found fame. I could see the frowns and murmurings among some of the folks. They didn't seem so happy about all the attention. They moved away from the others.

As I approached the group gathered around Peters, I heard her tell them how much she

"I appreciate your help," She said.

I approached her with a smile and a greeting.

"Ms. Peters, I think I may have some information you might be interested in."

That statement immediately caught her attention and she looked at me.

"Oh? And what is that information."

"Well, I thought you might be interested in what I've discovered."

"And who are you?" she asked.

"Me? Oh, I've been consulting on this case with the Miami-Dade Police."

"And how have you been consulting?"

"I have skills they call upon once in a while."

"What kind of skills?"

"That's not important," I replied. "I found out that the police have had one suspect on their radar this whole time but haven't been able to pin a thing on her thus far."

"What? What did you say? Did you say 'her'?"

"Did I say 'her'? No, I didn't mean to say 'her.' The police haven't been able to find any evidence that points to anyone in particular."

"You said the police were looking at a woman for this."

"I did?"

"You know you did. Wait a minute. You let that slip so I--"

"I didn't tell you a thing, especially that she's the daughter of a prominent businessman in Miami, did I?"

"No, you didn't. And what else did you not tell me?"

"I think I didn't tell you that they tracked the murderer to a yacht owned by this businessman and that he keeps the boat at a marina near the Epic Tower."

"Thank you," she said. "Um, I didn't catch your name."

"I told you that already."

"I'm sorry but I didn't catch it."

"I know. I told you."

"Ah," I said. "So, is there something else you aren't going to tell me?"

"Well, I've got a question that you probably won't answer."

"Oh?"

"How is it that you heard there were no suspects?"

"Well," I said stroking my chin. "Now that's an interesting question."

"You didn't answer that," she said. "But I'd rather you didn't."

"I think I'm a little tired of this game," I said

"Perhaps since I've helped you out more than you'll ever realize, why not allow me a little quid pro quo?"

"Between you and me," I replied. "I can't say except that it was from an official source. How about that?"

"That's all I needed."

"Will I ever not hear from you again?" she asked with a smile.

"Oh, you just might run into me again."

"I hope you aren't a policeman."

"I'm not ... now."

I quickly walked back to my car and drove off leaving Tanya Peters scrambling toward the van.

As I drove back to the hotel on South Beach, I called Sanchez and filled him in what I had found out.

"She got it from an official source."

"Official? Is that what she said?"

"Yep. Official. She has sources inside your office."

"I got that. Thank you, Perry. I'll look into it; and uh, you're official with me. Okay?"

I felt good as I drove to the hotel to get lunch.

CHAPTER FIFTY-TWO

One of the reasons people move to South Florida is simple. Fall and winter have days when the sun shines bright with no sign of a cloud in the sky.

The temperature averages around seventy-five degrees. There's just a slight breeze in the air that helps the temperature feel warm yet not hot.

This day was one of those wonderfully dry days. So, I decided to have my lunch out on the patio by the swimming pool. And there I sat most of the afternoon reading over the notes and ideas I had jotted down.

I thought through just how and why I was unable to put any evidence on the prime suspect. I hoped that maybe dropping that little bomb on the reporter might stir up some action and perhaps get Fara to make a mistake; maybe even give herself away. I needed that type of mistake to arrest her and, hopefully, put her behind bars.

I knew only by putting that spoiled little rich girl in the calaboose, the homeless in Miami would be much safer than they were at that moment. I continued hard on my research. About a half-an-hour later, I heard that familiar voice I had learned to dislike.

"Well, chief. It's good to see you again. I hope you're not too worn out from the other night."

I closed my eyes for a moment, realizing that she had decided I needed to be tortured. I knew that all I could do was just go with the flow.

"Sit down and join me, Ms. Flambeau," I said as I stood to my feet.

I extended my hand. She shook it and sat across from me. I sat back down and closed the file folder that held my notes.

"So, did you come to gloat or just to pass the time?"

"Gloat? Why on earth would I be doing that?"

"Oh, I don't know, maybe because you can?"

"We don't have to act like enemies, do we?"

"Well," I said slowly measuring my words. "Perhaps it's because we could be. And maybe we are."

"Oh, I understand; you know, you being gay and all."

I sat there totally not amused. I took a deep breath.

"Please. You don't have to be nasty."

"Oh, you have no idea. I haven't even come close to being nasty ... yet."

"What about the other night?"

"I was just flirting with you."

"Flirting?"

"Of course; I didn't know it was you. Otherwise I wouldn't have tried so hard."

That little dig brought on a sharp pain. I was just about ready to jump up and put my fist through her face when my good sense took over. I decided that discretion truly was the better part of valor in this situation. She was trying her best to get under my skin. I found himself fighting harder than I had ever done before.

"Oh. I thought you knew exactly who was there."

"I'm good, chief, but not that good."

"But I think you are."

The tension rose about forty degrees. I continued.

"Didn't you see the flashing lights?"

"What flashing lights? Are we talking about the same incident?"

"Of course, we are, my dear." I decided to dig it in hard. "Does your daddy know what you do for recreation?"

"Daddy hardly even knows I exist."

"He certainly knew you were up to something the other day at the warehouse."

"Oh, that. That was a miscommunication, that's all."

"Miss--" I stopped myself from saying something nasty. "I can see that. But, he didn't seem very amused by it all."

"Oh, daddy gets mad fast and calms down even quicker. You and he are so much alike, well except for the fact that he's filthy rich and you're--"

"On the right side of the law," I threw in.

"Now that wasn't nice, chief. I was thinking of introducing him to you. I think he would like you."

"We've already met. And he doesn't like me at all. I thought you already knew that."

"Not hardly. Daddy and I don't talk."

"I can believe that."

Fara looked at me with that "twinkle" I had seen before. She stood and walked away so fast I had no time to react.

"Here's hoping to see you again real soon," she said turning back to me. "In fact, how about this evening; would that be convenient?"

"Ms. Flambeau, I'm afraid that I'll be busy hunting a murderer tonight. If the murderer is you, I guess we will meet again this evening."

And almost as if by magic she was through the door to the lobby and out of the hotel. I had no time to get to my feet.

The waiter came to the table with a drink.

"Has the lady already left?"

"Yes. She's gone. But, leave the drink. I'll need it. Oh, and bring me my bill."

"The lady already paid the bill."

"I'm not surprised," I said in reply.

"You must be lucky, Mr. Savant."

"Why is that?"

"Well, Ms. Flambeau never pays anyone else's bill. She also doesn't tip well."

I sat there and shook my head smiling. As the waiter left, I took out my wallet, pulled out a twenty, and dropped it on the table. I could take a hint. Besides, the wait staff were always high on my list of people to treat well. I wanted my stay to e comfortable.

I walked back to my room intending to change into my swimming shorts and head out to the beach. But, as I walked through the door my phone rang. It was Royce.

"Okay, Royce. What you got for me?"

"Several things, sir; I've got the lab reports from the last several murders. I've analyzed all the reports from the murders we know of and have found some interesting discoveries that I'd like to discuss with you."

"Fine. You want me to come over there or do you want to come over here?"

"I'd rather drop by and pick you up and head for Chief Sanchez's office, if that's alright with you."

"Are you going to pick me up in that squad car you've been driving?"

"Oh, no. I've been given a new SUV to use. It's one we bought from the FBI. It has bullet proof glass and extra armoring in the doors. It also has those hidden emergency lights that you can only see when they light up."

"You sound excited about your new toy," I teased.

"Yes, sir; I guess I am. I'll be there in about twenty minutes."

"Fine I'll see you then."

I smiled as I thought about the irony.

CHAPTER FIFTY-THREE

Detective Adolph Sanchez had moved into his new office on the second floor just about a week before. So, I was pleased to see that the meeting would be in a nicely kept office with plenty of room.

The three of us could sit around a small table to discuss the evidence we had accumulated on the A1A murders.

"I've invited Laura Taylor to join us for her insights," Sanchez said pulling up a chair.

"Great," I said. "But, all I want to hear is that we have enough evidence to put this spoiled little rich girl in prison."

"The lab hasn't analyzed everything, yet. But so far what we have may be enough. I hope Laura has the pieces we need to put the whole case together."

"Shouldn't we have invited someone from the AG's office?" Royce asked.

"Oh, hell no!" said Sanchez quite sternly. "I'll present our case to the AG himself after we put it all together. I don't want our views of the evidence to be picked to pieces by a lawyer before we have a chance to even consider them."

"What evidence?" Asked Laura as we rose briefly from our chairs as she sat.

"I was speaking of lawyers, not evidence."

"Ah. But what about me?"

"What about you?" Sanchez asked.

I nodded at Laura.

"She's an attorney, Adolph."

"Crap."

"And that's why I rarely mention that I have a law degree and two years in the Attorney General's office," she added with a laugh. "I knew I needed to feel free enough to bust heads. They frown on doing that in the court room."

The four of us had a good laugh.

"Well," Royce began. "I spent the last couple of days going over every report I could get my hands on concerning these murders. That way I could share with you what I've found out."

"Good," Sanchez said. "We needed to have this meeting at least a month ago."

"That would have accomplished nothing since some of the most pertinent evidence was not found until a week or so ago."

"So," Royce continued. "It seems that the several pieces of plastic found at the sites all came from the exact same vehicle type, make, and model. In a different report, there was a note that assumed an error. It said that a piece of yellow plastic fit perfectly with a piece of plastic found at another site. This tells me that the same car was used at two different murders."

"That's good, Royce. The lab guys are not necessarily trained as detectives. They're scientific investigators. They report their findings, but don't necessarily make assumptions or draw inferences."

"If we have proof," Sanchez added, "That the vehicle was used in two murders, we can put that with the number of pieces of glass and plastic that are all from the same make, model and year; well, I think we can show that the same vehicle was used at most of the murder sites."

"I think a judge may find that compelling enough for a search warrant," Laura responded.

"Royce, tell us what else you have found," I added.

"Well, we thought there was no DNA. But, several reports indicate finding DNA samples that were never identified. So, I called the lab in Broward and here asking them to compare the DNA samples. The results were that the same DNA was found at all the crime scenes. So far, they have not been able to identify whose DNA it is; but the same person was in those places on all but two of the murders. That seems to be a bit more of a coincidence than one would normally expect."

"No kidding," said Sanchez. "Laura what do you have?"

Laura opened a file folder she had in her valise.

"I have a report that DNA found at one of the murder sites is identical to DNA found in the car and house at the Biscayne Point residence as well as on the boats we searched. So, we now need to see if those samples match the unidentified DNA samples found at the murders that Royce just referred to."

Sanchez picked up the phone and pushed one of the buttons.

"Charlene, get the DA on the line, please." He said before he hung up.

"Okay, I think we have enough. I'll arrange a BOLO on Fara with a location notice, but not to apprehend. We need to find out where she is."

"This evening, Laura added. "I'll have my people stake out the several parks on the island where she has struck before just in case we don't locate her before nightfall. It might be a good idea for Royce, Perry and I to meet up tonight for a possible sting."

"Great," I said. "If she's located today, please let me have a shot at her first. She came by my place this morning and taunted me about the other evening. I mean she was rubbing her clean escape in my face. Let me see if I can do a number on her head before tonight. Maybe, just maybe I can get her to make a mistake that would allow us to catch her red-handed."

"I like the way you think," Royce added.

The phone on Sanchez's desk sounded. He hit the speaker-phone button and we could hear his secretary.

"The DA's on the line, Chief."

Sanchez looked at us as we stood.

"Check in with me during the day. If you don't mind, Laura, I'd like everything funneled through my office until we catch her."

We all agreed and quickly left as Sanchez picked up the phone to speak to the District Attorney.

In the meantime, Royce and I drove back toward South Beach. Royce's phone rang. He mostly listened to a voice on the other end periodically making gestures about what he was hearing.

"Chief," Royce said. "I'm going to put you on the speaker, so Perry can listen in."

"I don't think it pertains to our meeting this morning," Sanchez continued. "That was Marva Berkshire at the homeless shelter who called earlier. She called to tell me that she was worried about Miss Flambeau. It seems she came in to help set up for the lunch crowd and was encouraging those folks like she often does. This guy came in and was hitting on her. After a couple of attempts, it seems that they got into a verbal exchange that ended in him slapping her."

"What?" I blurted out.

"Yeah. Well, Marva says that Fara became infuriated and pulled a gun out of her purse. The guy got upset and ran out. That's when Marva said she told Fara that she had called 911. Marva says that Fara went ballistic on her."

"Of course. She takes care of her own problems," I said. "She never wants the police involved."

"Marva wanted me to know since she knew we were concerned."

"Thanks, Chief," Royce said as he turned off the phone.

"That was smart, Royce," I replied." So, what time do you want to pick me up tonight?"

CHAPTER FIFTY-FOUR

Four o'clock that same afternoon, a small army of police and sheriff's deputies were issued search warrants for property owned by or occupied by Fara Flambeau or any of her immediate family members and corporations owned or affiliated with the Flambeau family.

The warrants were executed simultaneously at four thirty. The amount of evidence seized turned out to be damning and powerful. Everything seemed to point to Fara as the A1A murderer.

The officers were also armed with an arrest warrant for Fara; but, she was nowhere to be found at any of the normal locations she frequented. She had simply disappeared.

Sanchez called me after the warrants were executed and told me what they were up to. He explained why they decided not to include me in on the arrests and searches.

"Hey, Sanchez," I replied. "I get it. I'm not at all concerned."

"And another thing," he added. "Assistant District Attorney Ursula Burbank called Laura Taylor and reamed her out for having a leak in her office or among the officers she had selected. Of course, Laura insisted that the leak was not in her office."

"How did Fara find out?"

"Well, you can easily imagine what Laura said. Besides, Fara Flambeau's tentacles stretch long and far throughout the government. I suspect she owns several people in the DA's office."

"You've got to be kidding. Those ladies had it out?"

"Oh, yeah. And Laura called me right after that cozy little chat. We both had a good laugh since we both got the same call. But, we agreed that it would be the better part of secrecy not to inform the DA's office about this until we have Fara Flambeau in handcuffs."

"So, what are your plans at this point?"

"We're going to do some stake-outs tonight. How about you and Royce cruise the parks along the south end of A1A to see if she happens to be hiding there?"

"What about transportation out of town?"

"We had the airports, trains, and all buses covered before we even asked for the warrants; just in case, you know? And we had every automobile in the Flambeau arsenal either confiscated or under surveillance."

"So," I concluded, "If she got out of town it would have been through some means unknown to you."

"Right. My assumption is that we caught her off-guard."

I couldn't help myself as I laughed out loud.

"What?" Sanchez asked.

"That woman has never been caught off-guard in her adult life. She probably had some sort of escape plan ready and jumped to it as soon as she was tipped off."

"I just hope she hasn't fled the country."

"I doubt that happened. There was no way she could get anywhere unless--"

"Unless she was on a plane we were unaware of that was owned by a good friend. Man! If she got away, I'll never live this one down."

"Hey, Adolph, she didn't leave."

"How can you know that?"

"Because, well, just trust me. She's still around."

"Keep me informed of what happens tonight, even if it's nothing. Just stay in touch. Okay?"

"Okay, Chief."

I hung up the phone and walked down to the restaurant where I ordered an early dinner. I had skipped lunch to go over all the evidence and notes I had on the case. I had lost track of time and didn't realize it was so late when Sanchez called.

I half-way hoped that Fara would make an appearance at the hotel, so I could know for sure that she was still in town. Besides, she had made a point of keeping me informed and telling me that I was her target.

She was out to beat me at my own game. It seemed as if she had to prove she was the best at everything that she tried.

Now it was murder. If she didn't think she could get away with it, she would never have played the game. It was important to her. Thus, it had become important to me.

By seven thirty, I was finished with dinner and a cocktail to follow up the light flan I ordered for desert. As I walked out of the restaurant, my phone rang with an unfamiliar number. I answered reluctantly and heard a voice with which I was not familiar.

"Mr. Savant, my name is David Horowitz, from the Homeless Shelter in Overtown."

"Of course, Rev. Horowitz. What can I do for you?"

"You can come right over here as quickly as possible. I have someone here who needs to talk to you."

"Who?"

"I'd rather not say at the moment. How soon can you be here?"

"I guess I can be there in about twenty minutes." There was a long pause.

"Rev. Horowitz?" I continued.

"Yes. That will be fine. See you in twenty minutes."

He hung up the phone.

Feeling a bit perplexed, I was torn about what to do next. I had this gut feeling that the person I would be meeting was Fara Flambeau; yet I didn't know for sure. I wanted to call Sanchez and tell him, but tell him what?

I think Fara might be at the Homeless Shelter. And what if she was? What would happen? And would I get a chance to talk to her before the police arrested her?

I stood in the lobby for several minutes as I called Royce to tell him that I would be late. I took a deep breath and told the concierge to call for my car. When the valet pulled up, I handed him a ten, got in, and headed toward Overtown and the Homeless Shelter.

When I arrived at the meeting hall, the place was silent. I reached into my shoulder holster and pulled out my pistol. I checked to see if there was a round in the chamber. I carefully made my way into the kitchen area and into a back room that also served as a make-shift office for Rev. Horowitz.

I re-holstered my pistol and walked carefully back into the hall. Rev. Horowitz walked in the front door, reached out, and shook my hand.

"So, is she here?"

"No, sir. She left about ten minutes ago. I think she overheard me talking to the police."

"You called the police as well as me?"

"Yes, I thought it was my duty. But, I think she heard me and left immediately."

"Did she tell you where she was headed?"

"No. But, I hope she's going to make her way to a police station to turn herself in."

"Oh?" I replied.

My skepticism, I hoped, was obvious in my tone of voice.

"I have no idea where she is or where she's headed. I advised her to turn herself in. I hope she does. But, I don't know."

"I understand that. If you talk to her again, would you call me instead of the police? I mean, I'd like to accompany her to make sure she's safe. Oh, and to be sure that she gets a fair shake; you know? And you can tell her what you're going to do."

"Yes. I'll consider that."

"Consider what?"

Adolph Sanchez's voice penetrated the air like a gun shot as he walked into the room.

I hesitated a second too long and Rev. Horowitz jumped in with an answer to his query. "We were just talking about how we can help you take Fara Flambeau into custody."

"And?" Adolph said as he caught my eye.

"And," I said, "I guess we were also discussing having dinner together."

Adolph's face appeared as he burst into laughter. I didn't think my comment was all that funny.

Adolph continued.

"Okay, you guys. I'll bite. So, what did you decide?"

"We decided we'd wait to see if you wanted to join us, Rev. Horowitz said. "What about it?"

Adolph just shook his head as his smile grew larger.

"Okay. Perhaps that would be a clever idea. We can talk about how we're going to talk Fara into turning herself in, preventing a serious incident."

We left the hall. Each of us drove to a restaurant about two and a half miles from the shelter. There we had a sandwich and a couple of beers as we discussed our options in dealing with Fara.

Rev. Horowitz told us about the conversation he had with Fara.

"I was a bit surprised when she walked in since she rarely appeared when no one was around. You know, she always likes to make an entrance. But, this time she came to my office and looked scared."

"I believe that," I said.

"She told me that the police suspected her of the murders on A1A and that she had nothing to do with any of that. Well, I knew your suspicions and I told her the best thing she could do would be to turn herself in and let her lawyers sort it all out."

"Did she agree to that?" Sanchez asked.

"No; but she did say she wasn't ready to face the police. She left. I wish I could have talked her into staying here. Plus, I'm afraid for her being alone and on foot in that neighborhood."

"Good Lord," Sanchez added. "I didn't think about that. She has no transportation. And she would never blend in anywhere she went."

"We've got to find her," I said as I grabbed Sanchez's arm. "Now."

We each shook Rev. Horowitz's hand and left the restaurant as I threw a twenty on the table. In Sanchez's car, we cruised the area driving up several blocks, doubled back, moved in another direction, and doubled back.

Sanchez was using an old search pattern he had learned in New York. But after about an hour, I observed that she would not be walking, she'd be driving.

"What Car?" Sanchez asked. "We impounded all their vehicles."

"You don't believe that, do you?"

"Well, we impounded all the vehicles we could find out about."

"Right," I snickered. "I'll guarantee that family has numerous off-book vehicles they could grab at any time. So, why don't I run down Royce. We'll see what we can find at that warehouse and perhaps cruise by the park and her two condos in town?"

"That sounds fine," Sanchez agreed.

He pulled in behind my car. I opened the door, stopped, and turned back to him.

"Adolph, you understand--"

"I know, Perry. I hope you find her first. If we pick her up, you won't be able to get within a mile of her."

"What if--"

"If I get to her first, I'll do what I can to contact you and let you know. Other than that, you know I can't promise a thing."

"Right." I said as I walked to my car.

CHAPTER FIFTY-FIVE

I drove quietly with the radio off trying to make sense of what had happened over the last several hours. Fara's life had been turned upside down. I felt as though she was close to panicking.

I had seen this activity once before when I was attempting to catch a cop killer named Clark Davis nearly fifteen years ago.

After the police had fully analyzed the evidence in the shooting of a police officer in Queens, the only man who could have done it was Davis. Under my leadership, the police quickly closed in on him.

Unfortunately, I watched him elude every effort we made to track him down. After some careful police work, we got a break from a tip and surrounded a motel where he was last seen.

Lucky for me, Davis was there and surrendered without a fight. As the officers were bringing him out of the motel room in handcuffs, he looked at me in such a way that I knew I had not seen the last of this man's fury. I wondered what kind of look I would get from Fara when the police finally caught up with her.

It was nearly nine o'clock when I picked up Royce at the Sunny Isles Police Department. "In uniform?" I asked. "Really?"

"I saw no need to change clothes. Besides, being in full uniform might come in handy in a pinch."

Neither Royce nor I were hopeful of finding Fara. She could easily have slipped away using a prepaid credit card, a prepaid cell phone, and a car that was not directly related to the family or the business. Of course, she could always rent a car and leave the state. But, we persevered anyway setting up stake-outs at places she had been known to frequent.

We began at her apartment. But after an hour and checking with the doorman, we concluded that she had not been there all day. We drove over to her night club. No one there had seen her, nor had they heard from her. Upon Royce's insistence the manager took us to her office suite and allowed us to look around.

Of course, the police had already taken just about everything, but I guess I thought it would be good just to look. After about twenty minutes, I suggested that we move on to another location and just hope for luck.

As we walked out of the club, Royce noted that it was nearly midnight and they were no closer to finding her. So, he suggested that perhaps we head back to the station to drop him off.

But, I wasn't ready to quit.

"Let's check one more place," I said. "You know the pier where she keeps her yacht?"

"Yea. What about it?"

"She could easily have slipped back to that boat and taken up residence without anyone seeing her."

"I guess she could."

"Let's just slip over there and see what we can find."

"Okay; but I need to get some sleep tonight. I've got a real job, you know."

"No problem."

At this I turned back toward downtown Miami. I took the southern causeway on Treasure Island. I saw something that didn't seem right in the parking lot of a popular Japanese restaurant on the water.

Sitting at the north end of the empty lot was a car with its back pulled right up to the low guard rail next to the water. The lights were off. But Royce and I both could easily see that there was someone sitting on the driver's side behind the wheel.

I made a quick U-turn a block beyond and slowly pulled into the lot and stopped. We could see that the car was running, and the person seemed to be alone inside.

"Should I call for backup?" Royce suggested.

"No," I replied. "This is probably nothing."

"Maybe, but my gut tells me different. It just doesn't look right."

"You're the police here, Royce. You decide what needs to be done."

Royce pulled out his cell phone and dialed a number.

"This is detective junior grade DeShawn Royce with Sunny Isles, I have a possible murder suspect in sight and need immediate back-up."

He paused for several moments. He gave the address and situation to the person on the phone.

"We'll continue surveillance," he said. "Have the lieutenant contact me on TAC-3 when he arrives."

He turned his phone off and stared at the car ahead of us.

"They'll be here in about ten minutes," he said. "If not sooner."

We sat for four or five minutes watching the parked car.

"We need to get a closer look to be sure of what's going on," I said.

"No, Perry. If we're wrong, we'll just be embarrassed. But, if we're right, well, let's not blow it."

"I understand, but--"

"If the car tries to leave, we'll pull out and stop it."

"I know. I guess I'm just getting antsy."

"Antsy?" Royce said as he laughed.

"Yea. What about it?"

"Hey, nothing."

We sat there a few more minutes when I noticed that the car was slowly creeping forward. Royce saw it, too, and pointed. I shifted the car into drive and pulled out to block the exit. The driver hit the headlights on and bright.

I pulled out turning my front bumper to face the car just as it slammed on brakes. Royce jumped out, drew his weapon, and pointed it at the oncoming car. He pointed at the driver and yelled for him to get out. But, the driver put the car in reverse and backed up almost a hundred feet. It screeched to a stop.

The car immediately leaped forward headed directly at my car. A pistol appeared out of the driver side window exploding with several shots at me.

Moving like I did when I was younger, I jumped out and rolled away. As I looked back I saw the other car swerve toward Royce who attempted to jump out of the way without firing his weapon.

I pulled my pistol out and moved away from where I landed and ran toward the north end of the lot. I wanted to circle around and not allow the driver to find me until I was able to get a clear shot.

That's when I stopped cold. I could see Royce laying on the ground about ten feet from my car; and he was not moving. My stomach leaped in a violent reaction as I thought that I was retired from the police force and had already lost two police partners. I wondered if this was truly what people meant by being in hell.

I wanted to run out to see if I could help Royce, but my instincts told me to stay in the shadows and keep out of sight. I watched as the dark car pulled around and headed back toward where I had been sitting earlier. The car's headlights revealed that I had moved away from that spot.

The driver slowed and began sweeping the car's headlights into the areas of the shadows. I could see the headlights moving toward my location. I ran along the guard rail next to the water toward an area that was much darker.

But, the driver was quicker than I. And I found myself caught in the lights as the car sped directly for me.

Without thinking, I stood still until the last second jumped back toward where I was before the driver swerved toward me. The car barely missed me as it passed. It hit the guard rail with such force that I saw a couple of the posts that held the rail fly out into the water.

Two of the posts that had held another part of the rail gave way and bent ninety degrees over the water stopping and holding the car at bay. The passenger side of the car remained just barely on the lot's asphalt.

Lying flat on my stomach, I looked up to see the horrendous sight. The driver remained in the car perched in a precarious position over the water. The dirt and asphalt holding the posts cracked and snapped a little. The posts were slipping against the weight of the car.

I jumped up to the side of the car and grabbed at the door handle. Through the tinted window I could barely make out the face of the person inside. The driver was wearing a full head covering. The driver's hand reached up and pulled off the covering and looked at me. It was not Fara!

"Who the hell are you?" I said.

"I'm sorry," he replied.

I held onto the car but had to let go when I realized the car was slipping on the pylons pulling me to the blackness of the Intracoastal Waterway. That's when the posts and asphalt gave way and the car plunged into the water quickly sinking down and out of sight.

The momentum of the car pulled me for a few moments along the ground and nearly over the side before I let go of the door handle. The car flipped over on its top in the water and sank.

I lay there stunned as I watched the car slip into the water below me. I tried to ensure that I remember all the details about what had happened. But I felt woozy. My stomach ached.

I thought I heard sirens in the distance. I also had the impression of someone pulling me back from the edge. I pointed toward the water.

"There's someone in the car! Get him out! Help him! Fast!!"

I passed out.

I didn't know until later, but blood was flowing freely from a wound in my side. When I jumped from the car, the driver fired several shots. One of those bullets sliced through my arm and pierced my side just under the rib cage.

I woke up on a stretcher as the paramedics dressed my wounds and pumped fluids into my other arm. I looked back toward my own car. I saw numerous people gathered around Royce.

The driver must have hit him hard throwing him about twenty feet before he slammed onto the pavement. All that I could think about was *Is my new friend still alive?*

Moments later, I heard Sanchez's voice asking me how I was feeling.

"I feel like hell," was all I could say.

I could feel Sanchez next to me. I could tell that we were moving pretty fast. I felt the wheels under me give way as the doors to the ambulance caught my eye. I turned to someone beside me.

"My apartment is just off Central Park South. You can drop me off there."

I closed my eyes and dropped off into a deep coma-like sleep.

CHAPTER FIFTY-SIX

As the sun rose on the crime scene, Sanchez stood in the parking lot overseeing the recovery of the car that had flipped over into the water. A large crane pulled the water-logged car out of the water.

One of the divers that had helped to attach the cables to the car's frame under the water pulled himself up out of the water and called over to Sanchez.

"We found a body still in the car. The seatbelt was unbuckled, and the driver's side window was down. I can only assume that the driver tried to escape and drowned."

"What else did you find?"

"The CSI tech over there is processing the extra evidence that I bagged from inside the car. There were two shell casings and a forty-five-caliber pistol."

"That's a pretty big cannon."

"Yes, sir. I also found a head scarf and a black mask. And I also pulled the registration. It was a rental paid for by a Flambeau Corporation credit card."

Sanchez thanked the officer and walked over to where the CSI technician was packing away the items. He picked up the pistol and noted that the serial numbers were filed down. He walked back to his car where he dialed a number on the phone.

"Laura, Adolph. Are you at the hospital, yet?"

"I arrived about ten minutes ago."

"We found a body. It was not Fara. We're extracting it from the car as I speak. We still don't know who it was. If it's Fara's brother; well, at least we know it probably wasn't Fara who was involved."

"I understand." Laura replied. "Of course, Perry's going to be royally pissed off."

"How is Perry? Has he arrived?"

"An ambulance arrived several minutes ago. I'll let you know as soon as I know."

"Thanks, Laura. You gonna stay at the hospital?"

"I'll be here as long as it takes. This guy almost gave his life attempting to help us solve this crime."

"Yeah. What about Royce?"

"He's going to be just fine--badly bruised and in some serious pain, but he'll be okay."

"Glad to hear it. Tell Perry I'll be over to brief him on what's happened later today."

"Will do, Chief."

Laura hung up and walked over to the Emergency room desk.

Almost immediately, a doctor walked over to her.

"Is that Perry Savant who just arrived?" She asked.

"Are you a relative?"

Laura explained her position and why she was there.

"We have an Operating Room available," the doctor replied. "We're taking him there as soon as we get him prepped. You can wait in the OR waiting room on the second floor. I'll be out to let you know how it went. But, seriously, I don't anticipate any major problems based on the preliminary reports we got from the paramedics."

"Thank you, Doctor," Laura replied.

Laura walked to the public elevator and took it to the second floor where she got out and poured herself a cup of coffee. She sat down to wait on the doctor's report. That was when she noticed that she was alone. She sat on one end of a deep, cushioned sofa and felt a couple of tears roll down her cheek.

She sat for more than an hour feeling herself doze off a couple of times. She could feel the presence of someone standing near her. She opened her eyes with a start as she saw Adolph Sanchez pouring himself a cup of coffee.

"So, what of the Flambeau kid?" she asked. "Have you talked to the old man, yet?"

"No. I think I'll leave that to the Sheriff and mayor. I don't want to be in on that conversation. But, I will say, we got him dead to rights this time."

Adolph sat down on the sofa next to Laura. They both watched the television mindlessly for several minutes. The sound was off. But, neither of them got up to turn it up.

"What now?" asked Laura.

"I guess we close the file. It appears that Fara had nothing to do with any of these murders. I mean, she's a wack-job, but I don't think she's a murderer."

Laura thought about that for several minutes watching the TV.

"I can't wait to hear what Perry is going to say about this."

"Me? I can wait."

They smiled and looked at the television a few more minutes.

The large double doors into the OR opened as the doctor came out.

"Mr. Savant will be fine. We took out a small bullet fragment from his arm. The rest of the bullet must have gone through since we found nothing out of the ordinary. Oh, and the bullet missed all vital organs."

"Thank God," Sanchez sighed.

"What about his head?" Laura asked. "I thought he hit his head pretty hard on the pavement."

"There was no damage. He'll probably have a headache for several days, but that should go away. Do you have any other questions?"

Sanchez and Laura looked at each other.

"If you have any other issues or questions, just let the nurses know," the doctor said. "They'll be taking him to a room in a few hours. You can meet up with him there."

# # #

About four o'clock that same day, I blinked a few times to get my eyes focused. When the fog lifted I could see Laura smiling down at me.

"Well," I said a bit groggy. "I didn't quite expect to see you. But I'm glad you're here."

"Happy to see you alive and well."

"What did the doctor say?"

"I think he said that you should retire to Key West. You know, stay out of the crime-fighting business."

"That ain't gonna happen," I retorted. "Okay, tell me that you found the body."

"We did. Although the DNA testing has not been completed, I'm convinced that it must have been Fara's older brother. The old man has been informed that someone who used a company credit card to rent a Mercedes car died while attempting to kill two people."

"I wish I had been there to see the expression on his face. So, is he going to the morgue to identify the body?"

"No. He said he'll wait on the DNA test results then decide what to do. I think he didn't know his son was in town."

"Interesting, if it was his son. But, I guess we won't know a thing for sure for a while; We'll just have to wait and see."

"I'm headed to the coroner's office to see how they are doing in the search for a positive ID. You, on the other hand, are going to stay here for a few more days and write up your reports. After that you're going to Key West and get settled in your new retirement home. You hear me?"

"Yes, mother."

"Don't you get sassy with me, young man." Laura laughed just as Sanchez walked in.

"Okay, you two. This is a hospital. You're not supposed to have fun here."

I reached out my right hand and Sanchez shook it lightly.

"It's good to see you, too, Adolph."

"He's dead," he said straight out. "We have no idea who the hell he is. He might be the old man's son. But who can tell at this stage."

"Have you checked the data bases? I thought you had a large file on the Flambeau's."

"We're checking everything we can to this point, Perry. He just doesn't exist in any of our records. We're waiting on our request to the New York and New Jersey Attorney Generals' offices for confirmation on his identity. They should have some records."

"I wouldn't bet on any of that. His identity will turn up somewhere."

"I'm sure it will," replied Sanchez.

"Maybe you should get the old man to go to the Coroner's office and identify the corpse from the car," I suggested. "That should get quite a rise out of him. Might even bring Fara out of hiding."

"I hope so," Laura added.

"Okay. Now what about Fara?" I asked.

"Nobody's seen or heard from her in several days. The investigators we put on all of her hang-outs have reported nothing."

"Nothing?" I asked. "You mean you have no idea where she could have gone? There must be some record of her activities somewhere. No American citizen can just fall off the grid without leaving some small trace evidence somewhere."

Adolph just put his face in his hands and shook his head.

"Believe me, Perry. We're still searching. We'll find her someday. I promise you that the minute I hear of where she's gone to, I'll let you know. I'm sure," Sanchez said with a huge grin across his face. "You'll want to go visit her."

I couldn't help myself. I had to laugh. I relaxed.

"So, what's the plan?" I asked.

Adolph took a deep breath and turned toward Laura.

"You're the lead on this investigation, Laura." Sanchez said. "Tell him."

"I'm sorry, Perry, but we've closed the case of the murders on A1A. I believe as you probably do that all the evidence points to the driver of the car, not Fara. We still can only pin one murder on him. Everything else is still highly circumstantial at best."

"So, it's all done for now?" I questioned.

"Yes," Sanchez answered. "You go on to Key West and enjoy your retirement. Forget about The Flambeau family. We'll call you if we hear something worth investigating."

"Okay. But, I'll never forget the look on that young man's face as he refused to take my hand. He's the only one in my career that got away with murder; even if he did do it by dying."

I paused for a long moment as I realized that a tear was forming in my eye.

"What about Royce?"

"He's going to be fine. He's pretty bruised up and will definitely need a week or two of vacation in bed."

"Good," I muttered.

I felt the urge to close my eyes.

"I've got a terrible headache. I think ... I think, I'm going to sleep now."

I tried to say good-bye to everyone in the room. But instead, I slipped into a restful state. I finally got an undisturbed ten hours of regenerative, comforting sleep.

CHAPTER FIFTY-SEVEN

At the airport in Mexico City, a distinguished-looking gentleman of about sixty stood. He seemed anxious as he awaited someone arriving. He shuffled his feet and shifted back and forth on each leg. With him were two men who appeared to be escorting the gentleman.

The suitcoats worn by the men were bulging like they might had hidden weapons. Each man had an ear piece in one ear attached to two-way radios in their coat pockets.

Suddenly the door opened to the gangway leading to an airliner that had only landed moments before. A tall, beautiful young lady emerged from the gangway. She was immediately greeted by the gentleman who was waiting.

She stood for a moment taking in the reality that she was in Mexico City for the first time. She was dressed in elegant dress that flowed down her legs like a high-fashion model.

She wore little jewelry of note; yet, she carried herself as would a princess from a wealthy state. Her jet-black hair flowed down her back like silk. Her dark eyes seemed to pierce right through the minds of those standing nearby.

The waiting gentleman spoke in a very official voice. He spoke English with only a slight accent.

"On behalf of the president of Mexico, allow me to welcome you to our fair city. All arrangements have been made as per your father's request. A bank account has been set up in your name. A house has been purchased for you as requested here in the Capitol. And an apartment in Cozumel has been leased in your name. And here is your newly issued Mexican passport as well as your citizenship papers. Now, is there anything else that we can do?"

"No, Mister Secretary. I'm sure that you have made all preparations necessary for my stay."

"Your father and I go back many years. He was always kind to me and my family when I struggled as a political refuge. So, I consider it a rare privilege to be able to welcome his famous daughter to Mexico with full citizenship along with diplomatic immunity wherever you travel. Here is my card with my personal cell phone number on it. If you ever need anything, and I mean anything at all, please do not hesitate to call me at once."

"I will."

She leaned over, gave the gentleman a big hug with a kissed on the cheek. She walked out into the sunshine of Mexico City, pausing a moment to take in the warmth of the air. Then she stepped into the back seat of a large, black Mercedes limousine.

She opened a built-in icebox and pulled out a bottle of champagne. She opened a small cabinet built into the side of the car and pulled out a champagne glass. She poured herself a drink. Smiling, she seemed to give herself a toast. With a smile that stretched beyond her face, she drank the cool, sparkling nectar.

The vehicle then whisked Miss Fara Flambeau from the airport to a new life as the wealthiest woman in Mexico.

www.ingramcontent.com/pod-product-compliance
Lightning Source LLC
Chambersburg PA
CBHW031944260626
47157CB00017B/2314